Benjamin R. Curtis

Dottings Round the Circle

Second Edition

Benjamin R. Curtis

Dottings Round the Circle
Second Edition

ISBN/EAN: 9783337189990

Printed in Europe, USA, Canada, Australia, Japan

Cover: Foto ©Andreas Hilbeck / pixelio.de

More available books at **www.hansebooks.com**

DOTTINGS ROUND THE CIRCLE.

BY

BENJAMIN ROBBINS CURTIS.

SECOND EDITION.

BOSTON:
JAMES R. OSGOOD AND COMPANY,
LATE TICKNOR & FIELDS, AND FIELDS, OSGOOD, & CO.
1876.

University Press: Welch, Bigelow, & Co.,
Cambridge.

TO

ANDREW FISKE,

WHO ACCOMPANIED ME IN THE MAJORITY OF THESE WANDERINGS,

I Dedicate this Journal,

AS A TOKEN OF GRATITUDE FOR THE CONTINUAL
PLEASURE HIS COMPANIONSHIP
AFFORDED ME.

PREFACE.

It has been said of one of the greatest minds that the world has ever produced, that "he dotted round the circle of human knowledge." With all due modesty for making use of the comparison, I offer to the public these "Dottings," made in a journey around the world.

Starting immediately after my graduation at Harvard, I set out upon a tour of the world, equipped with a large number of desirable letters of introduction. By their means I was presented to some of the prominent people in the East, and by their kind favor I was shown what was deemed by them worthy of notice.

The result of my observations I now lay before the public. In the course of such rapid travel it cannot be expected that any deep political or ethnical investigations have been attempted. I simply offer a panoramic picture of several of the chief countries of the world.

I have said but little in regard to my wanderings in Europe. So much has been written of Italy and France and England, that I have merely noted my arrival in the different cities, and the impressions I derived from the most important.

If I can interest any to such a degree that they will wish to see for themselves these wonders of the world so imperfectly described, I shall feel happy in the thought that my past pleasure will be experienced afresh by others.

B. R. C.

Boston, October, 1876.

CONTENTS.

CHAPTER VI.

CHAPTER VII.

CHAPTER VIII.

CHAPTER IX.

CHAPTER X.

CHAPTER XI.

CHAPTER XII.

CHAPTER XIII.

CHAPTER XIV.

CHAPTER XV.

CHAPTER XVI.

CHAPTER XVII.

CHAPTER XVIII.

CHAPTER XIX.

CHAPTER XX.

CHAPTER XXI.

CHAPTER XXII.

DOTTINGS ROUND THE CIRCLE.

CHAPTER I.

FROM BOSTON TO SALT LAKE CITY.

1875, June 30. — Leaving Boston at 9 P. M. (by the Boston and Albany Railroad), I reach New York City at half past five o'clock the next morning.

July 3. — After spending two days in New York City and vicinity, I leave the Grand Central Depot at 10 A. M. (by the Hudson River Railroad) for Albany, where I have agreed to meet F——, my college classmate and travelling companion. The weather is fine, but decidedly warm ; but in spite of this, the journey along the bank of the Hudson is full of interest. The mountains rising from the opposite shore of the river, covered with a delicate bluish haze, look picturesque and refreshingly cool ; while the different steamers passing up and down, with here and there a sail-boat for variety, keep the eye continually occupied. We reach Albany at two o'clock, and I find I have an hour to wait before the "special express" on which F—— is coming will arrive from Boston. The time passes quickly by, and promptly at three o'clock the "special" appears, with F—— standing on the platform of the front car, waving his hat joyously. Soon after this we start for Niagara Falls *via* Rochester. Of course we have the traditional wedding couple on board; and of course the gentleman alights at every third station, eager to pour the entire contents of the refreshment-table into his wife's lap. As evening draws on (of course) the lady, becoming weary, rests her head lovingly and confidingly on her husband's shoulder, and, with his arm encircling her, they sit absorbed in themselves, forgetful of the outside world; while (of course) all the other passengers regard them with looks of half-pitying contempt. The train stops at Utica for supper, and we are soon again on our way. A grand railroad this New York Central, with its four broad tracks, its comfortable cars, its powerful engines, and its numberless trains! We are rushing continually on, through broad cultivated fields stretching away into the distance, past populous towns and cities, or, now leaving civilization for a time, we plunge into a thick wood, or dash round a sharp cutting in the rocks, and stop suddenly at some manufacturing village, whose inhabitants all turn out to give us a welcome. At 10.30 P. M. we reach Rochester, and here we must change cars for Niagara Falls. At 2 A. M. we arrive at our destination, and are shown to very comfortable rooms by the sleepy-looking clerk of the International, and, lulled by the ceaseless roar of the Falls, I drift into unconsciousness, thinking what a great State New York is, in which one can travel by express-train from ten o'clock one morning to two o'clock of the following, without leaving its limits.

July 4. — The ninety-ninth anniversary of our country's independence, though falling on a Sunday, is here ushered in by ringing of bells and an occasional fire-cracker; the younger portion of the community, however, evidently reserving itself for the morrow. After breakfast F—— and I start on foot for the Falls, successfully and completely routing the continuous attacks of the hackmen and guides by my truthful reply, "I have been here before," which stops each one's importunities, and apparently affects them as the sign of the cross does the Evil One. After wandering through Prospect Park we descend by the inclined railroad, and are ferried across the river to the Canada side by a remarkably muscular Charon of French descent. Two wedded couples accompany us; and when our little boat has reached the middle of the stream, the mighty roaring cataract above us, the clouds of rising spray, and the swiftly flowing river give great alarm to the ladies, and enable the husbands to exhibit themselves in the most heroic aspects. On the Canada side we are surrounded by traders of all kinds; but we have been wisely warned against purchasing, as a heavy duty is exacted by the United States authorities as soon as the article purchased is carried over the border. Indeed, one gentleman got thus into quite a serious difficulty; for having bought a tablecloth at a Canadian store, he was charged a large per cent by the United States customs officers; and, not deeming it worth such an additional sum, he was returning with it to the shop where he had purchased it, when he was halted on the other side by the Canadian officials, who declared that it was a product of the United States, and requested him to deposit the usual duty before bringing it into their country. The gentleman, however, succeeded in convincing them that he had bought it in Canada, and he returned it to its original owner, declaring that he wanted to have nothing further to do with the ill-fated article. After wandering along the Canadian side, we return by the new suspension-bridge, and, after an afternoon passed in quiet, seek sleep to prepare us for the journey of the morrow.

July 5. — We leave Niagara Falls at 1 P. M. by the Michigan Central and Great Western Railroad, and, after a somewhat tedious and rather uninteresting day's journey, we arrive in Detroit at 10 P. M., and drive at once to the Russell House for the night. To-day we made our first trial of a "hotel-car"; and although the dinner is hot and the food well cooked and of good quality, still the dust and cinders pretty effectually spoil the repast; for, as the kitchen occupies a large share of these hotel-cars, it is almost impossible to keep the windows closed.

July 6. — As Detroit is familiar to one of us, and as we are obliged to be in San Francisco by August 1 to take the steamer for Japan, and as there are, moreover, many new places which we wish to visit on the way, we decide to make no stop of any length at present, and a very hasty survey of Detroit is all that we can allow ourselves. Detroit has many fine business blocks, and Woodward Avenue contains some of the handsomest residences in the West. The large lake steamers lying at the docks give to the city an air of extended commerce which is very impressive.

We leave Detroit at 9.30 A. M. by the Michigan Central Railroad, and when we have travelled about two hours the aspect of the country through which we are passing has become thoroughly "Western." On both sides of the railroad the fences between the fields are far less numerous than in New England, probably indicating that these long stretches of rich grain are the property of a single proprietor. The towns and villages, too, look fresh and new, and the tall, keen-looking men, standing about in top-boots and flannel shirts, are strange objects to our Eastern eyes. At Kalamazoo our train rushes through a thick cloud of grasshoppers, who flutter and spread themselves over everything they meet, making it evident what serious damage they are capable of inflicting to crops over which they pass. At 7 P. M. we come in sight of Lake Michigan, and for nearly an hour our train runs close to the water, until, having rounded a curve, we see a great city spread out before us; clouds of smoke are pouring forth out of tall chimneys; the spires of churches stand out against the sky; our train rattles across several switches, rushes into a perfect labyrinth of tracks, gives a long shrill whistle, and at last comes to a stand-still; we alight and set foot in Chicago.

In 1833 Chicago was the name applied to a few houses near Fort Dearborn. In 1840 it had a population of 4,000; at present it has about 400,000. We enter one of the many omnibuses standing near the station, and soon have obtained most comfortable quarters at the Palmer House.

July 7. — After a refreshing sleep and most excellent breakfast, we walk out through the principal business street of the city. What a rush and whirl and hurry everywhere! Everybody walks rapidly along, rarely looking in each other's faces, each mind intent on its own business; each man, apparently, eager to get to a particular place before his neighbor, each fearful lest a moment's delay may upset his plans forever. This feverish haste is, it seems to me, far more noticeable than in New York itself. Some idea of the extent and variety of the trade of Chicago may be formed from the following: " In 1872 about 70,000,000 bushels of grain came to market, with 1,000,000,000 feet of timber, 400,000 cattle, 1,900,000 hogs, and 3,000,000 sheep. Enormous elevators shoot the grain into the vessels at the rate of 10,000 tons a day; one vessel can be filled in twenty minutes."

In the afternoon we take a carriage and drive about the city. The private residences, even on Michigan Avenue, do not satisfy my expectations. Many of the houses are built of wood, and a large majority of them look hastily constructed. The people of Chicago, however, can congratulate themselves on their fine "Boulevards," and the sight of them make me remember with regret how much Boston is in need of similar drives for her citizens. We drive next to the building containing the complicated and ponderous machinery which draws water from a point two miles out in the lake, for the use of the city; and, standing near this mass of iron, it hardly seems possible that it owes its very existence and movement to the comparatively small objects called men that circulate at its feet! From the neighboring tower a fine bird's-eye view of the city can be obtained.

We leave Chicago at 8 P. M. by the Chicago, Alton, and St. Louis Railroad, and reach St. Louis, our next objective point, at nine o'clock the following morning, after travelling with fearful rapidity.

July 8. — After breakfasting at a comfortably late hour at the Southern Hotel, we walk out to see the new bridge over the Mississippi River, and find it truly a wonder of engineering art and mechanical construction. We make a hasty survey of some of the principal streets of St. Louis, which seems to contain characteristics of both Northern and Southern cities; but as the heat is very oppressive, we soon return to the hotel, and endeavor to keep as cool as we possibly can, sitting quietly in doors.

We had intended to travel without change from St. Louis to Denver, but, owing to a recent "wash-out" on the North-Missouri Railroad, we find that we shall be obliged to travel to Kansas City by the Missouri Pacific Railroad, and change there on to the Kansas Pacific Railroad, which will carry us to Denver. So at 8 P. M. we arrive at the station of the Missouri Pacific Railroad, and enter the Pullman car only to find that our section (which we have previously engaged) is opposite a very colony of individuals. A mother with an elderly daughter, two small boys, a baby, and a maid, give all the rest of the passengers a mathematical as well as practical puzzle to decide how they intend to stow themselves for the night in places for a third of their number. The enigma is soon solved, however, by the mother remarking in a loud tone of voice that "she hopes some gentleman will give her a lower berth or take some of her children!" Before F—— or myself are called upon to immolate our night's rest on the altar of politeness, the conductor enters and informs us that our section is the corresponding one in the car ahead; so we leave the other gentlemen to attend to the lady's clearly-expressed wish, and make our way forward, congratulating ourselves that we shall now "have peace": but it is not to be. We find in our section in this car a young mother with a little girl and a very young baby, the latter of whom, overcome probably by the excessive heat and want of sleep, is crying heartily. This family are merely occupying our section till their own is prepared for the night; and this being accomplished, they retire, and we take possession. The poor baby cries all through the night with unfailing regularity, and when, at last, morning breaks, I am amazed to see the mother offer her children a breakfast of cold chicken, pickles, and Washington pie!

July 9. — We reach Kansas City at 8.30 A. M., and find the train for Denver waiting near by on the Kansas Pacific Railroad. We start at ten o'clock, and soon after are rushing over the desolate prairies.* Far as the eye can see, on either side of the train stretches one flat, unbroken, barren waste of land, with scarcely a living thing to break the intense silence and dreadful monotony. Once in about two hours the train halts at a "station," — consisting of one dwelling-house, a saloon, and a few lazy-looking Indians, — and, after taking in a fresh supply of water and coal, we leave all this behind us, with no great regret. Wearied with the monotony, I go forward on to the engine, and persuade the engineer to let me ride with him. From here I can at least see all that the country has to show. Once, as we dash along, a great eagle rises majestically in front of us, hovers a moment near by as if filled with a sort of sad wonder at being driven away from his

* In fact, in all my after-travel to San Francisco I did not find any more dreary, lonely, and uninteresting country than from Kansas City to Denver.

solitary haunt, and then floats gracefully off. A little farther along we scatter a herd of antelopes, which bound quickly aside. Having paused for half an hour at a characteristic "station" to discuss some dangerous-looking compounds called "dinner," we continue our journey. The afternoon wears wearily away; we stop again for "supper"; the sun sets in a mass of dark clouds, and a storm is evidently upon us. Soon the rain begins to patter down on the car-roof, accompanied by thunder, lightning, and hail. Still we rush on. Outside the car windows all is thick darkness, and the rain-drops striking against the glass can plainly be heard above the noise of the train. I look over at F——; he is fast asleep, and I strive to follow his example.

July 10. — We are due in Denver at 6 P. M.; but at the station where we halt for dinner we receive the annoying news by telegraph that the thunder-storm of yesterday has washed away two bridges between us and Denver, and a long delay is inevitable. To add to our misfortunes, it begins to rain again heavily, and a more desolate-looking car's company can hardly be found. Fortunately, however, we are halted at a little place (called Hugo) where food can be obtained. Another afternoon passes; evening closes in. What a comfortless position! Standing still away out on a desolate prairie in a drenching rain, — drenching, for the roof of our Pullman leaks badly, and all we can do is to follow the porter's advice and "wait till it swells"!

July 11. — Sunday morning dawns, however, clear and cool; and it seems as if Nature is determined to show us as bright a face as possible after her gloomy aspect of yesterday. After breakfasting on what the place affords, we stroll about and endeavor to pass the time as best we can; and I cannot help thinking how differently we are spending Sunday from those in Boston: for, instead of the musical church-bells, we hear only the discordant sounds from pigs, poultry, and cattle; and, instead of the throngs of well-dressed people bound to the different churches, we see only a few weary passengers, and an occasional Indian riding along on a mustang. By dinner-time we find that our unexpected and prolonged stay at Hugo has somewhat exhausted its culinary resources; and for this, as well as other reasons, we are delighted to hear, about 2 P. M., that the bridges have been repaired, and that we can proceed. After travelling slowly for one hundred and five miles, we finally arrive at Denver at 8 P. M., having been on the road from Kansas City fifty-eight hours! Every one coming to Denver hears, long before his arrival, of its excellent hotels, the best, indeed, between St. Louis and Salt Lake City, — the Grand Central, the Interocean, the Sargent House, and others. Not knowing, of course, exactly where they are located in the city, he will be somewhat surprised, immediately on his arrival at the station, to see directly opposite, across the square, a row of *small wooden* hotels, each one bearing one of these well-known names, its namesake being in reality located in a distant part of the town; and, unless one is on the lookout for this deception, it may happen that you take up your abode in one of these catchpennies before you discover your mistake. This state of things should be suppressed by the municipal authorities.

July 12. — We spend the morning in walking about the city, which is very pleasantly situated on the south bank of the South La Platte River, with the snow-capped peaks of the Rocky Mountains rising in the distance around it. The town covers a large amount of ground, but does not seem to possess a very large number of inhabitants. Denver is remarkable for the many elegantly appointed billiard and drinking saloons and cigar-stores that meet you at every turn. The climate is cool and delightful. We leave Denver at 3.30 P. M. by the Colorado Central Railroad for a short stay among the Rocky Mountains, bound first for Central City. After riding for about an hour, we change cars on to a narrow-gauge railroad, and from this point the scenery is of the very wildest description. The road itself, built as it is along the banks of streams, and through cuts in the solid rock which now rises so high above your head that it almost shuts out the sky, is a tribute to man's superiority to the obstacles nature has placed in his way. As we stop a minute before a very steep ascent, I go forward and ask permission of the engineer to ride by his side, believing that one cannot obtain an adequate view of the magnificent scenery through which we are about to pass while sitting in the cars. The engineer, however, says that, as the road is narrow-gauge, the cab is only just big enough for himself and the fireman. "But," says he, "many Eastern men ride up this cañon on the *cow-catcher*." After assuring me that it is perfectly safe, as he can by no means travel at express rate, he places a broad board on the cow-catcher; and, when I have taken my seat, with my hand firmly grasping the signal-flag, the engine gives a shrill whistle, and off we start. For the first five minutes I really enjoy my novel manner of locomotion. "This," said I, "is the very place of all others from which to view the mountains! — to be pushed slowly up the gorge with *nothing before you* on the track, a towering mass of rocks on the one hand, and on the other, far below, a quickly flowing stream, hissing and gurgling over stones and fallen trees and old mill-wheels. Another five minutes passes by. I begin to speculate as to what will happen to me if, getting a little dizzy, I leap off the engine. If I spring aside to the right, I shall be crushed between the train and the towering rock; if I jump to the left, I shall be dashed to pieces on the stones of the stream far below. The result will be the same in either case, — death. Still the quickly-throbbing engine pushes me on. As we pass through a village the inhabitants turn out and stare at the engine, amazed at the novel figure-head that it carries. The village is left behind; we are again alone, making our way up the cañon; the hot breath of the engine stiffes me; the continual swaying from side to side affects my head; I call aloud to the engineer, but the sound of my voice is drowned in the roar of the wheels. I try to grasp the little flag-staff more firmly; it turns in its socket, and I am compelled to trust to my hold on the bars of the cow-catcher. I do not know how long I can endure this. I almost feel that I may faint. A village is in sight! Do we stop? Yes, for our engine gives a loud whistle, the breaks are put down, the wheels turn more slowly; we come to a stand-still. I leap off the engine and seek the engineer.

"How far have we travelled since I got on to the engine?"

"Eight miles," is the reply.

Eight miles! I return to the car, much to F——'s satisfaction, who tells me that he happened to look out of the car window, a little while before, and, as the engine slowly rounded a curve, he was amazed to see me sitting bolt upright on the cow-catcher. At eight o'clock we arrive at the terminus of the railroad, a small mining town called "Black Hawk," where we find, waiting in the thick mist that has spread itself over everything, a comfortable omnibus bound for Central City and the Teller House, which latter spot, the best hotel in the vicinity, is to be our shelter for the night. The road winds directly up the mountain-side, and all along the way, a full half-mile, we pass straggling houses and mining buildings, with a saloon at every turn in the road. The inhabitants, however, seem to be a sturdy, honest-looking set, and the best of order prevails everywhere. We reach the Teller House about 8.45 o'clock, and find ourselves in a very comfortable-looking hotel, surrounded by a small mining village, with high mountain-peaks rising in every direction.

July 13. — After an early breakfast we ascend a neighboring spur of the mountain, and the view in every direction is wonderful. On all sides, and stretching away off into the distance, countless peaks, many snow-capped, thrust their heads upward, while a thin bluish haze floats around them, brought out into stronger relief by the excessive clearness of the air elsewhere. We visit a gold-mine near by, and find the miners very intelligent and polite. At eleven o'clock we take the outside seats on the stage bound for Idaho Springs, a neighboring town noted for its warm springs, where also you strike the direct railroad back to Denver. Going down a mountain in Colorado on a stage-coach is no light matter! The stage-driver shuts down the brake, and after taking a firm hold of the reins and giving a general caution to the passengers, "lets her run" away down to the foot, arriving there generally in perfect safety, but dashing and whirling round sudden turns in the road in a most alarming manner. The excellent stories, however, that one hears from these eccentric specimens of humanity almost excuse their apparent recklessness.

We arrive at Idaho Springs at noon, and go at once to take a bath in the waters for which the place is celebrated. We have our choice of a tub or swimming-bath, and both prefer the latter. We find this to consist of a large square room made into a sort of tank, with about five feet of water always in it, a pipe letting the water in, and another discharging it continually. The water is always very warm; the medicinal properties may be determined from the following analysis:—

Carbonate of soda .	30.80
Carbonate of lime .	9.52
Carbonate of magnesia .	2.88
Carbonate of iron .	4.12
Sulphate of soda .	29.36
Sulphate of magnesia .	18.72
Sulphate of lime .	3.44
Chloride of sodium .	4.16
Chlorides of calcium and magnesia, each a trace.	
Silicate of soda .	4.08
Grains	107.00

After dinner we take another stage-coach and drive to the railroad station, and soon after start in the cars for Denver. We have gone only about a hundred feet when a sudden and loud hissing sound, together with a peculiar grating motion of our car, causes every passenger to rush out of the train and look eagerly down the road in the direction of the unusual phenomena. We see before us our engine lying on its side in the water of the stream by which runs the railroad, the track twisted and broken up for a short distance, but all the cars standing safely in their places. The hissing sound is caused by the steam from the engine rushing out directly into the water. Soon the engineer (brave fellow!), who has gone down with his machine, emerges from the *débris*, a little but not seriously hurt. The fireman jumped before the engine struck the water. On going up to it I find that the broken mass of wood and iron was yesterday the very engine on whose cow-catcher I had ridden up the Colorado cañon! Another train is telegraphed for, which soon after backs up on the other side of the accident, and we are soon on our way to Denver, which we reach at 6.30 o'clock, and once more are quartered at the Grand Central Hotel.

July 14. — At 7 A. M. we say good-by to Denver, and start by the Denver Pacific Railroad for Cheyenne to meet the Union Pacific Railroad, which will carry us farther west. The day is very hot, the country flat and uninteresting, and we are glad when, at twelve o'clock, we reach Cheyenne and sit down to dinner. At 1.15 P. M. the Western train comes along, and, having engaged a section in the Pullman, we soon after start for Ogden. The prairie through which we are now passing is far more picturesque than that near Denver. The grass is greener, the land is undulating, and the landscape is frequently broken. Prairie-dogs gaze at us from their little mounds, and the graceful antelopes raise their delicate heads in calm contemplation as we rush by. At 8 P. M. a beautiful full moon rises over the prairie, and, taking advantage of a slight delay while the engine is taking in coal, I go forward, and, having easily obtained the engineer's permission, ride by his side (*in the cab*) for about an hour, the clear moonlight pouring over everything, making the night almost like day.

July 15. — After another long day in the cars we reach Ogden at 5.30 p. m., and find we have forty minutes to wait before the branch train will start for Salt Lake City. Ogden is the terminus of the Union Pacific Railroad and the starting-point of the Central Pacific Railroad. Here, too, is the point of departure of the Utah Central Railroad, which runs to Salt Lake City. Ogden is situated at the foot of some high and very picturesque mountains, and the air is exceedingly fresh and exhilarating. Three companies of soldiers from the United States military post at Salt Lake City are just leaving Ogden to proceed farther west to the scene of some recent Indian disturbance, and the full fighting-equipments of the men, the sharp commands of the officers, and the encouraging cheers from the lookers-on, carry one back, in memory, to the terrible days of our war.

Soon after six o'clock we start for Salt Lake City on the Utah Central Railroad. On either side of us a flat sandy desert stretches away into the distance. Soon we come in sight of the Great Salt Lake, whose unruffled waters, dull and metallic colored, are lighted up by the beams of the setting sun. At eight o'clock we reach Salt Lake City, and drive at once to the Townsend House, a hotel kept by a Mormon who takes great pains to give explicit information and even letters of introduction to strangers who take up their abode with him.

CHAPTER II.

FROM SALT LAKE CITY TO THE YOSEMITE VALLEY.

July 16. — What a peculiar place! The streets are broad and shady; the houses, mostly built of wood, are set a little back from the roads, and each one possesses its own plot of ground, where flowers or vegetables are cultivated. A city? No; rather a great caravanserai in the centre of a burning desert. The roofs of the houses are flat, and little gardens are sprouting from them, forming pleasant resting-spots for evening-time. The men look coarse and ill-educated, the women stupid, and the little children neglected. One can hardly believe he is in an American city. A strange moral atmosphere pervades the place. The passers-by seem filled with the consciousness of a Presence which is ever at their doors, whose laws they must obey, whose continual supervision they cannot escape.

The situation of Salt Lake City is extremely picturesque. It lies at the foot of the Wahsatch Mountains, whose snow-capped hills contrast beautifully with the deep blue of the sky. Considering its desert surroundings, it is well called by "the Saints" the "Eden" of the land. The population is about thirty thousand. A United States military post, Fort Douglas, overlooks the whole city, which could soon be laid low by the powerful guns which seem to be continually watching it.

Immediately after breakfast we go to the Mormon Tabernacle, situated in the centre of the city, not far from Brigham Young's house. On arriving at the grounds of the Tabernacle, we stop at a little lodge, where a guide — the custodian of the place — meets us and conducts us about, giving us full information in regard to every point of interest. The Tabernacle is a very large building, "oblong in shape, having a length of 250 feet from east to west, by 150 feet in width. The roof is supported by forty-six columns of cut sandstone, which, with the spaces between, used for doors, windows, etc., constitute the wall. From these pillars or walls the roof springs in one unbroken arch, forming the largest self-sustaining roof on the continent, with one notable exception, — the Grand Central Depot in New York City. The ceiling of the roof is 65 feet above the floor. In one end of this egg-shaped building is the organ, — the second in size in America. The Tabernacle is used for church purposes, as well as for other large gatherings of the people. With the gallery, which extends across both sides and one end of this immense building, it will seat 8,000 people."

We walk up on to the stage and sit down among the seats of the Elders. These form a semicircle directly in front of the organ; while a large chair in the extreme foreground, covered with a coarse fur rug, is the throne of the Prophet, or "the President," as he is usually called. To stand on the stage and look across over the almost countless rows of benches gives one a very good idea of the wonderful size of the hall; and when every seat is filled with "the congregation of the faithful," the sight must be very impressive. The entire exterior of the gallery is adorned with texts and maxims derived from various sources, the sentiments being partly Scriptural, partly political, and partly simply practical. They are as follows, each one being in large capital letters:—

OBEDIENCE IS BETTER THAN SACRIFICE.
SUFFER LITTLE CHILDREN TO COME UNTO ME.
WE THANK THEE, O GOD, FOR A PROPHET.
KEEP YOUR ARMOR BRIGHT.
GOD BLESS OUR TEACHERS.
BE TEMPERATE IN ALL THINGS.
IF YE LOVE ME, DO MY WILL.
HOLINESS TO THE LORD.
WHAT HATH GOD WROUGHT.
OUR OWN MOUNTAIN HOME.
UNITED WE STAND, DIVIDED WE FALL.
HEIRS OF THE PRIESTHOOD.
FEED MY LAMBS.
DO WHAT IS RIGHT.
OUR CRUCIFIED SAVIOUR.
THE MOTHERS IN ISRAEL.
UNION IS STRENGTH.
KNOWLEDGE IS POWER.
THE DAUGHTERS OF ZION.
OUR MARTYRED PROPHET.
GOD AND OUR RIGHT.

ZION IS GROWING.
IN GOD WE TRUST.
OUR LIVING ORACLES.
THE KINGDOM IS OURS.
THE HOLY PRIESTHOOD.
UTAH'S BEST-CROP CHILDREN.
BRIGHAM OUR LEADER AND FRIEND.
HAIL TO OUR CHIEFTAIN.
PROVIDENCE IS OVER ALL.
CHILDREN, OBEY YOUR PARENTS.
PRAISE THE LORD — HALLELUJAH!
HONOR THY FATHER AND MOTHER.
THE KINGDOM OF GOD OR NOTHING.
GLORY TO GOD IN THE HIGHEST.
THE PIONEERS OF 1847.

Having finished the perusal of this *pot-pourri* of precepts, we leave the Tabernacle, and make our way across the grounds to the site of the proposed Temple, of which the foundations only are laid. The Mormon Elders are building this Temple from the tithes received from the people, — for every Mormon is obliged to bestow a tenth part of his entire income upon the church, — and as these vary in amount greatly from year to year, the progress of the building has thus far been very slow, and it is doubtful if it will ever be completed. The proposed dimensions of the Temple are, at the foundations, 99 × 186½ feet. The Mormons intend it for a building in which they can perform the rites and ceremonies peculiar to their religion; the Tabernacle, as I have said, being only a place for general worship and assembly.

We visit next the Warm Springs, situated at the foot of the Wahsatch Mountains, about a mile from the centre of the city. We find here a swimming-bath, similar to the one at Idaho Springs. An analysis of these springs was made some years ago by Dr. Charles T. Jackson of Boston. The usual temperature is 102° Fahrenheit.

We now set out for Brigham Young's residence, to present a letter of introduction to him which we have received from a gentleman in Boston who has been instrumental in building the railroad from Ogden to Salt Lake City. Our way lies through the business portion of the town, and we are very much struck with the strange appearance of several things around us. Salt Lake City is, as I have said, situated at the foot of the Wahsatch Mountains, and the clear water from the neighboring hills is conducted down the sides of the principal streets in broad wooden troughs, which never serve, as do the gutters in our Eastern cities, as a repository for general waste, but are kept thoroughly clean by the citizens, who look to them for a daily supply of pure water. I saw a little boy lie flat down on the sidewalk, and, putting his mouth into the gutter, enjoy as pure and refreshing a draught as can be obtained anywhere in the world. This swiftly running water keeps the air cool and fresh, and tempers the summer's heat.

We see painted over many stores a large eye, with the following motto: "Holiness to the Lord." This is the distinguishing mark of the Mormon merchants, and is assumed at the special command of President Young, who endeavors to keep all the trade of the city in the hands of this "Zion's Co-operative Mercantile Institution." We have now arrived at the outer gate of Brigham's residence, and we pause a moment to examine it. It consists of a very large and curious stone house connected with several wooden buildings, in which dwell the Prophet's wives; the left-hand one containing many odd-looking peaked windows, the whole surrounded by a high wall. There are three entrances. Over the left-hand gate is a large stone beehive, — the emblem of the Mormons; over the middle and chief gate rests a great stone lion stretched at full length; while a stone eagle, with extended wings, surmounts the right-hand doorway. A porter is always in attendance at the middle gate, and having showed our letter of introduction to President Young (as well as one to Bishop John Sharpe, which we also have), he informs us that we have come too early, as "the President does not breakfast till eleven, and does not receive till half-past one." He tells us, however, that if we will call again later we will be received. So we return to the hotel for dinner.

Having finished our dinner, we set out again for the "Residency," followed by the respectful and admiring glances of all the attachés of the hotel, who evidently consider us of much importance, since we are actually to be received by the high authority of the place. Arrived at the main gateway, we are met by the porter, who conducts us under the sleeping lion into a sort of office, where many clerks, some of them sons of the " President," are busily at work on the affairs of Mormondom. Our guide, having seated us here, vanishes into the interior of the building. Returning soon after with a solemn face, he bids us, in a pompous manner, to follow him. We pass through the office into a wide hall, and crossing this, our guide halts us opposite a sort of double door, which evidently leads into the apartment of the Prophet. When our conductor decides that we have composed ourselves sufficiently to go into the presence of his master, he throws open the folding-doors in a manner which is intended to be impressive, and, bowing low, motions us to advance. We find ourselves in a long, high-studded room, plainly but comfortably furnished, at the upper end of which are seated a sort of semicircle of portly men, while a very large, elderly man with gray hair, distinguished from the others by a certain air of firmness and command, is seated a little apart from the rest in a large arm-chair. As we enter he rises, and when the genuflections of our little conductor have ceased, Brigham Young (for it is he) comes forward and greets us politely. Having presented us to Bishop John Sharpe and some other bishops whose names I do not catch, Brigham leads us to a sofa and converses with us pleasantly for about five minutes. He inquires especially about the gentleman who has given us our letter of introduction, questions us in regard to our proposed travels, and answers our interrogations in regard to Salt Lake City. At this point, thinking that we have remained long enough, we rise to take our leave. The bishops all bow politely, we acknowledge their salutes, write our names in a large "visitors' book," and receive Brigham's autograph in return, shake hands with the "President," and bid him farewell; the little mannikin guide reappears, bows low, throws open the folding-doors, and ushers us out. We emerge from the dazzling light of the presence of the Prophet into the light of day.

Brigham Young is now seventy-five years old; and though evidently the possessor of a strong constitution, he yet gives one the impression of being a very feeble man. His mouth is his remarkable feature; with closed lips it looks like a vice, and makes one feel certain that he always executes what he decides upon.

July 17.—We breakfast at six o'clock, and at seven o'clock take a train on the Utah Southern Railroad for a little settlement on the Great Salt Lake, called Lake Side. We wish to examine the lake more particularly, and also desire to bathe in its peculiar waters. The Utah Southern Railroad has lately been opened by Brigham Young. It is a narrow-gauge road, and extends southward from Salt Lake City for about thirty miles. The road runs directly across the desert; and the surrounding country, besides being flat and very uninteresting, swarms at this season with mosquitoes, that fall upon us without mercy. After travelling about two hours, the train stops at Lake Side. This consists of a small hotel, built directly on the water's edge, a long pier near which is a little steamboat, and several bathing-houses. Going up to the hotel, we sit down on the piazza, and, after conversing awhile with the proprietor, turn our attention to the lake, an immense sheet of water, one hundred miles long and forty miles broad! To-day it lies before us with scarcely a ripple on its surface. No fish leap up out of its depths, no insects scurry along its top. It is a *dead* sea. A naturalist, a correspondent of a New York paper, who has come to the hotel to make scientific investigations in the vicinity, assures us that he has repeatedly tested the waters. "No living thing," says he, "is there but the egg of a little fly, which is deposited near the surface of the water."

We take a bath in the lake. The water is so dense that it is impossible to sink, and so salt that it causes the eyes and even the skin to smart terribly. One can easily lie extended on the surface. When you lift your feet from the depths you might imagine you had trodden on a mass of india-rubber, so great is the buoyancy. We leave Lake Side at noon, and arrive back at Townsend's in time for dinner.

We have decided not to stay over Sunday, as there will be very little of interest in the Tabernacle. Neither Brigham Young nor Bishop John Sharpe are to preach. So at 4 P. M. we say farewell to the Saints, and, taking the afternoon train on the Utah Central Railroad, arrive at Ogden in time to connect with the train to the West on the Central Pacific Railroad. A pouring rain has set in, and while F—— is securing our section in the Pullman car, I am standing on the platform among a mass of trunks, vainly endeavoring to attract the attention of the baggage-master. At last everything is ready; the passengers have taken their seats, the baggage is checked and aboard, the engine gives a farewell scream, and we are off. We start ahead, skirt the northern shore of the Great Salt Lake, and disappear in the darkness.

July 18. — We pass through, to-day, broad prairies over which blows continually a fine alkali dust, very disagreeable to the eyes and intensely annoying to all the lady passengers. We stop at a "station" for dinner. Here we first make acquaintance with the Chinese waiter. A grotesque-looking Oriental stands between F—— and myself, and after enumerating the different articles on the bill-of-fare with astonishing volubility and without the slightest change of countenance, and being told that we will both take roast-beef, he goes to the side of the room and shouts out to his fellow-countrymen below, " Roastee-beef *twice*." Truly " the heathen Chinee is peculiar."

July 19. — Early this morning the passengers all crowd the platforms of the cars eager to see " The Horn," a deep chasm between two mountains, along the top of one of which our railroad is built. Far down below, fifteen hundred feet beneath us, runs what appears to be a small brook, — in reality a stream over fifty feet wide! The beauty of the spot is almost indescribable. The immense mass of rich foliage on either side of the chasm, the valley between, looking like a mere strip far below, and the many mountain-peaks which rise in various directions, all combine to produce an idea of immensity and far-extending space which is very impressive. The piece of railroad, indeed, on which we are now running, has a history in accordance with the wildness of the spot. The roadway was first dug out and fashioned by men let down in baskets from a higher point near by, and several lost their lives through the breaking of the rope while going to or coming from the scene of their daily labor. The scenery, indeed, from this spot to Sacramento City is one continuous panorama of exquisite views, broken only by the frequent snow-sheds (built for the protection of the road in the winter season) which line the sides of the hills. We reach Sacramento City at 9.30 o'clock, and after making only a short pause continue our journey, and arrive at Stockton, our point of departure for the Yosemite Valley, at noon. Here we leave the train and proceed to the Yosemite Hotel for lunch.

Stockton, situated on the San Joaquin River, contains a population of about twenty thousand. The city carries on a large grain trade, has several hotels, over a dozen churches, and many fine public buildings. While on our way from Ogden to Stockton we found three gentlemen, who, like ourselves, are bound to the Yosemite, and with whom we are very much pleased to make the trip. These are Messrs. H—— and R—— of Boston, and Mr. S—— of the West. There are two distinct routes to the Yosemite Valley. The tourist can either leave the Central Pacific Railroad at Stockton, go by a branch railroad to Milton (thirty miles away), where he will find a coach bound for the Yosemite, eighty-one miles distant, passing on the way the great trees of Calaveras County (considered the largest of the two groups of the West); or one may alight from the Central Pacific Railroad at Lathrop, go by a branch road to Merced, a distance of fifty-eight miles, and complete the journey to the Yosemite by stage, as before, a distance here of ninety-two miles, on a road lately constructed. If he selects the latter route he will pass the great trees of the Mariposa group. We decided to go by the Milton and Calaveras route, but to hire a three-seated covered wagon, and driver, and perform the journey, as it were, by ourselves. Having changed our money into gold, for California has always preserved a gold basis, we dine at the hotel, and soon after, about seven o'clock, a wagon, such as I have described, appears, drawn by four powerful horses, and guided by a driver "who has made the trip eighteen times this season, sir"! We put on board a very moderate allowance of baggage; the idlers in front of the hotel gaze at us curiously, almost sympathetically, as if knowing well the various hardships we shall have to undergo; the driver gathers up his reins, cracks his long whip, and we rattle off in a great cloud of dust. The road lies directly across the prairie, and the full moon, shining brightly over everything, makes the country almost as light as if it was the sun itself. Our evening ride is delightful, and at midnight we rumble into Milton, a small town which has been recently swept by fire and a tornado, and draw up before the Tornado Hotel (called so from the town's calamity), only to find that the landlord, probably not being in the habit of receiving guests at this hour, has closed his house for the night; but a shrill, weird scream from our driver (in imitation of the screech-owl) quickly rouses him, and, as we intend to continue our journey very early on the following morning, the whole party separate for the night.

July 20. — According to orders, our landlord rouses us at four o'clock, and after a cup of coffee (as we intend to stop for breakfast on the road), we start again on our way, getting in motion thus early, because, while the journey from Milton to the " Big Trees " of Calaveras usually occupies parties two days, on their way to the Yosemite, we being somewhat in haste, have decided, by changing horses at a point thirty-four miles away, to visit the trees and return to the main road the same day. Our track lies through a very wild and picturesque district, with scarcely a house anywhere about us. We pass great numbers of quail, pigeons, and " jack-rabbits," besides magpies and hawks innumerable. About noon we stop for a short rest at a small mining town whose principal citizen is soon in conversation with us. He says he was originally from Boston; but as he left that city twenty-five years ago, we find that he does not retain a very lively interest in regard to his former residence. Soon after this we reach Murphy's Camp, a mining town where we are to change horses for the Calaveras trees, and to which we intend to return for the night. After a wait of fifteen minutes, we start off with fresh horses and at once begin the ascent of the mountain, on the summit of which are the great trees. The dust is terrible and the heat intense. After grinding along for four hours, we reach the summit of the mountain, and see at once that even all the outlying trees, at a distance from the giants themselves, are of far more than ordinary size. We emerge from the woods into an open avenue, and see ahead of us " The Sentinels," — two of the big trees which stand one on each side of the road leading up to the hotel. What immense fellows! The mind almost fails to grasp their proportions, almost refuses to accept the testimony of the eye. We reach the hotel at last, and having turned our attention to dinner (for we have eaten very little since morning), we walk out into the neighboring grove and are lost in wonder at the giant trees that grow on every side. " There are only two species of this genus known to botanists: the *Sequoia gigantea,* or Big Tree, and the *Sequoia sempervirens,* or Redwood. The latter are very numerous, and are found all along the Coast Range. The former have been found only in the Sierra Nevada Mountains." The largest tree is called the "Father of the Forest," and measures one hundred and twelve feet in circumference, and four hundred and thirty feet in height. This tree now lies at full length, having been uprooted in a terrible storm some years ago. Upon a section of another tree twenty-five feet in diameter a house has been erected, and thirty-two persons are said to have danced there at one time. Another immense fellow eighteen feet in diameter is stretched on the ground, and persons on horseback, entering through a knot-hole, can ride into the tree for two hundred feet. Many of the trees bear well-known names, — Abraham Lincoln; Dr. Asa Gray; The Three Graces, etc. As our time is limited, we turn our faces homeward, and driving rapidly down the mountain, reach Murphy's Camp at ten o'clock and go at once to bed.

July 21. — We breakfast at six o'clock, and in an hour are again on our way. The road is immoderately dusty, the day one of the very hottest possible, and good water — not to mention ice-water — quite unattainable. Every half-hour one of us asks the driver, "How much farther to Sonora" (the place where we are to dine), and the patience of that worthy must be sorely tried. However, all drives, even the most uninteresting, have an end; and just before noon we drive into our wished-for village, where, waiting for dinner, we happen upon an old Harvard graduate of the class of '52, who

has drifted out into this part of the country, and, for the
sake of our Alma Mater, insists upon showing us all the
hospitality the place affords. We soon see that nothing gives
him so much pleasure as recounting his long-past college experiences; and we listen with interest while he tells laughable
anecdotes of his classmates, some of whom we have learned
to look upon with all the solemn veneration due from an un-
dergraduate to an instructor.

We resume our journey, passing all the afternoon through
small mining towns and scattered settlements, and at seven
o'clock we come to the foot of a high mountain, and, after giving
our horses a good rest, begin the ascent. The road runs for the
entire way along the edge of a very deep chasm, which separates
this mountain from its neighbor. At last we reach the summit,
and draw up before a little hotel kept by a thrifty Scotchman
and his wife, — the man an old "Forty-niner," who has become
a thorough Californian. A most enjoyable contrast is this
house to our other stopping-places along the road. The fresh-
est eggs, the most delicious bread and butter, together with
the very whitest table-linen, refresh us physically and mentally.
The house, from the proprietor, is called Priest's, and, certainly, its ministrations are not in vain. After tea we sit out
on the little piazza, on a level with the various mountain-peaks
around us, and witness a very beautiful sunset, the clearness
of the air greatly enhancing the loveliness of the picture. The
sun, a great molten mass, slowly sinks behind a curtain of pink

and gray; soon the pink disappears, the gray deepens into a dark blue border, the stars shine out one by one, night-hawks fly rapidly to and fro, and night has begun.

July 22. — We are on our way again at six o'clock, and, having stopped at the usual mining town for dinner, find ourselves at the foot of the mountain beyond which lies the Yosemite Valley. We intend to pass the night on the summit of the mountain, and enter the valley to-morrow. We continue our journey at 4 P. M., and almost at once begin the ascent. As the wagon winds wearily up the road, I alight for a walk, and, having distanced my friends by about a mile, I throw myself under a tree by the side of the road, and, regardless of rattlesnakes (which are plenty in the vicinity), lie still, struck with the silence and solitude of the forest. The wind murmurs pleasantly in the pines; a little mountain stream gurgles over the rocks strewn in its way; the sharp chatter of a squirrel is soothed by the gentle cooing of a dove; I can almost believe that I have strayed into the actual "forest primeval." A very prosaic-looking wagon, however, with four jaded horses, appears and recalls me to the presence of my fellow-men. We reach the top of the mountain and a little settlement called "Crane's Flat" at seven o'clock, and soon after supper seek sleep, lulled by the melodious voice of a tame "billy-goat," who continually haunts our neighborhood.

CHAPTER III.

FROM THE YOSEMITE VALLEY TO THE PACIFIC OCEAN.

July 23. — We rise early, and immediately after breakfast continue our journey, eager to accomplish the descent of the mountain and behold the long-sought-for Yosemite. The road down the mountain is frightfully precipitous, and we congratulate ourselves on having so careful a driver. On a sharp turn of the road, on the very edge of a deep chasm, we meet the regular stage-coach coming up out of the valley, and only the most scientific steering puts us by in safety. Soon after this we reach level ground, and are actually in the valley, with the grand mountains towering on all sides, and even in the first sight feel repaid for the various discomforts of the previous days.

"Yosemite is an Indian word, which means 'large grizzly bear.' The valley is a deep and wide fissure or gorge in the Sierra Nevada Mountains, within about twenty-five miles of their very topmost crest, and lying nearly due east from San Francisco. It is a little over seven miles in length by half a mile to a mile and a quarter in width. Its total area comprises 8,480 acres, 3,109 of which are meadow-land. The entire grant to the State was 36,111 acres, and includes one mile back of the edge of the precipice throughout its whole circumference.

"The altitude of the bottom or meadow-land of the valley is 4,000 feet above the sea; while on either side the walls — which are of beautiful gray granite of many shades — rise to the height of from 3,300 to 5,300 feet above the meadow, and are of every conceivable shape. Over these grand old walls leap numerous waterfalls, from 350 to 3,300 feet in height, and in forms of inexpressible beauty that change with every instant, or are changed by every breeze that plays and toys with them. A remarkably picturesque and beautiful river, — the Merced, — full of delicious trout, and clear as crystal, runs through it, and then roars and plunges down an almost impassable cañon, entering the San Joaquin River about sixty miles south of the city of Stockton. Patches and stretches of fertile meadow, covered with ferns and flowers and grasses in almost endless beauty and variety, open at intervals on both sides of the stream, their margins set with flowering-shrubs which, in early summer fill the air with perfume. Deciduous and evergreen trees — from the shade-giving oak to the stately pine — form picturesque groups over valley and river; in places presenting long vistas that seem like frames to many glorious pictures.

"The general course of the Yosemite is northeasterly and southwesterly, — a fortunate circumstance indeed, as it permits the delightfully invigorating northwest breeze from the Pacific to sweep pleasantly through it, and keep it exceedingly temperate on the hottest of days; and permits the sun to look into it from six o'clock in the morning until half past four in the afternoon, in summer, instead of only an hour or two, were it otherwise. In winter, however, the sun does not rise upon the hotels till half past one in the afternoon, and sets at half past three."

We drive at once to the Yosemite Hotel, — formerly Hutchings's,—and as we have previously telegraphed for saddle-horses, we mount directly (as our time in the valley is limited), and start with a guide for Snow's to see the Vernal and Nevada Falls. The trail, prepared by a man named Snow, — the pioneer of this spot, — winds precipitately up the mountain-side, and the ascent occupies about three hours, the party necessarily riding single-file. After enjoying a magnificent view, as we rise higher and higher, we come, about noon, into full sight of the Vernal Fall, four hundred feet in descent, the Indian name of which is " Pi-wa-ack," — Cataract of Diamonds. The guide restrains our expressions of delight by telling us to " wait till we see the Nevada Fall." So, pressing on, we soon emerge on to a little bridge crossing a rushing stream, and, looking up, we see directly opposite us the great Nevada Fall, seven hundred feet in descent, pouring itself over a smooth perpendicular rock, while clouds of spray rise continually upwards and float gracefully away. The Indian name of this magnificent waterfall is " Yo-wi-ye," — Meandering.

Near the foot of the falls is a little hotel, kept by Mr. Snow. Having dined here, and having thoroughly explored the neighborhood of the falls, we retrace our steps down the mountain with the aid of our horses, and reach the Yosemite Valley about five o'clock. The little mountain-ponies are remarkably sure-footed, and but for this the descent of these mountain trails would be attended with great danger; for the track runs, as I have said, along the very edge of a deep chasm, and in some places a stumble of your pony would hurl you far down on to the rocks below. Frequently, on arriving at a turn in the road, which was, for some little distance, perpendicular in descent, our horses would plant their feet firmly on the ground, and, like the mules of the Alps, slide down swiftly to the more level ground below; the high pommels of our Mexican saddles proving of decided advantage meanwhile.

We have arrived a day too late to witness the ceremonies attendant on the opening of a new road into the valley from Mariposa; but the ball of the evening before is repeated, and, to the destruction of our slumbers, the peculiar "music" of the band is continued unceasingly till morning.

July 24. — We breakfast at six o'clock, and at seven o'clock have mounted our ponies and are on our way to Glacier Point, — a very lofty peak from which a grand general view of the whole valley, with its surrounding mountains, can be obtained. Our road, as before, lies directly up the side of the precipice, and after ascending for about an hour, we come to a turn in the path, from which we can look across the valley to the beautiful Yosemite Falls, three in number, the first being sixteen hundred feet in descent, the second five hundred and thirty-four feet, and the third five hundred feet. Proceeding upwards again, we soon come to the "half-way spot," — a flat ledge of rocks, near which is Agassiz's Pillar. This is an upright mass of stone, about thirty feet high, standing on the very edge of the precipice. After resting for a few minutes, we continue our journey, and arrive, about eleven o'clock, at Glacier Point, where we dismount, leaving our horses tied to a tree.

Glacier Point, the Indian name of which is " Er-na-ting Low-oo-too," or Bearskin Mountain, is a peak three thousand one hundred feet above the valley, into which its side descends almost perpendicularly. The top is broad and flat, and from it the eye can review all the chief points of interest in the Yosemite; on this account a spot which should be visited especially by those whose time is limited. From here may be seen the Yosemite, Vernal, and Nevada Falls, looking like mere ribbons of water far below; here also one is in the immediate neighborhood of all the principal peaks, — Half Dome, five thousand three hundred feet high; Cloud's Rest, six thousand feet; North Dome, three thousand seven hundred and fifty feet; Mt. Starr King, five thousand feet; The Three Brothers, four thousand two hundred feet; El Capitan, three thousand three hundred feet; and many others.

Over the brow of the Point a flat ledge thrusts itself forward, and tourists with cool heads crawl out, and, lying flat, look far, far down to the valley below,—a feat which should not be attempted by every one.

Before leaving Glacier Point we have the pleasure of being introduced to General Upton and Major Sanger, U. S. A., who, with another officer whom they are to join in San Francisco, are sent out by our government on a tour of the world, to inspect the military forces of the various countries; and we are much pleased to learn that they will be our fellow-passengers across the Pacific. Leaving Glacier Point, we return to the hotel for an early dinner, and at four o'clock bid farewell to the Yosemite, and ascending a neighboring mountain, sleep once more on the summit at Crane's Flats.

July 25. — We make an early start, and, retracing our steps, arrive, after a long day's drive, at Priest's, where we are welcomed as cordially as before. On our way we pass some of the immense cones of the sugar-pine, several very fine specimens of which we carry along with us in the wagon. As we have taken the precaution to procure a good supply of ice in the Yosemite Valley, we do not suffer so much with the heat as before.

July 26. — As the day promises to be very hot, we start at 4 A. M., in order to reach Copperopolis — our halting-place for the night — before the sun has attained its full power. We have decided to stop at Copperopolis, as it contains a very comfortable hotel, and drive to Milton to-morrow, for there is only one train a day — at 10.30 A. M. — from Milton to Stockton and San Francisco. We reach Copperopolis at eleven o'clock, and drive at once to the quiet family hotel erected by the firm of Glidden and Williams of Boston, principally for their own accommodation when visiting their extensive copper-mines situated near by; but as the mines at present are not worked, the house, excellently kept, receives tourists coming from the Yosemite, who are so fortunate as to direct their steps thither instead of going to the regular hotel of the town.

On our arrival at Copperopolis we are surprised to hear that the stage-coach, which has just entered the town by a different road from ours, but one almost parallel to it and at no great distance off, was stopped near the Tuolumne River, about four o'clock this morning, by a masked robber, who appeared suddenly from behind some bushes near a turn of the road, and who, bringing a double-barrelled gun to bear on the occupants of the stage, demanded the express-box of Wells, Fargo, & Co., assuring those in the stage (as well as the occupants of a private team, similar to our own, which was immediately behind) that nothing further was desired. Besides the shot-gun, the robber was armed with a Sharpe rifle slung across his shoulders; but as there were eight revolvers in the stage-coach and six in the team behind, it seems almost incredible that somebody did not shoot the robber, since it is not likely that his gun covered everybody. It was urged, however, in excuse, that all were afraid that the robber, if shot, would discharge his gun in falling, and thus endanger the lives of several of the party, — an argument which I have been told by a military man is groundless, as the muscles of a man shot are suddenly and completely relaxed.

July 27. — We leave Copperopolis at seven o'clock, reach Milton at 9.15, and taking the train from there at 10.30, arrive at Stockton at noon, and, after waiting about an hour, join the regular express from the East, and continue our journey on the Central Pacific Railroad to San Francisco.

We roll swiftly along through broad fields of thick grain, by well-stocked orchards, and past prosperous farm-houses. The heat is intense. At five o'clock we reach Oakland, the actual terminus of the railroad, and, leaving the cars, embark on an immense ferry-boat which is to carry us to San Francisco. Here we find a great change in the temperature. A thin mist is about us, the air is cold, and overcoats are necessary. We have plunged, in an hour, from the heat of summer into the bluster of March. The peculiar costume of the West is now rarely seen. The dress of the ladies is tasteful and stylish; that of the men, strictly fashionable. A cosmopolitan air is over everything. After moving rapidly through the water for about twenty minutes, we see dimly through the mist a large city rising from the shore to the summit of a broad hill. In a moment more we have left the boat and are in the midst of a crowd of vociferating hackmen in the city of San Francisco. We arrive at the Occidental Hotel in time for dinner.

July 28. — The first house built in San Francisco — then, however, called Yerba Buena — was in 1835. The city became San Francisco in 1847, and now contains about 175,000 inhabitants, and enjoys a climate noted for uniformity and dryness, — the rain-fall being about half that of the Eastern States. Owing to the great fires which visited the city from 1849 – 1853, San Francisco is now largely built of brick, stone, or iron, particularly in the business portion. The city has many fine private residences, is amply supplied with schools, both public and private, and contains several theatres, and forty-six churches of various denominations, including several Chinese joss-houses.*

We go this morning to the Bank of California to obtain my letters, which I have ordered to be sent thither, and to present a letter of introduction to Mr. William C. Ralston, the president. Arrived at the commodious quarters of the bank, we hand our cards and the letter to Mr. Ralston, who immediately receives us with great politeness, and after talking with us for a short time, and urging us to make use of him in any way we desire, he complains of the press of business, and introduces us to Mr. Brown, the under chief. Mr. Brown extracts from a pigeon-hole a gratifying budget of letters for me (F——

---

* See Crofutt's Tourist.

expects his at Mr. C. Adolphe Low's), and proceeds to converse with us in regard to affairs in the East.

Standing in Mr. Ralston's private office and overlooking the multitude of clerks busily engaged with the affairs of the bank, one cannot but be impressed with the evident extent of the business, the diversity of its branches, and the power of the one master mind which regulates the whole.*

Having presented a letter of introduction to Mr. C. Adolphe Low (who assures us of his regret that his town-house is closed for the summer), we spend the rest of the day in walking quietly about the city. Montgomery Street, devoted to banks and bankers, contains many fine buildings. The same feverish haste which I noticed in Chicago animates the people here. Tall, keen-looking men rush frantically by, with an expression of anxiety on their faces. They elbow their way past each other as a matter of course, and give one the impression that with them the race for the almighty dollar is verily one against time, and the Devil take the hindmost.

At the upper end of Montgomery Street the houses rise to the top of a hill so steep that no carriages can ascend it. A flight of steps assists foot-passengers. From the summit a fine view of the city and harbor can be obtained. Many of the

---

* No one could have supposed, from merely observing the exterior of things, that a great crisis was at hand. Mr. Ralston himself looked perfectly calm and composed, and, except that he had not yet moved to his country place, no change had been made in his mode of life or his usual habits.

private dwellings are large and well built, while the first-class
hotels have few superiors even in New York City. The climate
especially surprises me. In the middle of summer I find here
the sharpness of fall.

July 29. — Soon after breakfast we engage a carriage and
set out for the Cliff House. This is a little hotel (somewhat
like Taft's at Point Shirley, near Boston), situated about six
miles west of the city, on the shore of the Pacific, near which
are to be seen (and heard) the famous sea-lions. Soon after
leaving the hotel we enter the city's well-kept Park, and pass
by several beautiful cemeteries, containing the monuments of
Senator Broderick, Starr King, Baker, and others. On the summit of Lone Mountain, near by, is a large cross, a well-known
landmark, which can be seen from far out at sea. Our road
presently climbs a hill, and beneath us we see, on our right, the
Golden Gate, "always open and inviting all nations to enter,"
but protected by a strong United States fort on the left-hand
side. Soon we reach the Cliff House; and even before we have
alighted we hear the peculiar roaring of the sea-lions, who are
continually jumping on and off a mass of rocks not far from the
hotel. These animals look somewhat like seals, but are much
larger, the biggest, called "General Grant," being estimated to
weigh three thousand pounds! Their cry is harsh and peculiar,
somewhat resembling the syllables "Yoi-hoi-Boyi," which is said
to mean (from the name of the champion), "Let us have peace."
Immense numbers of sea-fowl are perpetually hovering round

the rocks, apparently on perfectly good terms with their larger neighbors; while the broad Pacific, stretching far away, with the many different crafts passing in and out of the Golden Gate, forms a picture well worth coming to see.

On our return to the city we enter a horse-car and ride to Woodward Gardens, situated quite near the centre of the city. These gardens, which occupy about five acres of ground, contain specimens of almost every bird, beast, and fish under the sun. They are owned by R. B. Woodward, Esq., and "were laid out in 1860 for private use, but were thrown open to the public in the early days of the war, for the benefit of the Sanitary Fund, and in 1866 were opened permanently." The gardens are well worth a visit, the most interesting part to me being the trout aquarium, admirably arranged and most successfully administered. Rare plants, wonderful birds, and many varieties of animals occupy the visitor for a full hour in a hasty survey, while much more time could be profitably and enjoyably spent in careful investigation.

July 30. — As our steamer is to sail for Japan August 2, we occupy the day in making some final preparations for the voyage. In the evening we receive a call from Mr. Edward Simmons, a college friend and Eastern man, who is in business in the city.

July 31. — After a day passed quietly, at 10 P. M. we meet, by appointment, Colonel A——, a detective officer, who has been employed by the city for over twenty years, who has promised to take us through the Chinese Quarter, assuring us at the same time that we must expect the most disagreeable sights and the roughest surroundings. Leaving the main streets of the city, we arrive, before long, at the portion entirely inhabited by Chinese, and are at once in the midst of a chattering crowd of these foreigners, who are continually entering or leaving their various places of assembly along the way. Low, curious-looking buildings are on all sides, many hung with Chinese lanterns, or bearing large signs, which, with their odd figures and characters, give a strange air to everything about us. Our guide conducts us up the street and, pausing at the foot of a dark, villanous-looking flight of stairs, leads the ascent, we following close behind. At the top of the stairs we find a sort of hall, at the end of which are two large folding-doors, the entrance to the joss-house, or temple. The detective enters without ceremony, and shutting the doors after us, lights a candle at a small fire burning before a hideous idol directly opposite the entrance, and pauses a moment to let us look about the curious chamber. By the light of the candle we see we are in a large room hung with various kinds of gaudy ornaments, round the sides of which, in alcoves, are standing idols representing different Chinese deities, each one resting on a sort of throne, while a lamp burns dimly before all. The room is so long and wide that it is dark,

> "Save where the lamps that glimmered few and faint,
> Lighted a little space before some saint."

Opposite the entrance are the gods of Fire, Air, and Earth; near by sits the god of Commerce; while apart from the rest, shrouded in white garments, stands a melancholy looking figure, — the deity who disposes of the soul after death. Every good China-man, on the death of a relative or dear friend, feels obliged to make some present to this god, in order to secure good treatment for the soul of his departed brother; and we find some food, consisting of a thin wafer of bread, thrown down before the god, who evidently has not been hungry since its arrival.

After paying our respects — if I may use the word here — to the different silent divinities, we leave the joss-house, and retrace our steps through the dark alley which leads to the street. We see two men, of suspicious and repulsive appearance, standing in close conversation in the middle of the lane. The detective gazes at them earnestly, but the darkness is so thick about us that it is only by peering directly into their faces that he can satisfy himself as to their identity. One look is enough. He smiles grimly, says a word to them in a low tone; they pull their hats over their eyes and disappear in the darkness. "Who are those?" I inquire. "Two of the most dangerous men in San Francisco," he answers, "but I know them well, and can trace them like a dog." We go now to an opium-den situated in a street near by. Descending a flight of stairs, and going along a narrow passage leading under the street, we enter a small room lighted by several oil lamps and full of the peculiar smoke from the opium-pipes. The room is

lined with bunks arranged, berth-fashion, along the sides of the
walls; and upon these are lying, one over another, about a dozen
Chinamen, some smoking opium, while others, with their pipes
fallen beside them, are far away in the ecstatic dream-world,
free from the remembrance of care or toil. The faces of these
have a look of most perfect repose, as if every unpleasant
thought, recollection, or expectation has been forever annihi-
lated. Their features, however, are sunken: they resemble the
dead.

Our party takes a pull at one of the pipes, and soon after we
follow our conductor to a little hut, "where," says he, "I will
show you what amount of air is necessary to keep a Chinaman
alive." At the end of a foul alley we enter a little house
containing one room, with one window securely fastened and
entirely closed, the only entrance to the room being a swinging
door which shuts after each one who enters. We are almost
stifled by the horrible closeness of the atmosphere, which is not
to be wondered at, for, with the window thus always fastened,
the only fresh air that enters is brought in when some one
comes in or goes out by the swinging door; and around the
room, on their peculiar bunks, are lying eight men, besides a
sad object in the midst, — a man sick with the leprosy. Many
lamps and pipes are continually vitiating the air, and we are
all obliged to beat a hasty retreat in order to draw our breath!
We go next to the Chinese theatre, — a small building full of
plain wooden benches, with a little gallery overhead. The

scenery is of the very commonest character, the stage being adorned with cheap curtains, red joss-paper, and curious Chinese inscriptions. The orchestra sit at the back of the stage, facing the audience, and keep up the most incessant din of gongs, drums, and trumpets I have ever heard. The performance is largely made up of tumbling, of a very excellent and remarkable quality, interspersed with long processions of kings and queens, gods and goddesses, and the like. The players speak in a very high and disagreeable key. The "property-man" perambulates the stage continually, now picking up a mask which some actor has thrown down, now handing a false beard to another, with which to "disguise" himself. The audience do not seem to object to the absence of illusion. They sit silent for the most part; but when the orchestra succeed in making a peculiarly harsh sound, or a player an astonishingly hideous grimace, a ripple of shrill laughter runs through the assembly, and the next moment they are as grave and stolid as before. The play lasts from four o'clock of the afternoon till daybreak of the following morning.

We now visit a small house where we are initiated into the mysteries of the gambling game called "white-pigeon-paper." Every player as he enters receives a square piece of paper, upon which are printed various figures and characters. The banker, taking a piece similarly marked, puts a red stamp on twenty of these characters which he selects privately, the other players, of course, not being shown the different figures or squares which he has determined upon. When the banker has marked his slip, the other players' endeavor to select the same twenty squares which the banker has chosen, and so accurately do they calculate that they are required to find ten squares before receiving anything for their pains. If a Chinaman hits upon eleven of the squares that the banker has marked, he will receive from the bank the same sum that he staked upon the play; if he marks twelve squares correctly, he receives twice his original stake; and so on. If they do not mark at least ten squares correctly, their stake is forfeited. This game is played continually throughout the whole Chinese Quarter.

It is now long after midnight. Our guide conducts us to the broader streets of the city, away from the Chinese Quarter, and leaves us. We soon arrive at the Occidental Hotel, and go at once to bed.

August 1. — We pass the day in writing farewell letters. In the evening I dine with Colonel H. P. Curtis, Judge Advocate of the Department.

August 2. — The *Great Republic* is advertised to sail at noon, and an hour before that time F—— and I have come on board, and have stowed our trunks in our state-room, in readiness for our long voyage. As the hour for sailing approaches, the ship is crowded with friends of the passengers, who have come to say farewell; and the number keeps continually increasing, till the gong sounds, warning all who are not to sail to go ashore. Promptly at twelve o'clock Captain

Cobb takes his stand on the "bridge"; the ropes are cast off, the immense walking-beam starts into motion, and, amidst farewell shouts and waving handkerchiefs, the great steamer slowly backs out from the wharf, the paddle-wheels strike the water, and we move away from America. Our farewell gun is fired, a tug throws us its line, and we are soon opposite the United States fort near the city, where we lay to, and take on board three naval officers and one hundred seamen from a man-of-war anchored near by, whom we are to carry to China. Then the tug shrieks its farewell, we reply with shrill blasts of our whistle, our chief-engineer gives the signal to "unhook her," and we are fairly off for Japan. We pass out of the Golden Gate, and past the Cliff House, and soon a dense fog, rolling in from the sea, wreathes itself round every portion of the ship, and shuts the land from sight. We fall at once into the miserable "land-swell"; the ship pitches terribly; the lady passengers retire to their berths, while more than one gentleman hurries away from the dinner-table in silent communion with himself.

CHAPTER IV.

ACROSS THE PACIFIC TO JAPAN.

THE P. M. S. S. Co.'s *GREAT REPUBLIC.* — MY FELLOW-PASSENGERS. — THE LONG SEA-VOYAGE. — ARRIVAL AT YOKOHAMA.

August 3. — A cloudless sky, a bright sun, and a smooth ocean stretching away on every side, — all this puts the ship's company in a far different humor to-day. The ladies, indeed, still remain in their state-rooms, but all the gentlemen are in good spirits, and everybody begins to make each other's acquaintance. The number of passengers is between thirty and forty, made up of several nationalities: four young Japanese, who have just graduated at colleges in the United States, returning to their native country; three United States Army officers, — Generals Upton and Forsythe, and Major J. P. Sanger, sent out by our government, as I have said before, to inspect the infantry, cavalry, and artillery in the East; two Italian silk-merchants; five gentlemen (besides ourselves), making a tour of the world; the new American consul for Canton, going thither with his wife and child; several American gentlemen travelling on business; three United States naval officers, together with several young men intending to settle in Japan. Besides the one hundred sailors whom we took aboard off San Francisco, there are three hundred Chinese in the steerage; and these, together with the regular sailors, officers, and cabin-servants, make up a varied company for the long voyage. We have on board also a very fine pair of horses and a gorgeous carriage intended for the Mikado of Japan.

The *Great Republic* is a side-wheel steamer of four thousand three hundred and twenty-five tons, with capacity for one hundred and fifty cabin passengers, and twelve hundred in the steerage. On board all the boats of the P. M. S. S. Co. it is the custom to carry live cattle and poultry, which are killed when needed; and the consequence is that the most varied chorus comes from "between-decks" at all hours of the day and night, — the lowing of cows mingling with the bleating of sheep, the quacking of ducks, and the cackling of hens. These steamers are undoubtedly the finest line of ocean passenger-vessels in the world.* The state-rooms are large and comfortable; the dining-cabin high, wide, and airy; while the long deck affords a capital promenade, or, covered over with a huge awning, is a delightful place to read or write. Everything possible is done for the convenience and comfort of patrons. The table is, on the whole, excellent; the meats, for the reason stated above, being of remarkable flavor and quality. Every *attaché* of the ship, from lowest to highest, exerts himself to be accommodating and polite.

---

* My subsequent travel confirms this.

Captain Cobb (of Cambridgeport, Massachusetts) is a man of decided polish, a thorough seaman, and most agreeable talker. The first officer, though rather grave and taciturn, will meet you half-way in conversation, and will always prove interesting. The chief engineer won his place by a very brave act performed a short time ago, when he was in an inferior position. Our purser, belonging to a well-known New York family, dresses exquisitely, and always looks as if he was just stepping out for a promenade on Fifth Avenue. The steward, a comfortable sort of personage, whom nothing disturbs, regulates the movements of the corps of Chinese waiters by a tap of a bell, and comes to our table from time to time to inquire if we are well served. In short, the various elements which are around us, coalescing as they do, yet being often so utterly dissimilar, afford a wide field for quiet observation and amusement.

The boats of the P. M. S. S. Co. are not allowed, even if they have the most favorable passage imaginable, to enter the harbor of Yokohama before a certain number of days after leaving San Francisco. And if, as I have said, owing perhaps to very favorable winds and a smooth sea, a captain arrives off Japan before twenty-two days have passed since his departure from America, or reaches San Francisco on a return voyage before the specified time, he is not allowed to bring his ship into harbor, but must coast up and down till the particular day has come; and forty-five tons of coal is

the limit for a day's consumption. The reasons for the above,
as given by Baron Hübner in his " Ramble Round the World,"
are as follows : —

"A captain who should arrive before his time, even if it
were only by a few hours, would be dismissed the service. I
hear every one around me blaming these restrictions. I own
I think them wise and prudent. . . . . The consumption of
coal increases with the increase of speed, and that in a very
large proportion : without counting the expense, therefore, the
boats would have to be overloaded at starting. If the time
of the passage had not been fixed, the captains of the four
boats* would rival one another in speed, to the detriment of
the vessel and the machinery. . . . . Besides this, the merchants of Yokohama and Hong Kong depend on receiving
and expediting their correspondence on a certain day, and
that is only possible by giving such a margin to the boats as
shall make allowance for the insuperable delays which now
and then must arise from bad weather or contrary winds. On
their side the company is anxious that the steamers coming
from San Francisco and Hong Kong should not meet at Yokohama, because they would then have to be laden and un-
laden at the same time, and so they would need to double
the requisite staff of officials and coolies. Now this coinci-
dence would often happen if the Californian boat were less
than two-and-twenty days on the passage. Add to this that

* The number has since been increased.

the government of Washington, which has a right to interfere, as it pays the subvention, hearing that the boats might shorten the run by two days, would perhaps be tempted to force the company to do so, and thus reduce the time originally allowed by the contract."

For these reasons we do not expect to make long "runs," and consider that we have done fairly well since our start, having accomplished two hundred and twenty-five miles.

August 4. — The clear weather continues, but a slight head-wind opposes us. The lady passengers have recovered and are on deck to-day. At 4 P. M. the captain gave a false fire-alarm to drill the crew. The bells tolled, the whistle blew, and in a very short time each man was in his place with a bucket in his hand, the fire-extinguisher and hose were in readiness, and the officers appeared, prepared to command. The drill was very satisfactory, and went far to allay the apprehensions of the timid in regard to fire.

August 6. — The routine of our life is as follows: breakfast comes at nine o'clock, lunch at one, and dinner at six. The passengers pass the day in reading or writing, conversing with each other, walking the deck, or playing "ship's quoits." In the evening the consul's wife takes her place at the piano in the little deck-parlor, and plays accompaniments for lit-tle ballads which her daughter sings charmingly. This young lady, about twelve years old, is the life of the ship, and is a great favorite with everybody. The military and naval

officers are most interesting companions, and are great ac-
quisitions to our circle. General Upton, the author of our
"Tactics," is one of the most widely cultured men in our
army. He was at one time an instructor at the United
States Military Academy at West Point. General Forsythe
is one of the handsomest officers I ever saw; a little above
the ordinary height, with light hair and mustache, and piercing eyes which seem to read your very thoughts. Attired
in undress military cap and jacket, he may be seen at almost any hour pacing the deck in deep thought, as if planning an attack. Reticent as all truly brave men are about
their own exploits, he has told me, from time to time, sufficient to prove that he has already seen an unusual amount
of severe service. He is on General Sheridan's staff, and
was by his side, "twenty miles away," when the news was
brought of the outbreak at Winchester. He is experienced in
Indian warfare, and has been frequently wounded. Major
Sanger has been for the past two years Military Instructor at
Bowdoin College, and possesses remarkable firmness and decision of character. When, a year or so ago, the students of
Bowdoin attempted to throw off the burden — as it seemed
to them — of military instruction, and broke out into open
rebellion, Major Sanger, by taking a firm stand from the
very first, not only caused the troubles to cease, but brought
military training into such good favor, that many of the
students formed an extra "Elective." The naval officers,

too, are very agreeable companions, and to one of them, lately an instructor at Annapolis, I owe many useful hours of explanations in regard to the various problems of navigation that I see daily around me.

August 8. — To-day is Sunday, and at half past ten the surgeon takes his stand in the dining-cabin behind an extemporized reading-desk, — a large cushion covered with the American flag, — and reads the Episcopal service, the officers, passengers, and several seamen forming a congregation. In the psalm for the day are these words, which impress us, so far away from land, with their full signification: "The sea is His and He made it, and His hands prepared the dry land."

The moonlight nights, at present, are delightfully picturesque. The full moon shines clearly over the waters. Our steamer glides smoothly along through the glittering belt, leaving behind a long dark trail of smoke, while multitudes of stars of unusual brilliancy shine out from every part of the heavens above us.

August 11. — The Japanese are very bright, pleasant men. One especially interests me. He has just graduated from Princeton College, and has evidently used his time well. He is greatly impressed with the advanced state of our country, and hopes that many of our institutions will be adopted in Japan. He has been away from home for six years, — and at such a distance! He longs to arrive, and is rejoiced as each day closes. He explains to me the different theological beliefs in

Japan, and gives the preference to the abstract Shintoism, — the religion of the Mikado.

August 14. — The passengers are all roused at a very early hour this morning by perceiving that our steamer has come to a stand-still. Hastening on deck, we see a large bark lying to near by, flying the American flag and exhibiting a signal of distress. A boat is on its way to us, and when it arrives we see it contains two emaciated men, who tell us that the bark is the "J. W. Seaver" of San Francisco, bound thither from the Fiji Islands, from which place they sailed sixty days ago. They have lost their reckoning for days, and, worse than all, are nearly out of food, having only a small supply of fruit on board. We send them an ample stock of provisions, give them their position on the chart, and, having returned to their vessel, the bark dips her flag, and with every stitch of canvas set to catch the favorable wind, bears away to America, and soon has vanished beneath the horizon. Sailing-vessels are rarely encountered by the steamers, as they generally go above or below the steamer-track to catch the trade-winds.

August 15. — Service was held to-day in the cabin, some of the passengers forming a choir. By the captain's reckoning, we are 2,426 miles from San Francisco. We saw to-day several schools of porpoises and also multitudes of little delicate flying-fish.

August 16. — While sitting on deck this morning waiting for the breakfast-gong to sound, we saw several whales blowing quite near the ship, — a sight which greatly excited one of the ship's officers who had been on whaling voyages for many years.

August 18. — Although yesterday was Monday, to-day is Wednesday, and we have "lost" a day, for none of us have had a seventeenth day of August. We passed last night the 180° W. longitude, and hence the change; but few of the passengers (except the naval officers) seem to understand the theoretical reason, and the latter vainly endeavor to make it clear to us. This will make the week pass very rapidly.

August 19. — Every morning at eleven o'clock the captain, accompanied by the ship's surgeon and steward, makes an inspection of the whole ship, and to-day several of us go with them, by invitation. It is astonishing to find how every inch of room is utilized on board such a steamer as ours; and it is very gratifying, moreover, to see how clean every part of the ship is kept. We pass first through the steerage, where three hundred Chinamen are stowed. Plenty of fresh air is admitted through large open ports; the men are sitting round in groups, chattering Chinese, some gambling at dominos, while all appear comfortable and contented. One portion of the steerage is given up to the Chinese for an opium-smoking room. In another part they have prepared a joss-house. Thus the long voyage passes pleasantly for them. Near by, but apart from the Chinese, are the quarters of the one hundred United States sailors. The thorough ship-shape appearance of each one's berth and kit clearly indicates the American seaman.

We then take a look at the Mikado's horses, and cast a critical eye over several sheep and oxen which are soon to be sacri-
ficed for us; and after a short visit to the storeroom and kitchen,
we emerge once more on to the main deck. By the reckoning
to-day we are 3,114 miles from San Francisco.

August 20. — To-day is the hottest of any since we left
America. The sea is as smooth and glassy as a land-locked
lake, the sun beats down out of a cloudless sky, and all parts
of the ship are equally uncomfortable. After dinner, however,
it is cooler, and standing on deck, about nine o'clock, we watch
the full moon rise rapidly out of the water. The clear sky
dotted with the brilliant stars for which this region is noted,
the smooth ocean stretching far away on every side, and the
great yellow orb apparently emerging from some unknown spot
beneath the sea, and casting as it mounts higher and higher a
long trail of glittering beams in which the waters seem to dance
and leap, — all this forms a scene before which we linger long
in silent admiration.

August 21. — The great amusement of the passengers is
pitching quoits on the main deck. Besides this, the monotony
of the voyage is relieved by "betting on the ship's run," — a
bottle of claret or champagne being the prize each day of the
one who has estimated most exactly the number of miles accomplished by the ship during the last twenty-four hours. It
would be almost impossible to declare the number of bottles
that will be distributed on our arrival at Yokohama, some

believing that we shall reach that port Thursday night, while others fix Friday morning.

August 25. — Our run to-day was 256 miles, and our total distance from San Francisco is 4,496 miles. We expect to reach Yokohama to-morrow evening, probably in time to disembark. In company with the chief-engineer I visited to-day the engine-room and furnaces, and inspected all the machinery of the ship. The furnace-room is seventeen feet below the surface of the water, and contains twenty-four furnaces, into whose roaring mouths half-naked Chinamen are continually shovelling coal. The heat is tremendous, and a short visit is amply sufficient. These Chinese coal-heavers work four hours and then rest eight, the arduous labor performed in the intense heat making it necessary for them to rest at regular intervals. A balcony surrounds the furnace-room, and standing on it, and looking down upon the dark chamber lighted only by the glare of the fires, before which dusky forms like very fiends are running about, the spectator may well believe that he has strayed into the infernal regions and is witnessing the antics of some of its devil-inhabitants.

August 26. — At eleven o'clock to-day the welcome cry of "Land!" is heard throughout the ship, and it is impossible to describe our delight when, far ahead, "cloud-like, we saw the shore" of Japan, and realized fully that we were rapidly approaching the close of our long voyage. As we continue to advance, the shore grows more and more distinct, and by four o'clock we are opposite Cape King. The water surrounding us is absolutely at rest, and the great paddle-wheels of our steamer toss up high waves, which disappear as soon as we have passed by. The beautiful green hills sloping down to the sea are wonderfully refreshing to the eye so long accustomed to an unchanging view of sky and water. The passengers are all on deck, looking eagerly towards land, while the bows are crowded with a chattering multitude of Chinese, delighted at beholding a well-known country. We pass strange-looking crafts with odd sails, whose scantily clad occupants gaze at us curiously. We turn our marine-glasses upon them, and try to make ourselves realize that we are looking upon the inhabitants of the other side of the world from where we live. Dinner is served at six, as usual; but everybody leaves the table continually, unwilling to lose sight of the approach to Yokohama. On our left we see a lighthouse bearing a curious flag,—a red globe on a white ground, the flag of Japan. In the distance a conical mountain lifts its head above the clouds, while the beams of the setting sun cast a soft light over its base. It is sacred Fusiyama, the holy mount of Japan, which rises fourteen thousand feet above the sea. Now, far ahead, we can plainly distinguish the many different vessels lying off Yokohama, and, erelong, we are slowly picking our way through the various craft, our captain standing with the pilot in the bow, calling out every little while to the quartermaster at the wheel, now, " Port her handsomely!" now, "Starboard!" now, suddenly, "Steady!" each order being promptly repeated by the steersman, who follows it at the word. We pass the light-ship, fire our arrival-gun, make fast to our moorings at a little distance from the city, and come to a stand-still,—our voyage across the Pacific safely accomplished.

Immediately our ship is surrounded by multitudes of native boats,—*sampans*,—a long narrow sort of canoe, propelled by half-naked Japanese, with long oars, with which they scull the crafts to and fro with wonderful skill and precision. We seat ourselves in one of these *sampans*, and our boatmen, keeping time to a peculiar cry, row us quickly ashore. We are landed at a flight of stone steps which reach into the water. Ascending the steps, we find at the top a score of curious two-wheeled carriages, each drawn by a Japanese, who takes the place of a horse. These little vehicles are called in Japanese *jinrikishas*,—man-power-carriage,—and are very comfortable and convenient. Large numbers of them are to be found in waiting in all the principal streets of Yokohama, and, owing to the ingenious construction of the body of the carriage, the natives are enabled to propel them at a full run for a long distance and with little fatigue. They are used constantly by business men and others, and are now as indispensable in Japan as cabs in London. Indeed, the number of horse-vehicles in Yokohama is very small, and on this account there is very little clatter or noise in the city. All merchandise is transported on poles, which are carried by coolies on their shoulders. At night every *jinrikisha* is provided with a long Japanese lantern, bearing its number, and the many different lights darting up and down a thoroughfare form an animated scene.

There are three good hotels in Yokohama, — the Grand, the International, and the Hotel du Louvre. We have been strongly recommended to try the latter, and, though most Americans select one of the two former, we decide to accept the advice. The proprietor of the Hotel du Louvre calls *jinrikishas* for us, on our arrival, and we accompany him to the hotel. It looks very neat and comfortable. Having left our hand-bags, we re-enter the *jinrikishas* and drive at a rattling pace round the city. The curious Japanese houses, hung with gayly painted lanterns; the cool-looking rooms within, strewn with mats, on which are sitting different families drinking tea or smoking; the strange sound of the language spoken about us; and the long lines of Japanese carrying burdens slung on poles over their shoulders, — all these things interest us deeply, and make us realize that we are on "a strange and distant shore."

CHAPTER V.

FROM YOKOHAMA TO YEDO.

August 27. — We are awakened this morning by a confused sound in the street below, and on going to the window we see it is caused by successive gangs of coolies carrying burdens slung on poles, who walk in perfect step to the sound of a peculiar chorus. The heat is intense. The sky is without a cloud. After breakfast we go down to the " Bund," — a wide road and embankment built along the sea-shore, — and descending the stone steps where we landed yesterday, we call a *sampan* and order the boatmen to take us to the *Great Republic* as we wish to carry our trunks to the hotel. Our baggage being placed on the *sampan*, we visit the custom-house, situated on the " Bund," near the point from which we started. The officials are very polite, and having merely raised the lids, pass everything, and we engage several coolies to carry our possessions to the hotel. We now walk out through the city, to present various letters of introduction. Yokohama was founded by the first English merchants who arrived, after the signing of the treaties, to engage in trade in the Empire of the Rising Sun, which, until then, had been entirely closed to them. Whilst the English Minister, Sir Rutherford Alcock, was carrying on negotiations with the Shogun about the territory to be given to Europeans on which to dwell, the merchants chose, of their own accord, a spot near a small fishing village called Yokohama, or "Across the Sea-Shore." This site, indeed, was very accessible to ships, but it subjected the Europeans to the danger of absolute imprisonment by the Japanese. Sir Rutherford Alcock was well aware of this, but, in spite of his advice, the English merchants unanimously decided on the location. Sir Rutherford yielded to the wishes of his countrymen, and the new town sprung up. It was destroyed by fire, however, in 1866. No trace of the disaster now remains. The town is built in the form of a parallelogram. Three large streets run across it, and many little passages and alleys connect them. Along the sea-shore is the "Bund," a row of fine houses fronting a hard, broad roadway. This is the favorite promenade of the foreign population. The native quarter lies to the east. The palace of the Japanese governor is situated therein. Curio Street, a continuation of Main Street, contains the chief stores. Here may be found silk goods, lacquer-work, fine porcelain and bronze articles, and old armor. A long bridge, carefully guarded by native troops, leads to the interior. This road soon joins the Tokaido, the great highway from Tokio to Kioto. The houses of the foreign population are built, for the most part, along the "Bund." The foreign legations were formerly located in Yokohama, but they have been lately transferred to Yedo. To the right of the town is a high bluff, on the summit of which are many tea-houses belonging to foreigners and natives. The harbor is well adapted for rowing and sailing, and a foreign boat-club holds annual regattas. At night Yokohama is guarded by bands of native police, who patrol the streets, carrying lanterns and clubs, and uttering from hour to hour a shrill cry, which indicates to the inhabitants that "all is well." The streets of the city are clean, but very little attention is paid to keeping them in repair. Yokohama contains a population of about forty thousand, of which two thousand are foreigners, the English and Americans forming a large majority.

Having presented several letters of introduction, we are received and welcomed most kindly, and made members of the "Club" for the time that we remain. We are invited by Mr. Chandler P. Hall (of Walsh, Hall, & Co.) to accompany him in the evening to the theatre, and we engage him to dine with us previously at the hotel. F—— and I have been joined by one of our fellow-passengers on the *Great Republic*, Mr. E. U—— of New York City, who has planned a tour of the world very similar to ours.

Calling *jinrikishas*, we enter the native quarter of the city. It is a pleasure to look about us. The houses, the inhabitants, the odd costumes, the peculiar street-cries,—all arrest our attention.

Multitudes of people are passing up and down the streets.
There, a gang of coolies are carrying a heavy burden, chanting their strange song as they walk. Others are dragging
hand-carts full of vegetables; while successive groups of men,
women, and children form, to our unaccustomed eyes, kaleido-
scopic pictures which keep us continually interested.

The men dress in long flowing robes which nearly touch
the ground. The coolies, however, and the *jinrikisha*-men
wear only a white cloth around the waist. All have their
heads shaved, except a curious twist of hair which is trained
along the top of the cranium. They seem very good-natured,
and are continually laughing and talking with each other.
Frequently, when a foreigner appears on the street, a crowd
of *jinrikiska*-men scamper towards him, each eager to be employed; and the one who arrives first, having seen the stranger
safely seated in his carriage, looks round upon his disappointed
mates with a most comical expression of triumph; while one
of the unfortunates will make some comforting remark, at
which they will all laugh, and then they separate in search
of another foreigner or wealthy Japanese, before whom the
same performance is repeated.

The costume of the women is quite picturesque. The garments of the rich are elaborately embroidered, while even the
peasants seem to take pains in regard to the general arrangement of their toilets. Their hair, very black and very thick,
is braided into coils and kept in position by one or two long

tortoise-shell or metallic pins; and this is an operation so important and so tedious, that it is only done once in two weeks, — the women always using at night a peculiar pillow which is placed under the back of the neck and which does not disturb the *coiffure*. Their feet are bare, but they clatter along in clogs which are kept in position by a thong passed around the great toe. The married women cannot be called beautiful, for all have their teeth stained black, in accordance with a custom started by a wife of a former Mikado, who, being very beautiful, blackened her teeth as a sign of fidelity to her husband, and commanded all women throughout the Empire for successive years to do the same on their marriage-day. The young girls, however, are exceedingly pleasing in appearance and manners. Their complexions, though dark, are not yellowish like the Chinese. Their eyes are very large and expressive, and though almond-shaped, not disagreeably so.

After dinner, in company with Mr. Hall, we take *jinrikishas* and proceed to the native theatre. Following the invariable custom, our friend halts us at a tea-house directly opposite the theatre, and having addressed the proprietor in Japanese (for Mr. Hall speaks the language fluently), a servant of the tea-house leads us at once across the street and into the theatre, we not paying at the door, however, but simply mentioning the tea-house at which we stopped. The Japanese leads us up a flight of stairs to the balcony, which is divided into boxes, with low partitions between each one, every box

containing some straw matting on which to sit. As soon as we are seated, the Japanese servant leaves us, but returns immediately, bearing an immense gayly painted paper lantern with a sentence in Japanese on the front, declaring (as our friend tells us) what tea-house we are patronizing. Behind him comes another native with a teapot and exquisite little cups, and a *he-batchi,* — a sort of charcoal brazier from which the Japanese light their pipes. The servants hang the great lantern in front of our box (upon which the whole audience turns and stares fixedly for several minutes), pour out the tea, make us low ceremonious bows, and leave us to witness the play. The theatre is small, but the curtains and scenery, together with gorgeous flags and hangings surrounding the stage, give a bright and festive appearance to the whole interior. The majority of the audience are seated on plain wooden benches; a few Japanese ladies in an opposite box, lazily fanning themselves with immense fans, being the only other occupants of our part of the house. In front of them, like-wise, hangs a large lantern, which bears the sign of a rival tea-house to ours. The play itself, though rather uninteresting to us, is followed with the closest attention by the audience, and the efforts of the actors are rewarded at frequent intervals by a sharp "Hé!" and sometimes by clapping of hands. Be-tween the acts vendors of fruit, confectionery, cigars, tea, and *saki* (native wine) offer their wares, shouting out in loud tones as they walk about with great skill through the assembly on narrow boards raised a few feet above the backs of each score of seats. The orchestra sit on the stage; and although the cymbals and gongs are heard continually, still the music is not so deafening or disagreeable as in the Chinese theatre in San Francisco. Here too, however, much is left to the imagination; a wooden screen, for instance, doing duty as the wall of a house.

After witnessing two acts of the play, and being assured by Mr. Hall that there is no immediate prospect of its drawing to a close, we leave the theatre and cross the street to the tea-house where we first stopped. Here, having partaken of tea served in small cups by pretty Japanese girls, the master of the house presents his account, written in strange characters on the thinnest paper; and having paid the bill (which, including the theatre, tea, and attendance, is astonishingly small) and received the stamped receipt (which the Japanese are very particular to render), we are rewarded with hearty " Ar-ri-ga-tos " (thank you) from father, mother, and daughters, — the whole family falling on their knees and showing their gratitude by humble prostrations. Entering our *jinrikishas*, we return to the hotel.

August 28. — We spend the morning in Curio Street, and are delighted with the multitude of beautiful and useful things that are to be found everywhere. One of the first places a foreigner should visit is Shobey's silk-store, where silk articles of all sorts can be obtained at prices which seem incredible. Magnificent bed-spreads, with a monogram exquisitely embroidered on one side; elegant dressing-gowns and smoking-jackets of heavy quilted silk; handkerchief-cases, monogram pincushions, scarfs, embroidered handkerchiefs, sofa-pillows, screens, — all these are to be found, of the finest quality and the best workmanship. Near by one can find the largest stock of fans he probably ever saw, the choicest lacquer-work and bronze articles; while the antiquarian will be in paradise looking through collections of old armor, ancient Daimios' swords, and grotesque idols.

At 4 P. M. we meet again, by appointment, Mr. C. P. Hall, who has most kindly offered to accompany us on a trip to Inoshima and Kamakura, which includes a visit to the great idol of Daibutsu, or Buddha. The foreign treaties have by no means opened Japan. Europeans are simply allowed to reside and trade in the "treaty ports," and to travel from them inland for a short distance. The "treaty ports" are the following towns, namely, Yokohama, Hiogo (Kobe), Nagasaki, Niigata, Hakodaté, Yedo, and Osaka. In the vicinity of each "treaty port" are posts bearing signs marked in English and Japanese characters, "Frontiers of the treaty." Foreign officials, however, can obtain permission to travel in the interior, upon formal application to the Japanese government. At present foreigners can travel from any of the "treaty ports" fifteen miles inland; but even now, if a stranger attempts to penetrate farther, he will be promptly stopped, and, unless an official, probably put under arrest. All the places that we intend to visit are entirely within limits, although Kamakura marks the limit of the territory open to foreigners in that direction.

Our friend has sent his servant ahead, with two coolies, to carry a variety of food to Inoshima (where we intend to pass the night), as the native tea-houses afford little but tea, rice, and *saki*. Three *bettos* run ahead of us to take care of our horses when we stop by the way. These *bettos* are native hostlers, whom everybody employs, who run along near their master and hold his horse when he alights, take care of it over night, saddle it in the morning, and stand ready for another long day's run wherever they may be commanded to go. They are very fleet of foot, being able to keep up for many hours with a horse, and altogether are a most useful and necessary servant in Japan. The distance from Yokohama to Inoshima is about fifteen miles. The first part of our way lies along the Tokaido, — the great highway across Japan from Tokio to Kioto. The road is wide, shaded by trees, which form in many places a complete arch, while on each side are native houses with their heavy roofs of thatch. As we ride along we find the people are celebrating the day as a festival. The houses are hung with flags and lanterns, which latter, as evening draws on, are lighted, forming a brilliant sight. Near one cottage we see a group dressed in long white garments, chanting a prayer to the day's god; while every now and then one of them strikes a deep-sounding gong, which adds its reverberations to the measured voices of the worshippers. The inhabitants call out to us from all sides a cheery "Oh-hiyo" (How do you do), while small naked urchins show a "touch of nature" by shouting after us, "Onata oh-hiyo tempo shinjo" (Hallo! give us a cent), exactly as the street-boys of our own cities favor us. About dark we turn off from the Tokaido, and, taking a road to the left, soon reach Katasi, where we leave our horses in charge of our *bettos*, and strike across the sandy bar that joins Ino-shima with the mainland. The tide is nearly high, and we are obliged to walk in the heavy sand. After trudging along for about fifteen minutes, we arrive at the foot of the hill on which the town is built, and plunge suddenly into the chief street of the place. We find ourselves at once in the midst of a most varied crowd. The markets are all open. Many of the villagers are buying meat, fish, or rice. Little knots are standing here and there in earnest conversation, while grave Bonzes with shaved heads walk slowly past, accompa-nied by some of the numerous pilgrims who are always to be found in this holy isle. We go at once to the chief inn. The best rooms are already occupied by a party of English from Yokohama; but our friend, who is very well known in this vicinity, persuades the proprietor to give us one of his own apartments: to which, after a little debate, he agrees. We pass through a common room on the first floor, devoted principally to cooking, and ascending a flight of stairs reach a balcony extending round the inner walls of the house. Leading off from this are several rooms occupied by the proprietor's family, while in an adjoining portion of the inn are the apartments we should have obtained, now held, as I have said, by others. We are given, however, the best of the native quarters, being a large room spread with matting, with paper window-slides, and several inscriptions in Japanese around the walls. These paper window-slides are shut together at night, or in case of rain, while in ordinary weather they are shoved back, thus leaving the entire casement open for air.

After a cold and refreshing shower-bath in the native bathroom (a very primitive affair), we turn our attention to the food that our friend's servant and the coolies have brought from Yokohama; and after doing it ample justice, we soon after call for beds (thick blankets placed directly on the straw matting), and endeavor to get what sleep we can, our rest being continually interrupted by the peculiar dozing sounds from the Japanese in the adjoining room, and by multitudes of fleas, so common in the habitations of the lower orders throughout the Empire.

August 29. — The Japanese in the next room rise at daybreak, and soon after sunrise we follow their example, and make our way to the beach, where we enjoy a delightful bath in the sea, bright with the beams of the sun, while Fusiyama looms grandly up in the distance. After breakfast we proceed to visit the different temples and shrines that are found in various parts of the island. Inoshima is the most sacred spot in Japan. Every day is a *fête*. The houses are always gayly decorated with flags or religious sentences painted on cloth, while many banners are hung across the streets in honor of the gods. Ascending a long flight of stone steps, we come to an old temple filled with many curious and cherished articles, whose histories a pale priest relates at length. Here is a suit of armor, once worn by an old Daimio who performed prodigies of valor. Here is an immense sword which was carried by an ancient hero, and which slaughtered multitudes of the enemy. We are obliged to interrupt the old Bonze, for otherwise he will continue his romances forever. Passing on and ascending more steps, we come to another temple larger than the first, through which we are conducted in like manner by the resident priest. We examine thus a score of shrines and temples (none of which, however, are of special architectural beauty), and finally we descend a precipitous hill and enter a long cave, passing over several huge blocks of stone which are nearly covered with water. At the entrance to the grotto a small boy with lamps meets us, and shows us all the wonders of his domain. When we emerge from the cave we find a heavy rain is falling, so we take refuge in a cool tea-house at the brow of the hill overlooking the sea, and drink tea from minute cups while our friend con-

verses with the people. Soon a woman from our inn comes
clinking along in her wooden shoes, bringing an ample supply
of native umbrellas, which the people of the inn, believing
that we are exposed to the rain, have kindly sent to us. We
return to the inn, and, having paid the bill, depart with the
usual excessive thanks from our hosts. We recross the sand-
bar (for Inoshima is strictly only an island at high tide), and,
having sent on the coolies in advance with the food, remount
our horses and start off at a brisk canter for Kamakura, intending to visit the great idol of Daibutsu on the way.

We have not gone far, however, when the rain, which has
ceased for a while, once more comes down, and after waiting
under a shed in vain for it to stop, we decide to press on. After
riding for about an hour, we dismount at the foot of a flight
of wide stone steps, and, leaving our horses in charge of the
bettos, ascend the steps, and, passing under a huge stone gateway, stop involuntarily; for there before us, its face in deep
calm repose, is the bronze idol of Daibutsu, Great Buddha,
— the realization, in countenance, of entire rest and complete annihilation of care! This remarkable image is 44 feet
in height, 87 feet in circumference of base, $8\frac{1}{2}$ in length of face,
$3\frac{1}{2}$ in length of eyes, 6 in length of ears, 3 in width of mouth,
$3\frac{1}{2}$ in circumference of the thumb, and 34 in diameter of the
knee. It was erected, hundreds of years ago, with the desire
of displaying to the worshippers of the god a picture of that
perfect, blissful peace of the world to come for which all should

strive by a strict observance of the rules of the sect, and which is only to be obtained by a long and faithful probation in the body. This ideal has surely been realized in the bronze, and it seems to me it would be difficult to find another face expressing such absolute repose. The drooping lids, the serene mouth, and the calm joy in the expression of the whole, — as of one who has striven for a longed-for object for a lifetime, and at the last has obtained the result to which he has consecrated his whole being, — all this strikes the beholder, and keeps him long in silent admiration.

After talking for a few minutes with the priest who lives near by, we pass through a doorway at the base of the idol, and ascend a flight of steps leading up to the interior of the head. A little shrine has been erected here. Having descended to the ground, we remount our horses and continue our journey to Kamakura. As we are leaving the courtyard I turn to take a last look at Daibutsu. The expression of the face seems changed! The countenance is still, indeed, clothed with peace, but the mouth now has a scornful curl, indicating, as it were, that those who can reach the blissful state are very, very few.

After a sharp gallop in a pouring rain (passing over the bridge where the two English officers, Major Baldwin and Lieutenant Bird, were murdered, in 1862), we reach the chief tea-house at Kamakura at four o'clock, and, having changed our wet clothes, make a capital dinner of the food which has arrived before us in charge of our servants. Towards evening a young Japanese merchant who is acquainted with Mr. Hall comes to our apartment to pay his respects. He is very well educated and exceedingly polite, and our friend converses with him for half an hour. He accepts one of our cigars, and urges us to taste his *saki*. Finally he rises, bends his head low in a courteous salute with his arms extended gracefully, and, having said farewell, takes his departure. Soon after this we call for beds, which are brought, together with a large paper night-lantern always used in Japan, and with our heads on native pillows, — little blocks of wood on which is a small piece of cloth stuffed with straw, — we get what sleep we can, with multitudes of fleas holding high carnival over our arrival.

August 30. — We rise early, and after breakfast walk out through the town to visit the great temple. Kamakura is a city of the past. A long and wide stone avenue leads up to the massive steps in front of the temple. This structure is consecrated to Shintoism, — the religion now professed by the Mikado and his counsellors. In former times several Buddhist temples stood in the vicinity, but they have all been pulled down by express command. Kamakura was formerly the residence of the Shoguns. A long and wide stone avenue, and the great temple of Hachiman, founded by the Shogun Yoritomo towards the end of the twelfth century, are the only indications of the importance of the old city, once the second capital of the Empire. Many old temples, as I have said, have been destroyed; multitudes of houses and several palaces have been swept away; and tall trees and thick foliage are growing on the sites of wide streets once thronged with a busy crowd of courtiers, priests, officers, soldiers, and peasants. The perpetual silence of the present contrasts with the stir and bustle of the past.

The Mikado and his court profess Shintoism. This is an abstract faith which takes the mirror* as its symbol, regarding it as an emblem of purity. Shintoists believe in one supreme God, do not worship idols, or look upon them as representations of supernatural deities. The Mikado, being an advocate of progression, wishes to throw aside old superstitions, and prepare his people, little by little, to accept the wiser institutions of the West.

In front of the temple is a large stone *Torii*, — literally, bird-rest, — a sort of gateway found everywhere in Japan before sacred places.

After visiting the temple, we mount our horses and turn our faces towards Yokohama. As we canter along, we pass through little villages surrounded by broad rice-fields of a most brilliant green. The little boys wish us good morning; the young girls offer us their tempting little cups of tea; we leave the country, strike into more thickly settled districts, and finally emerge from the suburbs and find ourselves near

---

* In Shinto temples mirrors take the place of idols.

the great bridge of Yokohama, thronged with a vast number
of people moving hither and thither continually. We take
leave of Mr. Hall and return to the hotel.

August 31. — The railroad from Yokohama to Yedo was
opened on the 12th of June, 1872. The whole distance, however, seventeen miles, was not completed till afterwards. The
line was built under the direction and superintendence of
the English, and is most excellently constructed and thoroughly equipped. Several trains run every day between the
two cities, and large numbers of Japanese as well as many
foreigners travel continually.

We take the seven-o'clock train for Yedo. The following
description of the journey is from a recent "Guide to Yedo,"
which appeared in Yokohama in 1874, and which is invaluable
to all travellers: "Leaving the station at Yokohama (Cross
Strand), the Shinto temple at Nogi is seen on the hill to the
left. The ground to the right has been reclaimed by filling in
the shallow waters of the bay with clay, cut from the banks
seen on the left. The town of Kanagawa (Metal River) is
situated on a hill to the left. It was the place originally agreed
upon as a treaty port, and a number of foreigners lived there
for some time in 1858 – 59. For good reasons Yokohama
finally became the port of commerce, and the site of the
foreign settlement. At Kanagawa the railway crosses the
Tokaido (East Sea Road), the great highway which begins at
Tokio and ends at Kioto. The next station is Tsurumi (Stork

View).* The village lies to the right of the road, which passes through irrigated rice-fields. Kawasaki (River Point) is a village situated to the right of the road, lying near the Rokugo River, which is crossed by the railway bridge and another of native construction. Where the latter stands was formerly a ferry, by which, previous to the building of the railway, all travellers — Daimios with their trains of followers, foreigners from Yokohama, and people generally — crossed on flat-bottomed boats. On the river-flats will be noticed pear orchards, in which the trees are trained on trellises of bamboo. These pears are of inferior flavor, but new foreign grafts are being set on the old stocks. To the right of the road, before crossing the bridge, may be seen a small but famous shrine gayly decorated, and approached by a numerous series of sacred red portals. While crossing the bridge, a good view westward up the valley is obtained. The railway passes through fertile rice-lands, and the Tokaido, well planted with trees, is again seen on the right. Across the bay are seen the mountains of the provinces of Kadzusa and Awa. Several small temples and cemeteries are passed. Emerging from the clay-cutting and again crossing the Tokaido, we stop at Shinagawa (Merchandise River) station. To the left, in the bay, may be seen a number of forts, now dismantled, built

---

* As the train draws up to the platform, I see a curious example of Japanese progress. A young native stands gazing at the cars, clad in the long flowing robes of his country, with a black stove-pipe hat on his head, and a cigarette in his mouth !

by the Japanese under the direction of French engineers
for the defence of Yedo. Beyond them is the anchorage of
the Imperial navy. On the wooded bluffs to the left are
numerous temples and the old British Legation. A little
farther on may be seen a stone and sodded bank on either
side of the road, and two black gate-posts. The entrance to
the Japanese capital is at this place. Passing over the
causeway, and curving round the humbler portion of the
city, we pass the building and grounds of the En Rio Kan
(Hall for the Entertainment of Foreign Guests), formerly
called Hama Goten (Strand Palace, i. e. Summer Palace of
the Shogun). To the left may be seen the groves and pagoda
of Shiba. The train stops, and we are in the capital of the
Japanese Empire."

CHAPTER VI.

YEDO.

Description of the City. — Shiba. — Atago Yama. — Uyeno. — Asakusa.

"The city of Tokio,* formerly Yedo, is about nine miles long and eight miles wide. About one eighth of the area of the city is occupied by rivers, canals, and the moats of the castle. The Shiro (castle) is the centre of the city. It consists of a central citadel, and a large area of land within strong earthen embankments planted with trees and faced with stone walls, some of which are very massive, over fifty feet in height, and built in a manner well fitted to resist earthquakes and land-slides. The moats are wide, but shallow, and are crossed by wooden bridges. The citadel is now dismantled, and many of the old gate-towers have been torn down. The Shogun † (often called Tycoon by foreigners) formerly resided in the citadel. Many of the principal Daimios had residences called *Yashiki* (spread-out houses) within the castle circuit. In 1868 the Shogun was reduced to the rank of Daimio, and the Mikado took up his residence in the southern part of the citadel. In

---

* I continue to quote from a pamphlet recently published in Japan.

† Spelt also Siogun.

1873 the Imperial Palace was burned, and the Emperor now lives in the *Yashiki* which formerly belonged to the Daimio of Kishiu. The chief business quarter of the city is in that portion of it included in the area lying to the east of the castle, and stretching from Shimbashi * to the Kanda gawa (god's field river).

"There are a great number of temples in the city, belonging chiefly to the numerous Buddhist sects. The two principal religions of Japan are the Buddhist and the Shinto † (doctrine of the gods). The former is the popular, the latter appears to be the official, religion. There are also a great number of Buddhist monasteries and a few nunneries in the city. Nearly all the cemeteries are under Buddhist regulations. Pure Shinto temples contain no idols. Several thousand shrines in honor of Inarisama, the patron of rice, husbandry, and foxes, are found in the city.

"The climate of Tokio is in general very agreeable, though wind and dust at some intervals, and excessive rain at others, make travelling very unpleasant. There are now (1874) about two hundred and fifty foreigners living in Tokio, most of them English and Americans. The majority of the foreign residents in Tokio are in the service of the Japanese government. The European quarter of the city, called Tsukiji (filled-up or reclaimed land), lies to the southeast of, and near, the railway station. No foreigners are allowed to live in Tokio outside

---

* The railroad station.   † Spelt also Sinto, and Sintoo.

of Tsukiji, unless in government or Japanese employ. At Shiba, Kai Sei Gakko, Uyeno, and several other places are 'compounds,' in each of which a number of foreigners live together. Tokio is situated on a large plain called the Kantô (eastern plain), in the province of Musashi. The Japanese Emperor YAMATO DAKE NO MIKOTO in the second century conquered and tranquillized this part of the main island of Japan. Many temples in his honor are to be found in the Kantô. Yedo is not an ancient city. Up to the year 1600 there were on the present site of Tokio only a small castle and a number of straggling villages inhabited by farmers or fishermen. In 1355 Ota Dô Kan, a famous warrior and vassal of the Shogun Sadamasa, whose capital was Kamakura, twelve miles from Yokohama, built a castle, which still constitutes the western circuit of the present stronghold. The country around the castle and village of Yedo was still very wild until Iyesasu, the first Shogun of the Tokugawa line (who exercised almost imperial authority over Japan from 1593 to 1868), made Yedo his capital. In the time of his grandson Iyemitsu, the Daimios fixed their permanent half-yearly residences in the city, which assumed very much the appearance which characterized it down to the year 1868. The name Yedo means Door of the Bay, it being situated at the head of the bay of Yedo, shutting it like a door. In 1868, after the breaking out of the civil war, and the reduction of the usurping Shogun to the rank of an ordinary Daimio, the Mikado came to Yedo, which was called Tokio, or Eastern Capital. The name Yedo is now used only by foreigners. The appearance of the city has greatly changed since 1868. The castle and many *Yashikis* and temples have been burned, demolished, or have fallen to decay. New houses in what is called the "foreign style," and stone or brick barracks, have been built; the *jinrikishas* have made their appearance, and the *kangos* or *norimons* which were borne on men's shoulders have disappeared; beggars, naked coolies, men wearing two swords, Daimios' processions, and many other characteristic sights and scenes, — some very attractive, others very repulsive, — have passed away. The modern Japanese capital is, in a measure, both a Pompeii and a Paris, — a place of ruins and a newly founded city. Modern energy and civilization are everywhere found jostling the old indolence, ancient routine, and traditional custom.

"The old city was divided into thirty wards or districts, which still retain their names. That part of the city lying east of the Sumidagawa, or the river, is called Honjo. Shiba and Asakusa are also well-known divisions. Since 1869 the city has been divided into six great divisions and ninety-six subdivisions. It is a *Fu*, or Imperial city, and is under the direct control of the general government. The police force numbers thirty-five hundred uniformed men. The former Daimios now live privately in Tokio. Many of their old retainers are government officials. The old Shogun lives near the city of Shidzuoka, about ninety-five miles from Tokio. The military garrison of the capital usually consists of about seven thousand soldiers of the infantry, cavalry, artillery, and engineer corps. The population of Tokio, in 1872, was 789,000. It is doubtful whether the city of Yedo ever contained over one million souls. The vast extent of vacant space, as well as the lowness and perishable material of which the houses are built, will astonish most persons who see this city for the first time. For over two centuries the city has been well supplied with water brought from a pond and river several miles off in, and distributed by, aqueducts made of wood, which require to be renewed every ten years. After the great fire in 1872, the burnt district was resurveyed, new and substantial buildings of stone or brick were erected in semi-foreign style, many of which are very handsome."

Leaving the railroad station, we call *jinrikishas*, and proceed through the chief streets of the city on our way to Shiba, — the tombs of the Shoguns. The same street scenes are to be observed here as in Yokohama. The same crowds are moving about in various directions, the same cries and shouts are to be heard, the same curious buildings are on either side of the way. We arrive at the outer gate of the premises, and, ordering our *jinrikishas* to await us, pass in. "We enter a pebbled court-yard in which are over two hundred large stone lanterns. These are the gifts of the Fudai Daimios, one of the lower grade of vassals of the Shogun. Each lantern is inscribed with the name of the donor, the posthumous title of the deceased Shogun,

the name of the temple at Shiba, and the province in which
it is situated, the date of the offering, and a legend which
states that it is reverently offered. The following is the reading on one, and will serve as a specimen : —

TO THE

ILLUSTRIOUS TEMPLE OF LEARNING

(POSTHUMOUS TITLE OF THE SHOGUN),

This stone lantern,

Set up before the tomb at the temple of Zozoji,

IN MUSASHI,

Is reverently offered

by the

RULING DAIMIO,

Noble of the fifth rank,

MASUYAMA FUJIWARA MASATO,

LORD OF TSUSHIMA,

In the second Year of the period of Strict Virtue,

In the cycle of Midzuno ye Tatsu.

(1711.)

"Passing through a handsomely gilt and carved gateway, we
enter another courtyard, the sides of which are gorgeously
adorned. Within the area are bronze lanterns, the gift of the
Kokushiu Daimios, vassals of a much higher grade than the
Fudai. The six very large lanterns standing by themselves
are from the Go San Ke, the three princely families in which
the succession to the office of Shogun was vested. To the
left is a monolith lavatory; and to the right is a depository

of sacred utensils, such as bells, gongs, lanterns, etc., used only on *matsuri*, or festival days. Passing through another handsome gate, we enter a roofed gallery somewhat like a series of cloisters. In front is the shrine. Entering this,— either with or without shoes,— the walls and ceiling will repay study. Each panel of the wall is richly wrought in arabesques and high-relief, the patterns and objects in each case being different. Above some steps is another room, in which are splendidly gilded reliquaries, in which the posthumous titles of the deceased are treasured. Descending from the shrines, we pass up another court, ascend a flight of steps, and enter another pebbled court, in which is a smaller building called a *Hai-den*, formerly used by the living Shogun as a place of meditation and prayer when making his annual visit to the tombs of his ancestors. Beyond it is another flight of stone steps, and in the stone enclosure is a monumental urn. This is the 'simple ending to so much magnificence.'"

From here we go to an exquisite little temple near by, and, having removed our shoes, are invited by the priest to sit down near the shrine. Here it is delightfully cool, and we stretch ourselves out on the beautiful matting and gaze up at a large idol whose precincts we are invading. A high altar, directly behind us, conceals this part of the temple,— and well for us that it does! On the other side of the altar are several natives who are worshipping the god at whose feet we are lying in such disrespectful positions. We hear the murmured prayers, and see the pieces of money falling near us, thrown to the god by the faithful, who little suspect that some "barbarians" are taking their ease in the holy sanctuary of their god,—a place to which they themselves never penetrate. These beautiful Japanese temples! what a curious attraction they possess!

Having examined the other tombs in the vicinity, we return to the street, and, summoning our *jinrikisha*-men (who are smoking their curious little pipes while resting under some trees near by), we call out, "Atago Yama," at which they all smile and nod, thus assuring us that they comprehend perfectly where we wish to go. Atago Yama is a hill from which a fine view of Yedo and the surrounding country may be obtained. Two wide flights of stone steps lead up to the summit from the street below. One flight is built straight upwards, the other winds round to the right. The former is for men, the latter for women. This arrangement is not uncommon in Japan. The view from the top of the hill is, indeed, most beautiful. On one side is the bay with its junks, ships-of-war, and other vessels. A little beyond are the forts. In the distance are Kadzusa and Awa. To the south is Shinagawa. Looking towards the city, the railroad station and the houses of the foreigners may be seen. The great clearness of the atmosphere enables us to mark the different buildings with ease. Looking now to the west, we see the groves of Uyeno, the castle towers, few in number, that still remain,

the great temples, and the houses of the rich banker, Mitsui.
To the northwest is the Engineering College. From the west
side of the hill we see Fuji-No-Yama and the Hakone Mountains. At our feet lies a large cemetery. Looking from this
hill over the city, one is greatly impressed with the multitude
of houses which lie before you.

We sit down at one of the many little tables covered with
awnings, which are scattered over the summit of the hill, and
are served with a most refreshing drink, — a fragrant sort of
tea made from cherry-blossoms, called *sakura-yu*. Our wait-
ress is the most beautiful girl we have yet seen in the country. Her complexion, though dark, is so delicate that it is
very like one of our own brunettes. Her eyes are very large
and soft, her teeth very regular and white, and her thick
black hair is arranged in two high rolls, which are kept in
position by a long tortoise-shell pin. She has a flowing robe
of some cool-looking material, covered over with large Japanese patterns. A broad sash is tied about her waist, and her
bare feet are thrust into little slippers of braided straw. She
serves the tea in little cups, wishes us all a polite good-morn-
ing, and then retires to superintend the manufacture of more
sakura-yu. She is very graceful in all her movements, and
her manners are truly lady-like. We summon a native who
is standing near, who seems to understand English, and request him to act as interpreter. We call for more tea, and
thus bring our pretty attendant into our vicinity. Her name

is Otsuru. She is eighteen years old, and her father is the proprietor of the tea-booth in which we are sitting. She has tended it for several years, and has never been away from the city of Tokio. She is very glad to see us, for she knows we have come a long way from our home, and she is delighted that we enjoy her tea. We inquire if she has ever had her photograph taken, for we feel sure she must make a charming picture. At this, she covers her face with her fan, and, refusing to stay longer, runs off to her little kitchen near by. We send successive deputations of natives to demand her picture, but she waves them all away. Finally she goes to a little lacquered chest and takes out several photographs of herself, which she presents to us. We bid her farewell and take our leave. At the foot of the long flight of steps we look back. She is standing under her tea-booth gazing out over the city. Alas for your beauty, poor Otsuru! In a few years you will become the proprietress of the tea-booth where we found you. You will marry some small farmer or petty tradesman. You will stain your fine teeth black, and will no longer attract the notice of strangers.

We call our *jinrikishas*, and order the coolies to take us to Uyeno (Upper Plain). This is a cemetery similar to Shiba, where several of the Shoguns are buried. We pass along a wide and thronged street, and arrive at last at a small stream, crossed by three bridges. The coolies choose the middle one. This is the spot where, years ago, a man named Sôgorô hid himself, and as the *norimon* of the Shogun (who had paid his regular visit to the tombs of his ancestors) was passing over the bridge, Sôgorô thrust a petition suddenly into the hand of his sovereign. The grievance was redressed, but Sôgorô, his wife, and three children suffered death for the presumption.* Uyeno was the scene of a battle between the troops of the Shogun and the Mikado, July 4, 1869. "The Mikado's troops made rendezvous at the three bridges, in front of the black gate, the evening before. The adherents of the Shogun were strongly posted inside the enclosure and on rising ground. The battle lasted several hours, but by planting two field-pieces on the roof of a neighboring tea-house, the Mikado's troops were enabled to force the gates, and to drive their enemies into the temple, which they set on fire."

Having explored the grounds of Uyeno, and visited the tombs and temples therein, we continue our way to Asakusa (Morning Grass), a district of Yedo containing "the most popular temple in Tokio and the most celebrated in Japan." We enter a wide, paved courtyard. On both sides are little booths where people are buying and selling various kinds of small wares. A large red building called the gate-hall stands in front of the temple itself. Two colossal gods called Niô (Kings) guard the spot. "One is ever ready to

---

* See Mitford's "Tales of Old Japan," Vol. II. ("The Ghost of Sakura").

welcome the man who repents and endeavors to reform; the other 'is pleased when children are born who will become good men." Flocks of sacred pigeons wheel hither and thither, and the people buy grain to throw to them, expecting a blessing from the gods in return. Near the door of the temple is a tablet "hung up by a grateful Japanese who escaped death when the steamer *City of Yedo*, which used to ply between Tokio and Yokohama, was blown up in 1870."

The temple is dedicated to the god Kuanon. The interior is dimly lighted, but we can see that the main hall is unusually wide and high. Men and women are continually passing in and out on their way to or from the shrine. Let us watch these men at their prayers. They make their way opposite the altar and fall down on their knees, bow their heads to the ground, and stretch forth their arms. They clap their hands three times. At the third blow Kuanon will appear. They believe he is now before them in very reality. With downcast eyes they murmur their requests, then, dropping a few coins into a chest, make way for others, who go through the same performance. The worship is evidently so honestly and humbly rendered, that one cannot help feeling sure that the natives are thoroughly in earnest; and it is my firm opinion that the majority of them are as certain that they are doing their *full duty*, as is the most punctilious Christian who never misses a single service of his church.

"Stay for half an hour near these poor people, watch the expression of their faces, the play of their countenances, the fervor of their prayers, and then tell me if you don't think they really are believers. Doubtless their belief is the lowest superstition; but they *do* believe and pray; and in praying and calling upon God they draw near to him whom they ignorantly worship. That they may ask, one for the success of a commercial transaction, another for the fidelity of a husband, or a new dress, — what does it signify? *They believe.*" *

In the vicinity of the temple are various little theatres where a sort of Punch and Judy show goes on. Behind the main hall are some very interesting wax-figures called *ningiyo*. These are representations of miracles performed by the god Kuanon. Near by is a large garden where several rare plants may be seen.

Leaving the grounds of Asakusa, we go to a neighboring tea-house for lunch, after which we return to the *Shimbashi*, and, taking the train for Yokohama, arrive there about 6 P. M. In the cars we meet two of our fellow-travellers of the *Great Republic*, one of whom is in a great deal of trouble and perplexity. On our arrival in Japan we heard of the failure of the Bank of California, which occurred while our steamer was on the Pacific; and one of these gentlemen had deposited all his fortune in the bank shortly before he sailed, taking their

* Baron Hubner.

circular notes. He hears now that his property is all lost. He thinks of returning by the next steamer, but his friend urges him to await further news.*

We pass a delightful evening at dinner with Mr. Richard Irwin. His house is large and very cool, and a wide garden separates the premises from the street.

---

* Intelligence was soon after received that the bank would pay.

CHAPTER VII.

YOKOHAMA TO SHANGHAI.

YOKOHAMA TO KOBE. — OSAKA. — THE INLAND SEA. — ACROSS THE YELLOW
SEA TO CHINA. — SHANGHAI. — "CHIN-CHIN-ING THE MOON."

September 1. — We spend the day in walking through the
chief business streets, and visiting the principal stores, and
find it hard to make a selection from the multitude of exquisite articles that surround us in such profusion. In the
evening we dine with Mr. John Walsh, of Walsh, Hall, & Co.
What a charming establishment! Situated on the coolest part
of the " Bund," and surrounded with wide piazzas, the house
seems the perfection of comfort. Within, high, wide rooms, cool
mattings, and *chefs d'œuvre* of Japanese art. In the dining-
room, three attentive native servants, who seem to anticipate
their master's wishes. Everything easy, enjoyable, and *cool.*
To us fresh from America such a style of life seems Utopian.

September 2. — We devote another day to Curio Street. In
the evening we have the pleasure of Mr. Richard Irwin's
company to dinner.

September 3. — We pay a final visit to Yedo to visit the
shops, but find that the market at Yokohama is far superior.
On our return to Yokohama we find that we have failed to

deliver a letter of introduction to Minister Bingham, which we took with us to the capital; and as we start to-morrow for Kobe and Nagasaki, we shall be unable to make the acquaintance of our country's representative.

September 4. — Our trunks are packed and on the wharf; an export duty of five per cent has been paid upon all our silk purchases, and, thanks again to Mr. C. P. Hall, the customs officials are obliging and brief in their dealings with us. Our steamer is to start at 4 P. M.; it is now noon, and we go to the house of Mr. Gustavus Farley, Jr., for *tiffin* (breakfast). Afterwards, in a pouring rain, we make our way to the "Bund," call a *sampan,* and are soon on the deck of the P. M. S. S. *Oceanica,* Captain Harris, bound for Hiogo (Kobe), Nagasaki, and Shanghai. Just before we leave, our faithful friend Hall comes aboard to bid us farewell, introduces us to the purser, Mr. L. B. Hooff (formerly an officer in the Confederate Army), and soon after takes his departure. A starting-gun is fired from the deck of our steamer, and we are off. Yokohama quickly disappears behind the thick curtain of rain and mist. Dinner is ready at six o'clock, and we are delighted to find that the purser has placed us at his own table, F—— being on his left hand, and I on his right, while Mr. U—— sits next to F——. Of all the officers of a steamer, the purser is the one who has the most direct influence on the comfort of passengers. He it is who apportions the seats at the table, who obtains the most skilled and attentive waiters, and who often has at the last minute several choice state-rooms into which the initiated are slipped. After dinner we smoke a cigar with the purser in his office, and this over, as the sea has risen greatly, causing us to roll about in all directions, we take our leave, and wedge ourselves into our berths as securely as possible, to avoid having our brains dashed out by some sudden lurch of the ship.

September 5. — Although the rain has ceased, the sea is still very rough, and our vessel is tossed about, to the great discomfort of the passengers. Towards evening, however, we run into smoother water, and find that our captain expects to reach Kobe to-morrow at daybreak.

September 6. — Looking out of my state-room window at sunrise this morning, the scene is varied and beautiful. At a little distance off lies the town of Kobe, with high mountains rising directly behind it. The harbor, dotted with junks and *sampans*, is bright with the early beams of the sun; while near by I hear the monotone of the Japanese coolies chanting their peculiar cry while unloading freight from our vessel. Kobe is 349 miles from Yokohama. Although it is one of the treaty ports, it was only opened in 1868, and at present probably has not more than 500 or 600 inhabitants. It is situated a mile to the west of Hiogo. A railroad connects it with the great city of Osaka, the old capital of Japan, from which it is distant about sixteen miles.

After breakfast we call a *sampan* and go ashore to explore

the town.   Our steamer is to remain here twenty-four hours, and we have ample time to visit Osaka itself.   On reaching the "Bund" we inquire for the house of Mr. Robert Walsh, to whom we have a letter of introduction.   He lives near by, and soon we find ourselves at his door, and are welcomed most cordially.   He is an old schoolmate of our friend U——, and they have not met for years.   He proposes to guide us about Osaka; but as he cannot leave his business till one o'clock, he advises us to go at once to Osaka and occupy ourselves in visiting the Mint, and promises to meet us at luncheon; after which he will escort us to the chief objects of interest in the city.   So we walk slowly through the main street of Kobe to the railroad station, and after waiting a few minutes, enter the cars and start for Osaka.   The country through which we pass is similar in appearance to that between Yokohama and Yedo.   Broad fields of rice surround thatched cottages; many natives, with immense shade-hats, are working in the meadows; and flocks of beautiful white storks, disturbed by our train, launch themselves into the air and float away to some more peaceful marsh.

We reach Osaka at noon.   The city contains over 500,000 inhabitants.   Situated on four rivers (three of them branches of the Yodogawa), it is the receptacle of all foreign merchandise bound for the interior of Japan.   The rivers upon which it is built are so winding that nearly three hundred bridges span the various turns and angles.

We call *jinrikishas* and proceed to the "foreign concession," where we find a small hotel. Having ordered a lunch, we set out for the Mint. The streets are thronged; but the boats on the different rivers, carrying produce and merchandise of all sorts, are the most striking objects in the city. Having arrived at the Mint (a large, well-built structure), we are halted at the gate by a guard, who demand our cards. These being displayed to the authorities, they are returned to us stamped with the necessary order of admittance, after which we are given into the charge of a polite official who speaks English fluently, who conducts us over the establishment. We find the very best modern machinery throughout, and the different employés seem thoroughly to understand its manipulation.

On leaving the Mint, we return to the hotel for lunch. At two o'clock Mr. Walsh arrives, and after lunch we engage *jinrikishas* and are soon at the gates of the Castle. This fortification was the residence of the Tycoons up to the year 1868, when, on the breaking out of the rebellion, the Tycoon was deposed, and the Mikado was restored to his rightful rule over Japan. It was in this vicinity that the hardest fighting of those days took place, and the traces of the struggle can be plainly seen. The Castle is built of the largest stones that could be procured, without regard to labor or cost, some of the single blocks being thirty feet long and twenty broad! In many places fire has loosened one stone from another; there, large pieces have been chipped off, the stone steps are broken and scarred; while here, at the top of the mound, the residence itself of the Tycoon — inside of the very strongest portion of the walls — has been utterly swept away by the torch of the enemy. A fine view can be obtained from this spot, and one can look across over Osaka with its winding streams, while high mountains opposite add to the beauty of the picture. A sentry accompanies us back to the gate (for the place is held by a garrison, and the visitor must send in his card to the commandant of the post, who will detail a soldier to act as escort), and, passing out, we are nearly deafened by a dreadful discord made by three companies of buglers, who are all practising foreign bugle-calls at the same time. We next visit a very old and exceedingly sacred pagoda, called Tentoji, situated about three miles from the Castle. This pagoda is so ancient that the Japanese themselves are said to be ignorant of the date of its erection.

It is now half past five. We return to the railroad station and take the train for Kobe, which we reach at seven o'clock. We pass a very pleasant evening, dining with Mr. Walsh, and at eleven o'clock we return to our ship, which is to leave, as I have said, at daybreak to-morrow.

September 7. — Although a fine rain somewhat mars the view, the scenery along the Inland Sea is magnificent. Our steamer, gliding through calm water, passes within a stone's-throw of beautiful green hills, which rise boldly from the sea, cultivated in many places, with little villages nestling at the base, and many junks and *sampans* moving slowly in different directions. A fine sunset promises a clear day for the morrow.

Four new passengers have joined us at Kobe, — Ex-Secretary Richardson of Washington, with his wife and daughter, and Mr. George Hunter of London. This party have just arrived from Kioto, and only a few days ago Mr. Richardson was stopped in the interior, and was told that he had passed the treaty limits; but on summoning the proper authorities this was pronounced a mistake, and an apology was tendered by the officials.

September 8. — The bright day that succeeds yesterday's storm is gratefully recognized as most fitting in which to view the beautiful scenery that forms the approach to Nagasaki. There is much on each side of the steamer to interest us. Our course lies, as yesterday, very near to picturesque hills and hamlets. The water is without a ripple. At about four o'clock we pass Arched Rock, seven hundred and eighteen miles from Kobe. This is a huge rock planted almost in the middle of the passage, and cleft so as to form a sort of natural bridge. Soon after this we see Papenberg, a perpendicular wall of rock, from whose summit four thousand Christians were hurled in 1638. A portion of the island is covered with thick vegetation. At six o'clock we enter the beautiful harbor of Nagasaki, fire our arrival-gun, and come to a stand-still. Many vessels are already anchored here, among them a United States man-of-war.

Nagasaki is built at the foot of a semicircle of high hills. The European quarter is situated to the east. On the western side is Detsima, the former Dutch factory, and behind this stretches the native town. Nagasaki became a treaty port in 1858. Before this, the Dutch had entire control of the trade, but they were so restricted and so carefully watched by the natives, that they could only have regarded themselves as prisoners.

September 9. — We breakfast early and go immediately ashore. Having presented a letter of introduction to Postmaster Clarke (who kindly offers to show us the best tortoise-shell manufactories), we walk through the town with him and purser Hooff, and are delighted with the beautiful objects for sale on all sides. Exquisite tortoise-shell work and tasteful and delicate porcelain-ware are the chief productions. The prices asked seem very reasonable, but a little bargaining is always expected. At noon we hear the United States man-of-war firing a salute in honor of the visit of Ex-Secretary Richardson. At five o'clock we return to our steamer, and soon after we are making our way through the China Sea, bound for Shanghai.

September 10. — A steady rain which has continued unceasingly since daybreak prevents us from sitting on deck to-day,

and further annoys us by tossing up (with its accompany-
ing blasts of wind) a heavy sea, which puts the majority
of the passengers in an unhappy state of mind and body. I
have a long talk with the purser in regard to our late civil
war. The purser is a man of education and of the most varied
experiences of life. He possesses, as is natural, strong Southern sympathies. He speaks of the assassination of President
Lincoln, and characterizes it as a fanatical abomination, — the
most damaging occurrence that could have befallen the South.
The majority of Southerners feared that the North would regard them as instigators of the murder and supporters of the
murderer. On the contrary, it was viewed as a most grievous
calamity. In regard to the war itself, he says that he took
up arms in defence of a principle which seemed to him then
as sacred and as honorable as any which had ever driven men
into strife.

September 11. — At 9 A. M. we arrive opposite the light-ship
anchored forty-five miles from Shanghai, and, having stopped
to take on board a pilot, we proceed on our way. The water
surrounding us is now of a dirty yellow color, for we are in
the outlet of the great Yang-tse-kiang, which sweeps through
China for many hundred miles. At ten o'clock we see, far
ahead, a flat green shore, and soon we enter the Wang-poo
River (on which Shanghai is situated), and look with eagerness at the new country which we are rapidly approaching.
As we glide up the river we pass several merchant-junks and

one Chinese ship-of-war. What strange objects! Great eyes are painted on the bows; for the people firmly believe that a vessel without them is unable to see its way over the water. Their reasoning, expressed in "pigeon-English," is as follows: "Ship no have eye, no can see. If no can see, how can walk?"

At half past two we arrive opposite the warehouse ("go-down") of the P. M. S. S. Co. Our ship fires an arrival-gun and comes to a stand-still. We call a *sampan*; the boat-men row us quickly ashore. We leap out, and set foot on the Flowery Kingdom, the Celestial Empire!

September 12. — Shanghai, eleven hundred and ninety miles distant from Yokohama and eight hundred miles from Hong-Kong, was opened to foreign trade in 1846. The foreigners (in number about four thousand) live apart from the natives in a reservation which is composed of the American, the English, and the French "quarters." Shanghai contains probably the finest warehouses and private establishments of any city in the Empire. Indeed, the great houses of the merchants, stretching along the "Bund," are unnecessarily elaborate. An immense amount of money has been expended by the foreign residents, and the result is wide, clean streets, a superb club-house, an excellent race-course, theatre, public garden, and boat-house. The city is thoroughly drained, and a well-disci-plined police force and fire company, controlled by a carefully chosen foreign municipal government, preserve order and

CHINESE MANDARIN AND WIFE.

security everywhere. The Chinese city of Shanghai is situated about a mile from the foreign portion, and contains about three hundred and fifty thousand inhabitants. The harbor is crowded at all times with steamers and sailing-vessels bound to all parts of the world.

To-day being Sunday, several of our party attend the English church. Mr. George Hunter (whose arrival on board the *Oregonian* at Kobe I have mentioned) has decided to accompany us to Pekin. He has long wished to make the trip, but felt unwilling to start alone, knowing that the journey overland is exceedingly difficult, and, for a single traveller, dangerous. We are very glad of the addition to our numbers, and anticipate much pleasure from the companionship.

We have determined to start at once for Pekin, for, quite early in the fall, the trip is rendered uncomfortable by the coldness of the weather; and we are told on all sides that we shall accomplish the journey under the most favorable auspices if we set out immediately.

September 13. — As we are to leave Shanghai so soon, we only present a few of our letters of introduction, — one to Russell & Co., one to Olyphant & Co., one to the American consul, Mr. Seward, and one other. These gentlemen give us much information in regard to Pekin and the way thither, and urge us to call on them on our return.

September 14. — Fortunately for us, the favorite boat of

Russell's line — the *Shing King* — is to leave Shanghai for Tien-tsin (the port from whence travellers proceed overland to Pekin) to-morrow at daybreak; and, having filled our valises with our roughest clothes, we spend the rest of the day in packing the remainder of our possessions, which are to be left in charge of the manager of the Astor House. Early in the afternoon, however, a *chit* (note) is brought to us by one of Russell's servants, which informs us that the steamer will be unable to start till to-morrow at noon. This change will give us another evening on shore, and we can therefore witness the Chinese ceremony of "chin-chin-ing the moon." To-day is the middle of the Chinese month, and this evening the moon is to be "chin-chin-ed," with all the usual illuminations, explosions, and superstitions. To-day all Chinamen must pay their bills, balance their books, and make themselves even with the world. This being done, a grand illumination is held in honor of the moon's Joss, who, if the night is fine, looks down benignly with a full round face. At eight o'clock we leave the hotel, and, accompanied by Mr. H. B. Morse, walk along the "Bund," and turn down Nanking Road, and are soon walking by the houses of the Chinese, built close together on each side of the way. Every doorway and window is bright with the light of huge red candles, or red paper lanterns, while gold and silver "joss-paper" and brown "joss-sticks" burn slowly near by, throwing forth thick clouds of smoke, which the Joss of the moon can hardly consider a complimentary equivalent for the clear rays he is pouring over everything. Fire-crackers snap and fizz on all sides of us; the noise from cymbals, gongs, and drums is deafening; while every junk in the harbor, and every joss-house in the neighborhood is hung with red lanterns, — the color always used when "chin-chin-ing" a god. At an early hour, however, thin, hurrying clouds partially obscure the surface of the moon; in consequence of which the "chin-chin-ing" is to be continued and finished to-morrow evening.

Before returning to the hotel we visit the Chinese theatre, and, passing through the doorway, are met by a servant, who leads us down the main aisle to one of several small tables near the stage, and, having seen us comfortably seated, leaves us, but returns soon with four large cups of tea, some dried seeds, and some cigar-lighters, all which he places before us, and then departs to perform a like service for a party of Chinese merchants, who have seated themselves at a neighboring table. The theatre is small, but well lighted; the stage is large, but the scenery consists simply of curtains, on which are painted Chinese inscriptions of varied import. A balcony runs round the upper part of the house. The play is similar to the one we witnessed at the Chinese theatre in San Francisco; and after spending some time in trying to comprehend the plot, we are compelled to abandon the attempt, for the actions of the players are utterly unintelligible. Turning now to the left, we all raise our teacups, and, in our turn, toast a fat old Chinaman with immense spectacles, who from a neighboring table has recognized Mr. Morse (a resident of Shanghai), and has greeted him according to the custom of the country. Soon after this, the incessant noise from the gongs, drums, and cymbals of the orchestra (seated on the stage) induces us to make our way towards the door; but one of the ushers urges us so strongly to remain a little longer, "and see little boys makee fight," that we return to our seats. The "little boys" soon appear, dressed in fantastic costumes, representing dragons and devils, and, in the midst of flames of red fire, perform excellently with short sticks which they hold in their hands, — whirling them around their heads and about their bodies, and finally clashing them together. After this we leave the theatre and return to our hotel.

CHAPTER VIII.

SHANGHAI TO PEKIN.

SHANGHAI TO CHE-FOO. — A STORM IN THE GULF OF PE-CHI-LI. — TIEN-TSIN. — OVERLAND TO PEKIN. — A CHINESE INN. — ARRIVAL AT THE CAPITAL.

September 15. — At twelve o'clock, having left the larger portion of our baggage at the hotel to await our return, we go on board of the *Shing King*, which is to carry us to Tien-tsin. We find it a most excellent craft, built in Glasgow in 1873, with very comfortable cabin arrangements, and, as we are the only passengers, we have the whole boat to ourselves. We have the further good fortune to be in the charge of a captain who is as sincerely liked as he is widely known, — Captain Hawes of Searsport, Maine. Always on the lookout for the comfort of passengers, ready at all times for a story or a laugh, and, above all, zealous in the performance of every part of his profession, they are lucky, indeed, who come under his care.

At two o'clock the *Shing King* leaves her moorings and glides rapidly down the river. We pass another steamer of Russell's line coming up, whose captain gives us the gratifying news that "it's blowing guns outside." In spite of this, however, we continue on our way, reach the light-ship at six o'clock, and are once more navigating the Yellow Sea.

September 16. — The sea to-day is as calm as can be desired, and the hours pass quickly. A bright moon lights us on our way at night.

September 17. — At five o'clock this morning South Promontory is seen far ahead, and, after passing it in due time, our course lies all day within sight of various islands, uninhabited and desolate. At 8 P. M. we reach Black Rock, — ten miles from Che-foo, — and, having passed round the lighthouse, are soon making our way among the shipping, native and foreign, anchored off the town. At ten o'clock we drop our anchor, and two long whistles announce the steamer's arrival.

Che-foo is the summer habitation and watering-place of the foreign residents of Shanghai and Pekin. It is situated at the head of a beautiful harbor, has a fine beach, and a good hotel. Vessels of war find good anchorage here, and in 1860 the French fleet made it a rendezvous. The United States man-of-war *Kearsarge* lies at anchor near our steamer, and several other gun-boats — French, English, and Dutch — are in the vicinity.

September 18. — As our steamer is to leave at nine o'clock, we breakfast early and go immediately ashore, taking our Chinese servant (whom we obtained in Shanghai) as our guide. We walk through the streets of the native town, narrow, dirty, and full of the horrible odors which always pervade the habitations of these people. The men are dressed in the same pijamah-like costume that we observed on their fellow-countrymen in San Francisco. All wear the cue. The women are very plain and unattractive. Their garments are exceedingly unbecoming, and their poor little feet oblige them to hobble along as if walking on sticks of wood whittled down to a point. A half-hour's survey of this place is quite sufficient, and, having returned to the *Shing King*, we see the town disappear in the distance with no great regret. Our passenger-list is increased by two, — Colonel Eli Shepherd, United States consul at Tien-tsin, returning to his official residence, and an English merchant bound to Pekin on business. At three o'clock we pass the numerous islands which divide the Yellow Sea from the Gulf of Pe-chi-li, and are glad to find calm water in this place so noted for rough weather.

September 19. — At five o'clock this morning I am awakened by a confused noise, and, starting up in my berth, I see that the walls of my state-room are illuminated with a strange, dull light, entirely dissimilar to the beams from an ordinary sunrise. Going quickly through the cabin to the gangway, I find the majority of the passengers intently watching a spot in the heavens from whence a heavy squall is rushing rapidly upon us. The sun has just risen above the horizon, and its clear rays mingling with the sudden blackness cause the curious light I noticed on the walls of my state-room. Furious gusts of wind soon break full upon us, lashing the sea into angry waves. Little by little the darkness increases, the sun is blotted out, and we might almost suppose it was midnight. We are directly opposite the bar at the entrance

to the Peiho River, — a dangerous and difficult place in which
to navigate in a storm. The captain, seeing that it is impossible for the steamer to make any headway, decides to anchor
till the squall has passed, when we may take a pilot and
ascend the river. As he is leaving the wheel-house to give
the order to drop the anchor, a fierce blast lifts him from
his feet, and sweeps him across the deck. Fortunately he
grasps the railing, and, clinging to it with all his strength,
is saved. His loud cries to the sailors near the anchor to
"Let go!" "Let go!" the whistling of the wind through the
rigging, and the creaking of the ship, — coming as all this does
at such an early hour in the morning, — form an unpleasant
opening to the day. By this time, however, the worst part
of the storm has passed, and at nine o'clock the sun is shining brightly, the sky is clear, and the sea calm. The bar
at the mouth of the Peiho River must be passed at full tide;
and, owing to delay on account of the storm, we are obliged
to wait till four o'clock of the afternoon before proceeding on
our way. When that hour arrives, having received our pilot,
we resume our voyage, and, passing the Taku forts (near
which the English and French Allies were temporarily de-
feated in 1859 – 60),* we cross the bar, and begin the

* The Allied fleets, under Admiral Hope, captured these forts August 21,
1860. Commodore Tatnall, of the United States Navy, offered his assistance
to the English, adding the well-known remark that "blood is thicker than
water."

ascent of the river. We wind slowly up the narrow and crooked stream, past frequent villages on either bank, with houses built entirely of mud, the buildings and people looking dirty, squalid, and miserable. In some parts of the river, the stream, always narrow, bends at right angles to itself; and as steamers are obliged to run along a narrow channel through lines of junks anchored on each side,—whose owners are always ready to stone any foreign craft that encroaches upon them,—great care is necessary to bring a vessel safely to Tien-tsin. It is very unusual for a captain to escape hitting one bank or the other in running from the bar to Tien-tsin; and after we have navigated half-way, without any such delay, and are congratulating ourselves on the probability of an uninterrupted passage, suddenly, having turned round a sharp bend, we drift a little too far, and in a moment more our steamer lies still, fast to the bank, with one paddle-wheel firmly imbedded in the mud of the bottom, and the bow pointing directly into a little village near by. A boat is lowered at once; a long rope, with one end attached to the bow of the steamer, is taken to the other bank; and by the united efforts of eight men we are drawn little by little into deep water. This occurs twice again before our arrival at Tien-tsin, but at 2 A. M. we are safely tied to the dock.

September 20.—Tien-tsin is situated on the south bank of the Peiho River, and at the end of the Grand Canal. It is distant thirty-eight miles from the Taku forts, seven hundred and twenty-five from Shanghai, and eighty (as the crow flies) from Pekin. It contains two hundred thousand inhabitants, has a small foreign reservation, and, owing to its position on the Grand Canal, it receives immense quantities of merchandise destined for all parts of the Empire. Here, on June 21, 1870, occurred the abominable massacre of the French nuns and priests, as well as the consul himself. For this, Lieutenant-General Chung-how was responsible. Although certain apologies were made by the Chinese government for the outrage, and an indemnity paid, yet the actual guilty parties have never been punished.

The distance from Tien-tsin to Pekin — eighty miles by land and one hundred and twenty-five by water — can be accomplished in three ways. The traveller may engage a "house-boat," — a long, wide boat with a cabin, — and be rowed up the Peiho by coolies to Tung-chow, where donkeys can be obtained for the remaining fifteen miles of the journey; or one may ride across the country on ponies, stopping over night at the native inns; or one may hire a Chinese cart — *horribile dictu!* — and be driven to Pekin, which is sure to be reached, if travelling by this latter method, with scarcely a whole bone in one's body; for a Chinese road is only another name for a succession of deep ruts and a profusion of stones; and while a pony may be made to avoid at least some of these obstacles, the carts, built without springs, are sure to jolt over them all. The pony has an advantage over the boat, in going from Tien-tsin to Pekin; for while four or five days are required to push the boat up stream and for the traveller to afterwards ride from Tung-chow to the capital, the whole distance across country can be accomplished on horseback in two days by all who are accustomed to this method of locomotion.

For these reasons we decide to travel on ponies, and immediately after breakfast this morning we go to the office of the American consul, who has kindly promised to engage ponies and carts for us, as well as two *mafus* (who correspond to the *bettos* of Japan) to act as guides and to take care of the horses. The carts are necessary to carry our mattresses, canned food, plates, knives and forks, etc. (for none of these things are found at the inns), and also countless strings of native copper coins, called "cash." The consul has also applied to the *Tao-tai* of the city for the necessary passport for our party. Having made arrangements to start at an early hour on the morrow, we are kindly invited to *tiffin* by Mr. J. Twinem, commissioner of customs for the Chinese government, to whom we have a letter of introduction. Lunch over, we mount ponies, and in company with Mr. Twinem and an English merchant, ride outside of the city to the "Treaty Joss-House," or "Hai Quang Tsu," where the treaty between the Allies and the Chinese was signed in 1860 by Lord Elgin and Prince Kung. Besides the usual large idols, there are many small ones, formed of a sort of clay, and grotesquely painted, which are placed round the room at the feet of the larger deities. Calling an aged priest aside, F—— and I exhibit small silver coins, and, pointing at a little joss near by, demand "two piecee god all same like that." The priest, making sure that we are unobserved, thrusts our money under his cloak, and, snatching two of the gods from their places, hands them to us, and we quickly put them out of sight. On our return to the city, Mr. Twinem insists, with great hospitality, upon our dining with him. At the conclusion of the dinner he introduces us at the foreign club, where we meet an officer of an English gun-boat (lately arrived at Tien-tsin), who gives us information which rather discourages our intended overland trip to Pekin.

In the summer of 1874 Augustus Raymond Margary, a young and promising member of the China consular service, was sent from Pekin by the British Minister with a special passport, to meet a small embassy, under the leadership of Colonel Horace Browne, which had been ordered by the government of India to proceed into Yün Nan, crossing the frontier from the Burmese side. Though frequently molested along the road, as his published journal attests, Margary joined Colonel Browne in safety at Bhamo. "The mission had entered China, and was but a short distance from Manwyne, when Mr. Margary pushed on (alone) to that town. He had passed a week in it on his journey southward. At Manwyne, according to testimony too strong to be doubted, he was murdered on the

21st of February. An attack was made on the following morning on Colonel Browne's party, which, however, after a sharp struggle, was enabled to draw off without serious loss."*

Ever since poor Margary's death, the British Minister at Pekin has continually pressed the Chinese government for reparation; and although many promises have been made, the Chinese are apparently determined not to consent to the full demands of the English. Matters, however, have now reached a crisis. The English Minister, wearied and annoyed with the procrastination, has formally notified the Chinese government that the 22d of September will be the last day he shall allow them for consideration; and if they have not acceded to his terms by that time, he shall withdraw his legation from the capital and shall consider friendly negotiations at an end. Moreover, the English admiral (in whose fleet our informant is stationed) has been requested by Mr. Wade to hold several ships-of-war in readiness off Tien-tsin, either to receive him on his arrival at the coast, or, in case of extreme necessity, to march the men across country to his relief.

Such is the political state of the country through which we are about to travel. As the common people do not distinguish between English and Americans, both being obnoxious "foreign devils," our reception in the different villages is likely to be rather inhospitable. The English naval officer even counsels us to abandon the expedition, and urges us not to expose our-

---

* See Preface to Margary's Journal.

selves unnecessarily to danger or insult. On the other hand, we have made all our preparations to go; our party, including guides, hostlers, and servant, numbers nine persons; we possess passports from the *Tao-tai* of Tien-tsin, giving us full permission to travel to Pekin (and beyond, to the Great Wall), and warning all Chinamen against molesting or hindering us; we hold letters of introduction to three ministers at the capital, — the American, the English, and the German; furthermore, the Chinese may yield at the last moment to the demands of the English, tranquillity may be restored, and the threatened troubles averted. We *cannot* give up our visit to Pekin! We will start as planned!

September 21. — At six o'clock we despatch the carts (containing our baggage, food, mattresses, etc.) in charge of our servant, and we ourselves start soon after on ponies, our *mafus* leading the way. Passing through the native city as quickly as possible (for the dirt and odors are sickening), we strike across a barren plain covered with innumerable graves, — little conical heaps of earth and bricks which cover the coffins (laid on the surface of the ground) from sight. These curious graves may be seen in the vicinity of every city and along almost every road in China. As we wish to reach Pekin in two days, we must accomplish forty miles each day. We ride along at a steady, brisk gait, for several hours. The country is cultivated only in the vicinity of wretched mud-villages scattered here and there, and everything about us looks neglected and

大清

照得據天津定約第九款內開：凡美國民人欲前往內地各處遊歷、通商等因，現有美國領事官[illegible]給執照[illegible]蓋印，定以一年為限[illegible]地方官隨時保護[illegible]不許留難[illegible]美國領事官[illegible]協助可也。須至執照者。

右給美國人[illegible]收執。

光緒[illegible]年[illegible]月[illegible]日給執照

加印照

大清欽命[illegible]江南海關兼管蘇松太[illegible]兵備道[illegible]

desolate. At noon we reach the town of Yang-tsin, distant twenty miles from Tien-tsin, and proceed slowly through the filthy streets on the lookout for a native inn where we may eat luncheon and give our horses a rest. The people gather on each side of the street in crowds to see us pass, gaze at us with intense curiosity, and make it evident that our appearance causes them great amusement. When we have arrived at the inn and have dismounted, they press round us from all sides, examine and criticise the texture of our clothes, look wonderingly at our shoes and hats, and finally burst into a loud laugh at our general aspect.* Leaving Yang-tsin immediately after lunch, we continue our journey, and after much delay, on account of a rise of the Peiho, which has overflowed the usual track and which obliges us to make a long *détour*, and after a half-hour's chase for the runaway pony of one of our party who was unseated, we reach Ho-see-woo, our resting-place for the night, at eight o'clock, having accomplished forty miles since morning. Our carts arrive soon after, and, having made a very excellent supper of our canned food, and rice and eggs procured in the town, we stretch our mattresses on the brick *congs*, and, lying down in our clothes, are soon asleep, our long horseback ride proving a capital soporific.

A Chinese inn is decidedly uninviting in its general outward appearance, and a closer acquaintance with its interior arrangements is scarcely more encouraging. A wall of mud

---

* One man even *tasted* of one of our riding gloves.

and bricks, about eight feet high, shuts in the premises from
the village street, and passing this you find yourself in a sort
of quadrangle with low brick buildings on three sides, partly
devoted to cattle and partly to men. Being a foreigner, you
are met, on your arrival, by the proprietor, and, after exchanging
most obsequious *chin-chin-ings*,* you are led at once to the best
room. This turns out to be a little chamber about fifteen by
twenty feet, in which is a table, four chairs, and a brick *cong*, —
a sort of platform, about six feet long and three feet high.
Upon this you are to stretch your mattress, which (of course)
you have brought with you. The very next partition to yours,
possibly, may be a simple stall in which are quartered horses,
mules, camels, or sheep! The whole quadrangle is thus filled
with men and beasts; and early in the morning or at evening one may see an indiscriminate crowd of Chinese and Mon-
golians, who, with their beasts, have just arrived or are pre-
paring to depart. Rice, eggs, mutton, and tea may be obtained,
but everybody brings food with them. In cold weather a sort
of stove under each *cong* is filled with charcoal, and the bricks
are comfortably warmed. The proprietors of the best inns place
in their "foreigner's room" various pictures illustrating Chinese life, together with Confucian maxims painted in large
red characters on long narrow strips of thick paper. The usual
Chinese inn is dirty and thoroughly uncomfortable, and a for-

---

* The closed fists are placed together and raised up and down to correspond
with low inclinations of the body ; the two men performing the ceremony look
into each other's eyes and ejaculate, "Chin-chin!"

eigner is sure to have at least a quarter of the village surrounding his door from the first moment of his arrival, watching his every movement, and gazing in deep astonishment at
his peculiar method of conveying his food to his mouth. An
empty bottle or sardine-box is highly prized, and a fierce
wrangle is caused by tossing one out of the inn door. It was
at Ho-see-woo, indeed, that we lost one of our forks, and,
having sent our servant to inquire for it, we received the information that the villagers, never having seen such an article
before, wished to preserve it as a curiosity!

September 22. — It is impossible for a traveller to sleep un-
interruptedly at a Chinese inn. From hour to hour one hears
loud cries from men, shrill blasts of horns, the beating of
drums, the explosion of fire-crackers, and a peculiar noise
made by the town watchmen by striking together two sticks
of wood. Chinamen delight in harsh sounds, and even in their
daily occupations they roar and shout at one another as if
they were all stone-deaf. Soon after daybreak, moreover, the
whole inn is astir. The courtyard is filled with a crowd of
men and beasts, and further sleep is out of the question.

For these reasons we breakfast at sunrise, and have soon
mounted our horses and are on our way. Our track lies, as
yesterday, through a flat, uninteresting country, with squalid
mud-villages here and there, and hundreds of graves heaped
up along the road. We planned to lunch at Chang-chea-wang,
half-way from Ho-see-woo to Pekin, but, owing to a delay of

our carts, we are obliged to stop at a wretched village near by, where we make as short a stay as possible, and press on to our final destination. At two o'clock it begins to rain heavily, and we canter rapidly along, all of us soon being drenched to the skin. At half past three we reach a high nine-story pagoda, and a little farther on the road runs by several large monuments standing in a grove of tall trees. The houses increase in number as we advance; many of them are far more solidly built than those in the villages through which we have been passing; in short, there is every indication that we are approaching a large city. We enter now a broad road lined with trees, thronged with multitudes of people on horses or mules bound for Pekin; while many carts, and quantities of coolies carrying burdens slung on poles, add to the general entanglement. At four o'clock we see far ahead of us, through the rain and mist, a high wall which looks like some strong fortification. Our *mafu* pauses for a moment in his rapid canter to point before him with his riding-whip and cry out, "Pa-ching!" (as the natives pronounce it,) and urging on our horses we soon arrive at the great outer wall, and at quarter to five we pass through the *Sha-who-men*, or *Sha-who* gate, and look with curiosity on all around us. We make our way along a broad street, once well paved with wide blocks of stone, but now full of holes and ruts. On each side of us is terrible waste, and filth of every description; the mud is a foot thick, the odors around us are various

and nauseating. Low houses are built on each side of the
road, the doorways swarming with men, women, and children,
who peer wonderingly at us as we go by. After riding for
another mile we come to another wall, which divides the outer
Chinese city from the Tartar city, and, passing under the *Harto*
gate, we soon arrive at the French Hotel. We find, however,
that the proprietor has recently died; and as we are deliberat-
ing what we shall do, a gentleman comes up and introduces
himself (an *attaché* of the German Legation), and kindly conducts us to the only good hotel in the city, a house kept by a
German, called in Chinese *Poo-Kwo-fan-tia*. Here we are
received; but as the gates of the city are closed at sunset, our
mafu tells us that our carts and baggage cannot enter till
morning, so we are obliged to borrow garments of our landlord. Afterwards we sit down to an excellent dinner, and
converse with our host in regard to the probability of political
disturbances in the city. We are somewhat alarmed when he
informs us that he has made every preparation for a hasty
flight. "The time is up to-day," says he, "for China's consideration of England's demands; and as Mr. Wade will probably be obliged to declare war, I have ready Chinese dresses
for my wife and myself, and a ladder to scale yonder wall;
for all foreigners will be regarded alike, and will be shut into
the city and killed!" We go to bed with the high Tartar
wall in sight from our window, fully expecting to be murdered
before morning in a sudden *mélée* of native cut-throats.

CHAPTER IX.

PEKIN TO THE GREAT WALL.

September 23. — We are rejoiced to find ourselves awake and safe this morning, and immediately after breakfast we decide to seek, by means of our letters of introduction, some definite information in regard to the anticipated troubles. In order to reach the fountain-head, we will call first at the English Legation. Passing through several wide but dirty streets, we arrive at the grounds of the Legation, which are surrounded by a high wall. At the entrance-gate we are met by two native servants, dressed in the usual official livery (black cloaks and scarlet hats), who, taking our cards and the letter of introduction, request us to be seated till our names have been submitted to the minister. In a short time they return, and, bowing politely, invite us to enter. We follow them across a large, well-kept quadrangle, surrounded with neat-looking buildings, which vary in size and ornamentation. Approaching the largest and handsomest, we ascend a short flight of stone steps, and crossing a hall, enter

a very wide, lofty apartment, richly furnished and adorned
with various works of art. The servants motion us to be
seated, make low bows, and retire. In a moment there enters an elderly man, rather below the middle height, with an
intellectual and careworn face, and restless, piercing eyes.
This is His Excellency T. F. Wade, C. B.* He greets us
pleasantly, and after the usual commonplaces, we inquire if
he thinks there will be any danger in a stay in Pekin, or,
furthermore, in a journey inland to the Great Wall. "Although I cannot be interviewed on political matters at this
time," replies Mr. Wade, laughingly, "I will say that you may
anticipate no immediate danger; for, even if war is declared,
several months will be required to put troops in the field,
and long before serious hostilities have begun you will be
out of the way." This diplomatic response, like a Greek
oracle of old, while relieving our minds of much apprehension,
does not entirely remove our uncertainty; but, after further
conversation, we agree that it will be wisest to start for the
Great Wall at once, and explore Pekin on our return. At
this point Mr. Wade kindly offers to introduce us to a young
member of his Legation, who is thoroughly posted in regard
to the journey to the Great Wall; and we accompany the
minister across the grounds to a neighboring building, where
we are presented to Mr. Hillyar, who gives us full information in regard to the trip to the Wall, and advises us to

* Now Sir Thomas Wade.

start immediately. Before taking our leave, we are also introduced to Honorable Mr. Grosvenor. As the day is advancing, and we have other visits to make, we say farewell, promising to call on our return from the Great Wall.

We now make our way to the German Legation, situated near by. Again we are received by neatly dressed servants, who conduct us through ample grounds to a well-furnished apartment. Minister Von Brandt puts us at once at our ease, produces some Havana cigars (a great rarity in China), and advises us to set out promptly for the interior, and visit the points of interest in the city on our return. He lends us a book of very useful maps, and assures us that we are about to start on a trip of unusual interest ; he says, furthermore, that we need apprehend no immediate hostilities. We now take our leave, having accepted his kind invitation to dine with him at the Legation on our return.

Passing now up the street and turning to the right, we arrive at the grounds of the American Legation, and halt, as before, at an outer gate. Instead of the well-dressed servants who met us at the other legations, we find, after some searching, two common coolies, in the usual unbecoming blue garments of their class. One of them receives our cards, and requests us to wait till he has presented them to Mr. Avery. We look about us. What a contrast to the embassies we have just quitted ! The buildings are low, poorly built, and, apparently uncomfortable. Absolute meagreness is called republican simplicity! "Is it possible," says our English fellow-traveller, "that this is all your government can furnish to its representative in this great Empire?" What can we reply? We are sure the United States *can* take better care of its representative, but why it *does not* can only be answered by the politicians at Washington.

The servant returns and asks us to follow him. Crossing the yard, we see Mr. Avery walking up and down in the sunshine. He advances, greets us politely, and invites us into his house. The room is small and scantily furnished. We consult him in regard to our proposed inland trip. He says we need anticipate no serious trouble, but advises us to avoid all roving bands of native soldiers, who care nothing for the laws of the country. Soon after, we rise to take our leave. "Gentlemen," says Mr. Avery, "I should like to ask you to dine with me, but I gave up entertaining some time ago. My salary, little enough before, as my surroundings indicate, is, I hear, to be still further diminished. If the sensible ones at Washington could look upon these places with their own eyes, I feel sure that the country would not allow us to be subjected to continual mortification." *

Having returned to the hotel and deliberated, we decide to start for the Great Wall on the morrow, and explore Pekin on our return.

* Mr. Avery died soon after. He is succeeded by Mr. Seward, late Consul-General at Shanghai.

September 24. — We make an early start, having sent on our carts in advance. As we pass through the city, we meet, near the Imperial grounds, a mandarin riding along in his chair of state. Two horsemen, with great red plumes in their hats, lead the procession, and shout at the crowd to make way for their master. Then come six well-dressed servants bearing the old fellow's sedan-chair, in which we can see the official sitting at his ease, while two horsemen, dressed like the ones in advance, bring up the rear. On a cushion in front of the mandarin is his full-dress hat, with a red button on the top, indicating that he is of high rank, — for buttons of different colors belong to the various grades. When we are about three miles from Pekin, the horse of one of our party gives a sudden start and tosses his rider off his back. Away dashes the pony, and three of us after him, through gardens and fields, past houses, and across roads, our horses in pursuit seeming as eager to capture the runaway as we are ourselves. After a brisk half-hour's chase we succeed in grasping his bridle, and have hardly started again, when the pony which our servant is riding shakes him off, and we have another gallop longer than the first; at the conclusion of which we push on as rapidly as possible towards the Bell Temple. A priest meets us at the gate, and crossing a court-yard, we enter the temple, where hangs the Great Bell, second largest in the world, — that at Moscow being its only supe-rior. This immense bell is eighteen feet high and thirty-six feet in circumference, and was cast A. D. 1400. It is covered all over with Chinese inscriptions referring to the circumstances which caused its production, besides various sentences in praise of its guardian deity.

From the Bell Temple we continue our way towards the ruins of the Summer Palace of the Emperors, called in Chinese Wan-shou-san.* This magnificent residence was destroyed by the Allies in 1860, in return for indignities offered by the Chinese to the English Minister, Sir Harry Parkes.† As we are crossing a little stream, not far from the ruins, the horse of the "unlucky one" of our party suddenly lowers his head to drink,—which causes his rider to slide gracefully to the ground. Off goes the pony, this time straight through a potato-field, two of us following at full gallop. The owner of the field—a tall Chinaman of forbidding aspect—rushes at us with uplifted hoe, motioning to us to go back. We gesticulate frantically towards our pony, now far ahead, quietly

---

* I. e. Sans Soucis.

† "The rooms were completely filled with gold, silver, and bronze gods of gigantic dimensions (one of which, a Buddha, was seventy feet high); some were stored with bales of the finest silk fabrics. A sum of £32,000 was found in solid ingots of gold and silver, which gave each private in the Allied forces prize money to the amount of about £3 5s. The French officers presented to the Emperor, Empress, and Prince Imperial of France the whole of the most valuable articles which they carried off from the palace. A superb green jade baton, of great value, mounted with gold, was selected by Lord Elgin as a present to Queen Victoria; and a similar one was likewise sent to the Emperor Napoleon."

grazing on potato-heads, and, in spite of the native's threatening movements, do not pause till we hold the runaway securely by the rein. We now proceed without interruption to the ruins of the Summer Palace, and dismounting in the outer court-yard, now full of weeds and decay, we lunch near a marble gateway, in the midst of a half-circle of gaping Chinese, who watch our every motion with evident surprise and amusement. While sitting here we see a party of foreigners galloping rapidly towards us. When they draw near and dismount, F—— and I are delighted to find that one of the number is a friend and fellow-citizen,—Mr. R. S. Russell of Boston. Strange and enjoyable fortune, to meet a Bostonian in the interior of China!

Lunch over, we set out to explore the ruins, and pass first through a succession of gates, each shutting in what must formerly have been beautiful pleasure-parks. Beyond these, we emerge on to a broad stone walk shaded by grand old trees, with a large pond on the left, full of lotos-flowers, over which is built a beautiful marble bridge. On our right hand are the ruins, extending to the top of a high hill, on the summit of which — its Imperial yellow roof and tiles glistening in the sun like gold — stands the only once-inhabited building that remains from the terrible desolation that was spread over the whole.

The front of this structure contains innumerable little Buddhas, standing in niches very near together. The view

from the top of the hill, where the building stands, is one of
the finest in the vicinity of Pekin, and the varied prospect
of lake, valley, and mountains must have pleased even an
Emperor. Half-way down the hill, on the right-hand side,
stands a beautiful bronze pagoda, which was untouched in
the bombardment. It is at the base of the hill, between it
and the lake, that the most evident traces of the destruction
are to be seen. Here palace walls are crumbling to pieces,
stone lions, bronze gods, and marble pagodas lie heaped in an
indiscriminate mass, covered all over with fragments of the
blue, yellow, and green bricks of which the royal buildings
were mainly constructed.

Leaving Wan-shou-san, we make our way slowly towards
Hai-lung-tan, a town where we are to pass the night. At
six o'clock we come in sight of a village built at the foot of
a hill, on the summit of which is a picturesque temple with
a yellow roof,—which indicates that the Emperors worship
therein at certain seasons. We are informed that the joss-
man of the temple has kindly offered us accommodations in
the sacred precincts, and, having dismounted and "chin-
chined" our host, we are shown to very comfortable quarters,—being the very room occupied by some of the official
staff of the last Emperor during the royal visit. In company
with the priest we visit the temple. Among the various ugly
divinities enthroned herein is one—the god of war—of uncommon hideousness. He holds a thick, knotted club in his

hand, which we temporarily deprive him of and examine at our leisure. Leaving the temple, and retracing our steps through the grounds, we suddenly find ourselves on the bank of a clear, deep pond, and, having received permission from the joss-man, we enjoy a refreshing swim, to the great astonishment of a crowd of Chinese, who, apparently, feel sure that we are possessed of a devil.

After supper, about ten o'clock, F—— and the New-Yorker being asleep on their *congs*, I am sitting with my other companion, when our servant enters and informs us that the joss-man has received intelligence that a band of thieves from the village below are planning to fall upon us during the night, and the priest warns us to make preparations to defend ourselves. Our servant finishes the message with a word of advice from himself, that we "better makee pistol all proper." Going into the next room, where our attendant sleeps, we find that he has determined not to be taken by surprise. He has erected a high barricade against the only door, formed of the various furniture of the apartment, and has placed his mattress near by, so that he may surely be aroused if the door is pushed open from without. Indeed, if the barricade is disturbed, it is highly probable that our faithful ally will be crushed to death. By his bed also are matches and a candle. Our door has no lock, and the windows are simple sheets of oiled paper.

I approach the New-Yorker and inform him of our threatened danger. He mutters something very uncomplimentary to the robbers, hands me his revolver, and turns over to continue his nap. F—— makes no sound.

Ever since our departure from Tien-tsin, our English fellow-traveller has repeatedly informed us of a remarkable pistol which he is carrying. I now congratulate him on the opportunity for employing it which has arrived. He removes it from its case, looks at it tenderly, and loads it. An expression of admiration escapes our servant, who is looking on, and I almost fear that the tempting sight may cause him to join our expected foes. We have now made ample preparations, and are about to extinguish the lights, and follow the example of our other companions who are sleeping quietly, when we decide to question the servant a little more particularly. We summon him and submit him to a cross-examination. His answers, expressed in "pigeon-English," require some consideration, but his ideas are eventually conveyed to us. The message of the priest becomes now of a different import. He wished us to be informed that "a party of foreigners who lodged in our rooms two months ago were robbed by villagers during the night." This intelligence modifies matters, and, having stretched ourselves on our *congs*, we are soon asleep. Quiet reigns throughout the premises, and we are undisturbed till morning.

September 25. — The various temples or joss-houses in China belong, for the most part, to the Emperor. The joss-men are supported either by a direct salary from the government, or, as in the case of our host, by voluntary contributions from the people of the neighborhood. These joss-men are not allowed to marry, and are forbidden to eat certain articles of food; but the joss-man of Hai-lung-tan was certainly not scrupulous in regard to the strict performance of his vows. Not only did he make a hearty meal from the remnants of our supper and breakfast (smoking some of our cigars afterwards), but he even had the audacity to charge us a large price for our accommodations, — a "squeeze" which even our Chinese servant assured us was atrocious; for the buildings did not belong to him, and we brought along our own food. Having, therefore, paid him two thirds of his demand (presented with some unadulterated Americanisms), we continue our way.

Our road lies over a flat, poorly cultivated country, with the usual mud-towns placed at certain intervals apart. We meet constantly small bands of common soldiers going towards Pekin, armed with long guns of very inferior construction. They stare at us insolently, but, remembering Mr. Avery's advice, we pay no attention to them. About noon we approach a village, built on the top of a hill, and drawing near (for our path runs through it), we see that the inhabitants are making great preparations to receive us. As we pass through the town in single file, the men cease their work, range themselves on each side of the street, and, snatching up gongs, drums, and cymbals, beat them furiously; the little boys explode cannon-crackers; and the women, hurrying to their doors with their children in their arms, burst into shrill peals of laughter at sight of the strangely dressed objects who are moving slowly by.

We lunch at Cham-ping-chow,* one of the dirtiest and most squalid "cities" we have yet seen. A company of native cavalry are occupying the best inn, and we are obliged to dismount at an inferior one. We hurry off as soon as possible, and passing out of the city, make our way round a range of low hills, into a vast valley beyond. We see ahead of us several lofty buildings, standing, for the most part, at the base of the distant mountains, which enclose the other side of the plain. Proceeding across the plain, we come first to a marble gateway, ninety feet wide and fifty high, containing some fine *bas-reliefs*. Passing through this, we next reach a lofty brick arch with the Imperial yellow roof, and a little farther on, after crossing several marble bridges, now rapidly falling into decay, we emerge on to a broad stone avenue, on each side of which are colossal figures of blue marble. Two pairs of lions, unicorns, camels, horses, and elephants compose the group, all most finely carved, and next to these are ranged colossal priests, and warriors, some with huge swords, who seem to be guarding these precincts of the dead. The elephants are thirteen feet high and seven long; and our horses, in turn, shy violently at sight of them. After passing over

---

* Called by foreigners "Jumping Joe."

the long stone avenue,—which once must have been a grand approach,—we come to the tomb of Yung Lo, the founder of the Ming dynasty,* which stands in the centre, while the others stretch along the base of the mountain, on each side.

The site of these Ming Tombs is exactly in accordance with the most approved principles of *Feng-shui.* To explain this, I will quote from a very interesting pamphlet which appeared recently in Hong Kong:† "The common people have the notion . . . . that the souls of their ancestors are by their animal nature chained, as it were, for some time to the tomb in which their bodies are interred, whilst by their spiritual nature they feel impelled to hover near the dwellings of their descendants; whence it is but a natural and logical inference to suppose that the fortunes of the living depend in some measure upon the favorable situation of the tombs of their ancestors. If a tomb is so placed that the animal spirit of the deceased supposed to dwell there is comfortable and free of disturbing elements, so that the soul has unrestricted egress and ingress, the ancestors' spirits will feel well disposed towards their descendants, will be enabled to constantly surround them, and willing to shower upon them all the blessings within reach of the spirit world.‡ . . . . Naturally, therefore, every

---

* 1368 – 1628.

† Feng-shui ; or, The Rudiments of Natural Science in China. By Ernest J. Eitel, M. A., Ph. D., of the London Missionary Society.

‡ "So deeply ingrafted is this idea of the influence of the dead upon the

Chinaman takes the greatest pains to place the tombs of his
relatives in such a situation, that no star or planet above, nor
any terrestrial element below, no breath or subtle influence
of nature, no ill-portending configuration of hills and dales,
should disturb the quiet repose of the dead, for upon this depend the fortunes and misfortunes of the living. It is consequently important to know the rules by which the luckiest
spot for a grave can be found. . . . . There are in the earth's
crust two different, shall I say magnetic currents, the one
male, the other female; the one positive, the other negative;
the one favorable, the other unfavorable. The one is allegori-
cally called the azure dragon, the other the white tiger. The
azure dragon must always be to the left, the white tiger to
the right of any place supposed to contain a luck-bringing site.
This therefore is the first business of the geomancer on looking
out for a propitious site, to find a true dragon, and its complement the white tiger, both being discernible by certain
elevations of the ground. Dragon and tiger are constantly
compared with the lower and upper portion of a man's arm;
in the bend of the arm the favorable site must be looked for.
In other words, in the angle formed by dragon and tiger, in

living, that Chinese wishing to get into the good graces of foreigners will
actually go out to the Hong Kong cemeteries in the Happy Valley, and worship there at the tombs of foreigners, supposing that the spirits of the dead
there, pleased with their offerings and worship, would influence the spirits of
the living, and thus produce a mutual good understanding between all the
parties concerned."

the very point where the two (magnetic) currents which they individually represent cross each other, there may the luck-bringing site . . . . be found. I say it *may* be found there, because, besides the conjunction of dragon and tiger, there must be there also a tranquil harmony of all the heavenly and terrestrial elements which influence that particular spot, and which is to be determined by observing the compass and its indication of the numerical proportions, and by examining the direction of the watercourses."

The site of the Ming Tombs possesses the exact requisites declared above. The two chains of hills enclosing the valley form, by their junction, a complete horseshoe; and this spot, crossed by the two necessary magnetic currents representing the dragon and the tiger, was selected as thoroughly propitious for the interment of Imperial remains.

Crossing now a court-yard, we enter a large chamber containing many pillars of teak-wood, each twelve feet in circumference and thirty-two feet high. This room is two hundred and ten feet long and thirty wide. Passing through this, we cross another court-yard and enter the building which contains the bone of the illustrious Yung Lo. A colossal tortoise, bearing on its back a tablet with inscriptions referring to the Ming dynasty and its founder, marks the spot where the remains are deposited. The whole place is neglected. A very garden is sprouting from the roof, the court-yard is full of coarse weeds, and only a few beggars, or a solitary merchant bound to Pekin, are to be seen in the vicinity. A more beautiful spot for an Emperor's cemetery could hardly be obtained. The wide valley, enclosed by high mountains, looks secluded and peaceful, and an air of rest and quiet seems to pervade the whole place. These Ming Tombs testify very unfavorably against the Chinese. The nation does not even preserve the grand works bequeathed to them by their ancestors, but their fine roads and lofty buildings are suffered to fall into ruin and decay. They declare, however, that they are the only truly civilized race on the globe, and regard all others as "barbarians."

As the tomb of Yung Lo is a type of the others, we strike across the plain towards Nan-kow, which we reach at sunset. Here we find the best inn we have thus far seen. The "foreigner's room" is clean, and the walls are hung with pictures of Chinese life and moral maxims of Confucius. It is true that a drove of sheep are quartered in the very next partition of the building, but to this we are accustomed. Our landlord, a fat, jolly-looking Chinaman, meets us on our arrival, offers us his snuff-box, and "chin-chins" us till he grows weary. As he understands no English, we address him as "Kolooz-leum," — which seems to please him greatly.

September 26. — The Great Wall is met at a distance of fifteen miles from Nan-kow, at the end of a pass of the same name. The pass is so rocky that the distance must be accomplished on donkeys. Soon after breakfast we mount these

patient animals, and start on our way, intending to return to
Nan-kow for the night.   Passing through the town we ride
under the great gate which marks the opening of Nan-kow
Pass.   The structure contains, on each post, some fine carving.
From here our path lies over stones and rocks and across
streams;* here, too, we meet frequently long lines of ladened
camels, coming from Mongolia or going thither, with an armed
man in front and in the rear.   Large flocks of black-headed
sheep pour over the road, plunging through rivulets and across
stones, and creating great confusion.   Several mule-litters — a
sedan-chair carried by mules — go by, bound for Pekin, with
indolent-looking Chinamen stretched at their ease within,
while innumerable donkeys and mules and vast droves of
horses increase the general disorder.   At the foot of a precipitous spur of the mountain we see a woman kneeling on the
ground, bending herself to and fro, sobbing, and wringing her
hands, and pouring out a wild lament in a piteous voice,
which echoes from hill to hill.   On inquiry, we are told that
she has recently become a widow, and is mourning at her husband's grave, according to the custom of her country.   Along
the pass are built little joss-houses, before which are hung
gongs which the priests strike on the approach of a traveller,
who is expected to contribute a few "cash," in return for a
prayer offered for his safety.

---

* "Genghis Khan followed it when he invaded China." — BARON HÜBNER.

After riding about four hours, we emerge from the pass, and soon arrive at the Great Wall, which stretches over the hills far off into the distance. At certain intervals steps lead up to the top. The wall is about forty feet high and twelve feet wide. It is built of a hard gray stone. Against modern artillery it would be of little avail, but at the time of its construction it must have been, if well defended, a serious obstacle to an opposing band. The wall was begun B. C. 200. It is about twelve hundred miles long, and surmounts the highest and most inaccessible peaks in the vicinity.

We lunch, sitting on the summit; the view on all sides is superb. Along the high mountains, stretching away into the distance, can be distinguished the thin gray line of the wall. On the plain below, a long procession of heavily loaded camels is winding slowly on, the shouts of the drivers echoing through the hills. Except this, all is quiet and still. Before us is an Asiatic picture which will never be effaced from our minds.

We retrace our steps through the pass and arrive back at Nan-kow at 6 P. M.

September 27. — We return to Pekin, stopping, on our way, to see the Llama pagoda, situated about two miles from the Chaen-men gate, which is the finest piece of sculpture in the vicinity of the city.

CHAPTER X.

PEKIN.

September 28. — The city of Pekin* possesses three walls. The outer wall encloses the Chinese city; the second divides off the Tartar city; and lastly, there is the Imperial wall, which shuts in the Yellow City, — the residence of the Emperor, the Son of Heaven. Foreigners are allowed to visit certain parts of the Yellow City, but only the highest ambassadors are suffered, at stated times, to pass through the royal gateway and cross the long avenue which leads to the Hall of Audience. The streets of Pekin are unusually wide for a Chinese city; and if it were not for the total absence of sewers, and the abominable habits of the people, who have no idea of decency or cleanliness, the pure air from the neighboring hills would render it quite a desirable residence. As it is, every street is full of mud and shocking waste;

---

* It is impossible to state the population of this city. Of one fact I am sure; the "3,000,000" of the geographies is an absurdity. It is doubtful if the number reaches 1,200,000.

deep ruts, which grow worse daily, nearly swallow up all
carts that jolt over them; and in spite of fresh breezes, the
odors from all points are sickening and almost unendurable.

We start this morning to visit the great Llama temples,
where Buddha is worshipped by fifteen hundred resident
priests. The buildings, situated near the Custom House, are
fully two miles from our hotel, and, as the day is very warm,
we engage carts, and sitting forward on the shafts (where the
least jolting is felt), we are bumped along the Harto-men Street,
through a wondering crowd who stare at us as we go by.
When we have accomplished about a mile, we meet a long
funeral procession. The dead man was a rich merchant, and
his wealth and importance are attested by the vast number
that are following his remains to the grave. One hundred
men, walking two by two, lead the way, dressed in full
mourning garments of white, and bearing in their hands tall,
broad wands, painted red and covered with inscriptions. Then
follow ten men bearing the body on a litter, over which is a
handsome canopy. The body itself is protected by a richly
embroidered cloth, which falls in graceful folds around it.
The procession is closed by another hundred men dressed in
white, some carrying banners and others gongs, drums, and
cymbals, with which to mark time for the whole. The Chinese consider themselves polluted if they have any contact
with a corpse, even so much as touching the litter on which
it is lying. On this account, all the dead are carried to the

grave by men whose caste or calling is not held respectable, — the beggars, the barbers, and the offal-carriers. The richest prince is thus often borne to his last resting-place by beggars.

On our arrival at the wall which surrounds the temple grounds we pass through a gate, and are met in the court-yard by a priest in long yellow garments, who is to serve as guide. We are very glad to find that we have arrived at service-time; and on approaching one of the buildings, we hear a noise like the loud buzzing of countless swarms of bees, and looking into the temple we discover the cause. About three hundred priests,* with long yellow robes and shaved heads, are seated on wooden benches, facing a large, richly decorated altar, before which an elderly priest is stand-ing, and chanting a prayer to the accompaniment of a gong; the others repeating it after him in a loud chorus, at the same time passing their hands over strings of curiously carved beads, which they wear round their necks. At the conclusion of the prayer they all rise, and putting on their heads tall yellow hats, pour into another temple to perform another portion of their daily devotion. We find that this temple (which they have just left) contains large collections of valu-able articles, — rich carpets, gold, silver, and bronze vessels, fine carvings, and costly tapestries. In a neighboring building is a great wooden figure of Buddha, seventy-five feet high,

---

* Moguls.

and twenty feet across the chest. Near by, some priests are chanting a song to their god, and one magnificent bass voice rings out above all the others.* After taking a cup of tea with the priests, we return to our quarters for *tiffin*, as we plan to visit, or attempt to visit, the Temple of Heaven this afternoon.

The Temple of Heaven (where the Emperor worships at a certain time of the year) is not open to foreigners, but many, through bribery, corruption, or force, gain admittance. With our landlord (who speaks Chinese fluently), we start soon after lunch, and passing out of the *Chaen-men* gate, and crossing the "Beggars' Bridge," are soon in sight of the temple wall. As we walk along I hear for the first time the epithet *hong kueitzu* (foreign devils) applied to us; and from this and other little occurrences, our landlord assures us that the crowd know perfectly where we are going, and will probably do all they can to hinder us. By this time we are near the temple gate, and a multitude of men and boys are following steadily behind us; suddenly one starts ahead, reaches the temple gate before us, says something rapidly to the gate-keepers, and disappears. We make a rush forward (for we know he has given warning of our approach), but too late; the heavy doors swing together, the interior bolts are shot into their sockets, and our further advance is checked. The crowd, which has rapidly

---

* We afterwards heard that this man's voice is famous throughout the city.

increased, raise a shout of derision, and evidently consider our repulse but another evidence of the inferiority of the "barbarians." Our landlord cannot contain himself. Pouring forth a volley of abuse in Chinese (which evidently surprises them), he seizes a short stick, and, grasping the nearest native by his cue, he thrashes him till he howls for mercy. Matters now begin to look serious. The natives, incensed at the treatment of their comrade (for which act our landlord could be summoned before his minister), pick up stones* from the street, and mass themselves together more compactly. The New-Yorker, with complacency, lays his hand on a pocket in his vest from which a small loaded pistol protrudes. Our landlord is determined not to be outdone. He hurries us rapidly along till we arrive at a part of the wall where some bricks have fallen out, and where it can easily be scaled. In turn we scramble up, and drop down into the párk beyond. Our difficulties are not yet over. In the distance, across the park, we see another high gate tightly closed. Having arrived there, however, we hold a long parley with the keeper, who consents to admit us for a silver dollar. The second obstacle is thus surmounted, but still another gate remains. Through the crevices we can plainly see the blue roof of the temple. A half-dollar, thrust under the sill, causes the heavy doors to swing

---

* Only three weeks previously, Dr. Bushell and his wife, of the English Legation, while walking quietly by this very spot, were severely stoned by the populace.

inwards; we cross a grass-plot, ascend some beautiful marble steps, and see the hidden building before us.

The Temple of Heaven is a pagoda-like structure, covered with blue tiles. Three umbrella-like roofs rise, one above another, from the blue walls below. These walls are elaborately sculptured and enamelled, and are inlaid with glass-work. Three white marble terraces, finely carved, surround it. Near by are three large bronze vessels, in which the papers of criminals of high rank are burned. Behind, is the spot where cattle are slaughtered for the yearly sacrifice, performed by the Emperor after worshipping in the temple.

The door is bolted, but we can easily look in through the windows. No idols of any sort are to be seen. The interior pillars and wood-work are solid but plain. Once a year in this place he who calls himself Ruler of Earth bows down before the Sovereign of Heaven.

We leave the temple and retrace our steps, expecting to find the gates closed upon us, but, apparently, our unceremonious entrance has so astonished the natives, that they are glad to get rid of us. We return to the hotel unmolested.

September 29. — We spend the morning in Curio Street, examining different articles for which Pekin is noted, — fine *cloisonné* work, and beautiful devices of jade-stone; ivory carvings, bronzes, and old porcelain, and great varieties of fine furs, which are brought principally from Siberia. The lacquer-work does not compare favorably with the Japanese.

The prices asked are ridiculously exorbitant, and the purchaser must make a reasonable offer and hold to it firmly.

In the afternoon I present a letter of introduction to Rev. Henry Blodget, D. D. a leading Protestant missionary, who, with his wife, has resided in Pekin for many years. I pass a pleasant half-hour, and promise to lunch with them before my departure.

September 30. — We go this morning to pay another visit to the English Legation. Mr. Hillyar congratulates us on our good fortune at the Temple of Heaven, telling us that a friend of his, who recently obtained admittance to the grounds, with his wife, was shut in, on returning, by the keeper of the outer gate, who stubbornly refused to allow the "barbarians" to pass; and it was only when a loaded pistol was held close to his head, that the native changed his mind.

In regard to political matters the Chinese are again temporizing. Prince Kung has agreed to furnish special and extraordinary passports to three Englishmen who will proceed to Yun Nan, and, after investigating the entire circumstances of the murder, will join with a Chinese commission in making a formal report to both governments. The Honorable Mr. Grosvenor is the chief of the English commission, and, in company with the others, is to start at once for Shanghai. All danger of immediate hostilities is therefore at an end.

In the afternoon we receive a visit from Mr. R. S. Russell of Boston, who is about to start for the Great Wall.

October 1. — We visit this morning the old Observatory and Imperial College, erected under the directions of the Jesuits in A. D. 1279. The Observatory is built on the City Wall, and the College near by in the city below. Some of the bronze astronomical instruments are of elaborate and exquisite construction. The entire premises have been unused for years.

From here we proceed through the city back to the hotel. It is nearly one o'clock, and I am due at the Blodgets'. Arrived there, I am cordially welcomed, and, after lunch, Dr. Blodget conducts me to his church, and relates many interesting anecdotes, and gives me much useful information in regard to his long labors among the natives. In the church (which is open through the day) we see a converted Chinaman (a member of the church) lecturing to a little knot of his fellow-countrymen, who are gathered around him; and I cannot help noticing the expression of the lecturer's countenance. Instead of the careless insolence which is generally stamped on the faces of the Chinese, the speaker has a look of quiet manliness and serenity which is unusual.

At 7 P. M. (preceded by our servant with a lantern) we pick our way carefully through the horrible streets till we arrive at the German Legation. We are met, as usual, by a polite servant, who receives our wraps, and announces us to the minister. Dinner is served immediately. Six or seven gentlemen of the legation are at table. All talk English fluently, and the charming manners of our host put us thoroughly at ease. The lofty dining-room itself in which we are sitting is not unworthy of its cultivated possessor. A heavy carpet is on the floor, the table is adorned with costly silver and glass; and behind the minister, on the wall, a large and valuable collection of Japanese and Chinese daggers and swords is tastefully arranged. Noiseless servants quickly remove the courses, each of which is a triumph of culinary art. In short, we have stepped from the discomforts of a people of the past into the luxuries of modern society. Beyond the threshold is neglect and decay; within, is order, refinement, and progression.

After dinner, we adjourn to a large parlor adjoining. From all foreigners that I have met in Pekin I hear one unvarying complaint. "The discomforts of the city," they say, "we can endure; but the lack of polished society is keenly felt." Besides the dreadful uncleanliness, however, the climate, except during the month of October, is disagreeable and annoying. In November, December, January, and February a little snow falls, which, however, is quickly removed by a cutting northeast wind, which blows continually at this season. In the spring the dust is overpowering; and the heat in summer is only tempered by heavy rains, which form long avenues of deep mud.

By the kindness of the minister, a servant with a huge paper lantern conducts us back to our lodgings.

October 2. — We are to devote this morning to an inspection of the Emperor's marble bridge and the Roman Catholic cathedrals. The marble bridge spans a wide stream, running close to the Imperial buildings, full of lotos-flowers and great masses of decaying weeds and general rottenness. With proper care, this rivulet might be kept clear and fresh, and such was undoubtedly the intention of the Emperor, who planned the surrounding pleasure parks and grounds, but it is neglected, along with so much else in China.

From here we proceed to the new Roman Catholic Cathedral. It is a large, handsome edifice, and testifies favorably to the result of the labors of the Catholic missionaries. An extensive ornithological museum is attached to a school for natives, which is conducted by the priests. The old church, which we next visit, is smaller than the new, but it contains a tablet, erected on the back of a large stone tortoise, on which is an inscription in Chinese, placed there by an old Emperor, which commands the citizens to spare this building, even if the rest of the city is destroyed.

Towards sunset we ascend to the top of the Tartar Wall to see the sun disappear behind the distant hills. At our feet lies the city, teeming with life, and the eye can roam over the multitudes of buildings stretching far away in every direction. The beams of the setting sun are shining full on the Imperial palaces, which, with their yellow roofs, glitter like gold. Flocks of carrier-pigeons, with tinkling bells tied to their wings, wheel round and round over our heads, and the various sounds of the city below come up to us pleasantly from afar. At last the sun sinks down behind the hills, long lines of men and animals pass in through the closing gates, and taking a last look around us, — for we have planned to leave Pekin on the morrow, — we descend to the street and return to our hotel.

CHAPTER XI.

PEKIN TO CANTON.

October 3. — At half past seven this morning, having placed
our baggage in carts and obtained donkeys for ourselves, we
bid farewell to Pekin and start for Tung-chow. We have
decided to return to Tien-tsin by boat; for, dropping down
the river with the current, the distance to Tien-tsin (one
hundred and twenty-five miles) is easily accomplished in two
days, and is, of course, far less fatiguing than the long horseback ride. We reach Tung-chow at noon, and find that our
servant, whom we sent on ahead, has already engaged a "house-
boat," and four men who are to row us down stream. We
start immediately, and having skirted the town, are soon gliding along through a flat, thinly cultivated country, while the
measured sound of the oars alone breaks the silence around
us.

These "house-boats" contain a sort of cabin, in which four
persons can sleep, and in another part of the boat is a small
kitchen, which our servant superintends. The crew disappear
at night into a locker in the bow. They have solemnly prom-

ised us to work, in turn, through the night; at 2 A. M. I am awakened by loud, confused shouts. Starting up, I find that our craft is tied securely to the bank of the river, and the crew are nowhere to be seen. The New-Yorker is calling fiercely to our servant, who, in turn, delivers our complaints to the half-unconscious crew down below. At last three of them appear, and, receiving a fresh volley of abuse with Oriental stolidity, they untie the boat and work steadily till morning.

October 5. — We reach Tien-tsin at seven o'clock this morning, and find the steamer *Shing King* lying at her moorings, ready to start on the morrow. We go at once on board, and are delighted to be again in charge of Captain Hawes.

October 6. — We start at ten o'clock. Among the passengers are the English Commission, who are bound to Yün Nan *vià* Shanghai, to inquire into the circumstances of Margary's death. The Honorable Mr. Grosvenor (whom we met in Pekin) is the chief, and to him I owe much information in regard to the curious people in whose country we are travelling. Our fellow-citizen, Mr. R. S. Russell, is also on board.

October 7. — We arrive at Che-foo at 10 A. M., and remain till afternoon. We are joined here by several passengers, among whom is Mr. William M. Evarts, Jr., of New York.

October 9. — At eight o'clock this evening we come in sight of Shanghai, after a smooth and pleasant run from Che-foo. As we move slowly up the river, the bright lights along the

"Bund" and in the various residences make us almost believe that we are approaching a city of our own land.

October 13. — Ever since our start we have planned to go from Shanghai to Foo-chow, and thence to Canton and Hong Kong. We have several letters of introduction to Foo-chow, and wish especially to make the acquaintance of Commissioner Drew, a Harvard graduate, who has been in the employ of the Chinese government for twelve years. We find, however, that we shall be unable to make satisfactory connections with the steamers for Hong Kong, and we are therefore obliged to give up a visit to Foo-chow. As we wish to reach India during the Prince of Wales's visit (and have much to see on the way), we decide to take passage on a steamer which is to start for Canton to-morrow at daybreak, and we are therefore compelled to leave undelivered several letters of introduction to people in Shanghai.

At midnight we go on board the steamer *Glengyle*, bound for Amoy and Canton. The *Glengyle* is a fine vessel of thirteen hundred and seventy-five tons, and, with wind and tide in our favor, we move rapidly down the Wang-poo River and enter once more the Yellow Sea. Only three passengers besides ourselves are on board.

October 16. — At daybreak this morning we are off Amoy. On our left we can dimly see Formosa. Around us are a score of swiftly sailing junks, whose piratical owners are always on the lookout for disabled vessels, which they plunder without mercy. Indeed, our captain tells us that we are in the most dangerous waters of the Chinese seas. The course, he says, is but imperfectly marked on the chart; hidden rocks abound, and the various pirate-junks, for which the region is noted, are perpetually hovering in the neighborhod. If a steamer strikes a rock, the passengers are often obliged to fight their way ashore.

We change our course and approach Amoy. On our right is the reef of rocks where the steamer *Hector* was wrecked a few weeks before, and we can plainly see the remains of the deck rising above the waves. We come to anchor between the native town of Amoy and the little island Koo-lun-soo, where the foreign population dwell.

Amoy is a picturesque place, containing, however, but little of interest to the traveller. It is distant five hundred miles from Hong Kong, and contains a small foreign population and about two hundred thousand natives.

We go ashore and make our way through the dirty streets to the custom-house, where we find Mr. Spinney (a recent Harvard graduate), who is employed by the Chinese government. Afterwards we obtain a guide and walk about the city. Amoy is by far the dirtiest place we have yet seen. The natives are quite different in appearance from their countrymen in the North. They wear heavy turbans, which give them a fierce, piratical look. Here one may buy necklaces and bracelets, exquisitely carved from olive-stones. A stranger should, however, invariably refuse the specimens first offered in the shops, as the best goods are only brought out when the inferior are rejected. Here, too, are lace and silk factories, and large quantities of artificial flowers are exported every year to various parts of the Empire.

In the afternoon Mr. Spinney comes aboard to return our call. He says his work in the custom-house is continuous and rather uninteresting at present, but as soon as he obtains a little knowledge of the language he shall progress more rapidly.

At midnight we weigh anchor, and in the light of a full moon resume our journey to Canton.

October 18. — At five o'clock this morning the first officer rouses me and informs me that the ship is just entering the harbor of Hong Kong. Going quickly on deck, the scene in the early morning light is very beautiful. The sun has not yet risen, and the various lights of the town shine clearly forth from the base of the hill, which rises perpendicularly eighteen hundred feet. As soon as we drop anchor we are surrounded by multitudes of *sampans*, on the lookout for employment. We intend to visit Hong Kong on our return from Canton and Macao, and at ten o'clock we are once more on our way, steaming rapidly up the Chu-kiang, or Pearl River, past beautiful scenery on each side of us, while gayly painted junks and fishing-boats are tossed up and down unceremoniously by our steamer's waves. At one o'clock we

pass the Boca or Bogue forts, the scene of a conflict between
the English and the Chinese in 1857. Beyond, on our left,
is Whampoa, where heavily loaded vessels are obliged to anchor, on account of the shallowness of the stream above. At
five o'clock we reach Canton and anchor opposite Shamien
(the foreign reservation), in the midst of a perfect flotilla of
junks, "flower-boats," "snake-boats," and *sampans*. These
boats are the homes of a large portion of the population of
the city. Women and young girls take the place of the men
(who for the most part are employed elsewhere), and mothers
with their babies strapped on their backs wield a long oar
with wonderful muscular power. Often, too, the mothers tie
their very youngest children to the deck by a long cord, while
those of a few years tumble about with a bamboo float fastened around them, which serves at once for clothing and life-
preserver. Canton River swarms with life. Regular streets
are formed by the "house-boats," which are placed side by
side, and the multitude of men, women, children (of all ages),
dogs, ducks, and chickens that are packed away in them for
the night is appalling! The little children, however, are wonderfully well-behaved, and look healthy and contented. Indeed, I have never seen better behaved babies than those in
China. Early in the morning, as I have said, they are either
strapped to their mothers' backs, or tied by a cord to the deck,
and no further notice is taken of them,—a fact they seem to
be perfectly well aware of, and hence do not seek to attract
attention.

Canton is distant ninety miles from Hong Kong and eighty from Macao. It contains a population of one million in the city proper, while two hundred and fifty thousand live in boats. A large foreign population still dwell on the reservation, but the number has been considerably diminished of late years, owing to the stagnation of trade. Canton is situated in exact accordance with the rules of *Feng-Shui.* " It is placed in the very angle formed by two chains of hills running in gentle curves towards the Bogue, where they almost meet each other, forming a complete horseshoe. The chain of hills known as the White Clouds represent the dragon, whilst the undulating ground on the other side of the river forms the white tiger." *

October 19. — We go ashore soon after breakfast. F—— and I are cordially received by Messrs. Russell & Co., to whom we have letters; while Mr. U—— and our English companion are comfortably installed at the house of the Commissioner of Customs. Indeed, letters of introduction are absolutely necessary in Canton, as the place contains only one second-rate hotel. The house of Messrs. Russell & Co. stands on the site of the old East India Company's Factory, destroyed by a mob in 1856. Our host kindly places his private boat at our disposal, and we return to the *Glengyle* for our trunks. Having obtained them, we bid the captain and officers farewell.†

---

* Eitel's Feng-Shui.

† It was farewell indeed. The *Glengyle* returned safely to Shanghai, and

After landing our baggage we spend the rest of the day in walking slowly about the city. We find, on all sides, vast quantities of ivory and sandal-wood articles, many handsome cups of silver and gold, covered with grotesque designs, while silk goods of the best quality can be bought at very reasonable prices. In the course of our wanderings we enter a large emporium of fire-crackers, and I perceive that I am in the very store whence comes a certain brand of fire-crackers, — the Golden Dragon Chop, — which was always the favorite among my companions at home. Opposite the house of Messrs. Russell & Co. I see the warehouse containing the prepared ginger which is exported from Canton in large quantities.

October 20. — With a guide in advance, we start this morning for a walk through the city, intending to visit some of the chief objects of interest. The streets of Canton are scarcely wide enough for two sedan-chairs to pass along, but, contrary to the usual state of things in China, the thoroughfares are really very clean. Large painted signs, suspended perpendicularly, and gorgeous lanterns, improve the outward appearance of the houses and stores; and in spite of the vast crowds of people hurrying hither and thither, the best of order prevails. Every one seems to treat his neighbor with courteous consideration; oftentimes when, on account of the

on her next trip down the coast to Amoy she struck on Namoa Island (off Amoy), on November 9, and sank in seven minutes. Captain Carnell, several under-officers, and many of the crew were drowned.

After landing our baggage we spend the rest of the day in walking slowly about the city. We find, on all sides, vast

courteous consideration; oftentimes when, on account of the

on her next trip down the coast to Amoy she struck on Namoa Island (off Amoy), on November 9, and sank in seven minutes. Captain Carnell, several under-officers, and many of the crew were drowned.

excessive narrowness of the streets, two coolies carrying a
heavy burden meet two other coolies similarly loaded, and
produce for the moment a complete block, one pair quickly
moves aside for the others, while a large crowd at each end
quietly wait till the road is clear, without any pushing or
ill-temper, so often seen at home.

We visit first the markets, where we see, dressed and exposed for sale, rats, cats, and puppies, besides various other
articles of food. As we are passing a native restaurant, the
proprietor lifts the cover from a sort of stew, at the same
time calling my attention to it, in hopes of alluring me to
taste. "What b'long?" I inquire. "This b'long cat-hash,"
he replies, at the same time stirring up the mess with a
long chopstick. I shake my head in disgust. The proprietor
looks at it with delight, but remarks philosophically, "Some
people likee, some people no likee?" "Yes," I reply, "me no
likee." And I walk on.

From here we make our way to a silk-weaving establishment, and can but wonder how such beautiful fabrics origi-
nate in such disagreeable quarters. We then stop in at an
opium-den. Owing to the early hour of the day, it is thinly
patronized, but two poor wretches are even now under the
influence of the drug. The room is similar in appearance to
the one we visited in San Francisco. From here we proceed
to the Temple of the Five Hundred Genii, called in Chinese
Wa-lum-tsz'. Canton contains one hundred and twenty-four

temples and other religious edifices. This Temple of the Five Hundred Genii is full of small gilded images, five hundred in number, which are placed around a large room, called the Hall of the Saints. Beyond, is the "Triple Representation of Buddha," and near by stands a figure of the Emperor Kien-lung, who reigned from A. D. 1736 – 1796. In the immediate vicinity of the temple, also, is a beautiful marble pagoda, about thirty-five feet high.

Our guide takes us next to the Temple of Longevity, called in Chinese *Cheong-shau-tsz'*, where we are shown a colossal figure of Buddha in a recumbent position. We now leave the Chinese city proper, and enter the Tartar city, and soon arrive at the Tartar city temple, called in Chinese *Kwong-hau-tsz'*. Here are three colossal images of Buddha, about twenty feet in height, and two small granite pagodas of great antiquity. This temple was built A. D. 250. Continuing our way, we visit next the Flowery Pagoda, called in Chinese *Fa-Cap-tok-yong-tsz'*. This building is over two hundred feet in height, and from its summit we obtain a fine view of the city. On our way back we stop at the Mohammedan Mosque, said to have been founded by Arabian voyagers in A. D. 850. It is called in Chinese *Kwong-Cap-wai-shing-tsz'*. Having removed our shoes, we enter, but, except some rich carpets and a few curious tablets, it contains little of interest. We finish our morning's tour by an inspection of the Temple of the Five Genii. The Chinese name is *'Ng-sin-kon*. Here there

is much that will well repay investigation. As we enter we
see a large idol. This is the supreme god of the Tauists.
Near by is a very large bell, which was struck by a cannon-
ball from an English man-of-war during the bombardment of
the city, in 1857. The bell is said to have been placed in
this temple hundreds of years ago, and a prophecy was then
uttered, declaring that evil would fall upon the city when
the bell gave forth sound. While doing our best to accept
this statement, we are led by our guide to a little court-
yard of the temple, in which is a large rock, with a curious
impression on its surface, somewhat like the print of a gigantic foot. This is declared by the priests to be the mark
of the divine Buddha. Before passing out we are shown five
stones which represent five holy rams, from which Canton is
said to have derived the name of the "City of Rams." From
here we return to *Ki-chong* (Russell & Co.'s residence).

After *tiffin* and a good rest we set out again. Embarking
in our host's boat (for every merchant possesses a well-built
boat for the use of his establishment), we are rowed rapidly
across the river to the great Honam Temple, called in Chinese *Hai-chong-tsz'*. It was built about A. D. 1675, by the
son-in-law of the Emperor Kang-hi. Among the various idols
is an image of Koon-yam (the Japanese Kuanon), the Hearer
of Prayers. A handsome pagoda, of white marble, stands in
the main hall. Near the temple, in an adjoining building,
are some sacred pigs, enormously fat, kept by the priests as

an example to the people to obey the command of Buddha, forbidding the destruction of a single living creature. For the same reason a quantity of fish are fed daily in an artificial pond near by.* Going now through the temple grounds, we are conducted to an immense urn, in which the ashes of the priests belonging to the temple are placed after cremation. Our guide assures us that the urn now contains the ashes of eighteen hundred and thirty-two. As we retrace our steps by one of the halls of the temple, we see the priests at supper. Several act as waiters, and walk round the room, filling each one's bowl with an uninviting stew of a sort of herb. The long line of priests with their flowing robes — not too clean — and shaved heads, eating rapidly with chopsticks, is not a pleasant sight. They offer us some refreshment, but we shudder and decline.

Having returned to the boat, we recross the river and make our way to the Execution Ground, called *Tin-tsz'-ma-lan*. A more dismal spot from which to make exit from the world could hardly be obtained. On landing from the river, we are led through a neglected garden into a small plot of ground, enclosed on one side by a high mud-wall, and on the other by the rear of a pottery manufactory. This is the

---

* I have been told, however, that Buddhists allow themselves to eat fish, on the ground that they themselves do not actually put them to death; for, having removed a fish from the water, it dies without any interference from man.

Execution Ground of the city. A narrow alley connects it with one of the principal streets. Several skulls are strewn about; and in the centre of the place a large pool of clotted blood, and a head covered with a piece of matting, give certain evidence that some criminal has very recently paid the penalty of his crimes. On inquiring, we are told that a man was executed only twenty-four hours before. At one end of the Execution Ground are two tall upright poles on which the heads of notorious malefactors are displayed. As we are leaving the grounds we meet the executioner, — a fat, happy-looking native, calmly smoking his pipe. Our guide addresses him respectfully. He tells us that he receives for his services "half-dollar one piecee," and is evidently satisfied with his lot. We ask to examine his official sword, but he replies that it is kept in the neighboring Yamen, and only brought to him when a criminal is to be killed.

Leaving this place of death, we follow our guide to the city prison. Here we are immediately surrounded by a crowd of miserable prisoners, some chained together, others with a ball and chain on their legs, all of them clamorous for a few "cash." Among the convicts is a wretched woman who has poisoned her husband. For this deed she is to be cut into thirty-six pieces on the Execution Ground. The Chinese believe that if the body is deprived of any member or part at or before death, that very portion will be lacking in the next world; consequently there is no worse punishment, in their opinion, apart from the physical pain, than to undergo a separation of limb from limb. A gentleman who witnessed this terrible torture told me that nothing could be more inhuman; for, beginning with the extremities, the less vital parts are lopped off, until the victim either dies from pain and loss of blood, or endures the agony till the heart itself is destroyed.

We next visit the Examination Hall, called in Chinese *Kung-ün*. This contains about 8,650 cells, in which the candidates are locked and left entirely alone for two days, till their answers to the given questions have been handed in to the authorities. Similar examinations are held at certain times in all the provinces and districts, and by means of these, and a final and much more severe one held triennially at Pekin, various high offices of the Empire are apportioned. Any one may be a candidate for the lowest or district examination. If he passes this and is still ambitious, he must then apply for the provincial examination, and the chosen few from each province strive in the Imperial examination at Pekin for the button of a powerful mandarin, or some other magistracy, and sometimes return as rulers of the province from whence they came.

We now proceed to the Temple of Horrors, called by the Chinese *Shing-wong-miu*. It contains a large number of figures, which were made to represent the tortures of the wicked in hell. About a dozen small chambers, enclosed by a sort of wooden wicker-work, are filled with devils who are causing sinful wretches to pay the penalty of crimes committed in the body. In one room an unfortunate man is exhibited jammed in a wooden vise; in another, several imps have just thrown their victim into a pot of molten lead; in another, they are slowly strangling a man; while in each compartment a large statue of the Devil himself looks down joyfully on the various performances. This temple is evidently regarded with awe by the common people, for we saw little knots come up in turn and gaze through the bars with a look of horror on their faces.

On our way back we visit the water-clock, called *T'ong-u-tik-lau*, a very old and curious machine. Then, striking rapidly down a side street to the river, we call a *sampan*, and are soon landed at the dock of Russell & Co.*

In the various Buddhist temples that we have visited in China I have observed an entire absence of that reverent and heart-felt worship which is noticeable in Japan. The priests and people perform the ceremonies of their sect with an air of decided carelessness, regarding them evidently as forms which must be discharged to insure their safety in the world to come. The buildings themselves, and the various sacred utensils, are ill kept and neglected.

The service in a Buddhist temple is astonishingly similar

---

* The temples and other objects of interest in Canton are so located, that, with a good guide, one may visit the majority in a single day.

to the form of worship in a Roman Catholic church. Processions of priests march up and down, swinging censers, and bowing before richly decorated altars on which are several tapers burning dimly. A little bell or gong, struck from time to time, increases the resemblance. The following graphic description of a Buddhist temple I copy from a most interesting pamphlet, recently published, which I obtained in Hong Kong:—*

"As you turn towards the principal entrance to the building, you remark, a yard or two in advance of the flight of steps leading up to it, figures of crouching lions carved in stone and resting on pedestals, placed on either side. You will be told that these are emblems of Shákyamuni, whose cognomen Shákya-simha (lit. Shákya, the lion) indicates that he is, by his moral excellence, the king of men, as the lion by his strength is the king of the beasts. Perhaps your guide will even quote a passage from his sacred scriptures, 'As a lion's howl makes all animals tremble, subdues elephants, arrests birds in their flight, and fish in the water, thus Buddha's utterances upset all other religions, subdue all devils, conquer all heretics, and arrest all the misery of life.'

"If it is a sunny day you will find gathered on the entrance steps a motley assembly; priests and beggars, lying lazily in the sun, or engaged in entological pursuits, mending their

* Buddhism; its Historical, Theoretical, and Popular Aspects. By Ernest J. Eitel, M. A., Ph. D.

clothes, cobbling their shoes, cleaning their opium-pipes, smoking, gambling, and so forth, and your appearance will be the signal for a general clamor for an alms-offering in the shape of a foreign cent, or they will offer their services as guides. But if it should happen to be a feast day the steps and the whole open space in front, with the court-yards inside, will be crowded to excess by a busy multitude, men, women, and children, who have come to worship or to consult the oracle, hawkers of fruit and other edibles, booths with fancy articles of all kinds, stalls opened by druggists, wandering doctors, fortune-tellers, tents for the purpose of gambling, in short, a complete fair, which pushes its lumber and its clamor close to the very altars of the divinities worshipped inside the central temple.

"As you enter the front door, a martial figure, with defying mien, armed to the teeth and sword in hand, confronts you. It is the image of Vêda, the patron and protector of monasteries. Inside the door there are to the right and left niches for the spirits of the doorway, who are supposed to keep out all evil influences, and for the Nâga (dragon) spirits, who are looked upon as the tutelary deities of the ground on which the sacred buildings are erected.

"Having passed the first court-yard, you are led through a second gateway, when your eye is arrested by four gigantic images, two being placed on either side of the gateway, guarding, as it were, with flaming eyes, the entrance to the sanctuary beyond. Your guide will inform you that they are the demon-kings of the four regions (Tchatur Mahârâdjas), who guard the world against the attack of evil spirits (Asuras); that each of them is posted on a different side of the central mountain (Méru), engaged in guarding and defending with the assistance of large armies under their command the corresponding quarter of the heavens. You will find incense lighted at the feet of these giants, and the images themselves almost covered with slips of paper, containing either a record of vows to be performed in case of prayer answered by these heroes, or a record of thanks for favors already bestowed. For you will be told, or may witness it, perhaps, with your own eyes, that these demon-kings are daily worshipped by the common people, who ascribe to them the power of healing all those diseases, and of preventing or averting all those calamities, which are supposed to be the work of evil spirits.

"After crossing a second court-yard you reach the principal temple by ascending a small flight of steps. On entering this building you see before you five little altars placed in a row, with a small image on each; and if it is the hour of prayer you may find a number of priests in full canonicals, resembling so many Roman Catholic priests, chanting their monotonous litanies and responses to the sound of bell and a sort of wooden drum. . . . .

"Step nearer. You need not fear to give offence or to disturb the devotion of men, who, whilst mechanically con-

tinuing their monotonous litany and chanting their responses,
will stretch out a hand to examine the texture of your clothes,
to receive an alms, or offer to light your cigar or criticise in
whispers the shape and size of your nose. Glance over the
shoulder of one of those priests and examine his 'manual of
daily prayer.' It is neatly printed in large-sized, full-bodied
native type and in the native character, but totally unintelligible to him, for it is Sanskrit, pure grammatical Sanskrit,
systematically transliterated, syllable by syllable. Listen to
him, as he chants, rhythmically indeed, but in drowsy monotonous voice: '*Sarva tathâgatâ schœmâm Samârasantu buddhyâ buddhyâ siddhyâ siddhyâ bodhaya bodhaya ribodhaya
ribodhaya mochaya vimochaya vimochaya sodhaya sodhaya visodhaya visodhaya Samantâm mochaya Samanta,*' etc., etc.
Poor fellow, he has not the slightest idea of the meaning of
these words, though he may have been chanting these Sanskrit prayers day after day for ever so many years. But he
has a notion that these strange sounds have some magic effect,
beneficial for himself and for the salvation of his soul. There
is, however, tolerably good sense in the words of his prayer
which reads, when translated, as follows: 'May all the Tathâ-
gatas (i. e. Buddhas) take up their abode in me! ever teach,
ever instruct, ever deliver with all knowledge! with all knowledge deliver, deliver, completely deliver! purify, purify, purify, completely purify! deliver, O deliver all living creatures'! etc.

"Pass on from these poor deluded souls that grope in the darkness for the light of a Saviour whom they know not. . . . . Visit some of the smaller buildings; you will probably see in one of them a fine marble pagoda reaching to the very rafters of the roof. It is built in strict Indian style, tastefully decorated, and forms the receptacle of some sacred relic. There may be in it perhaps a hair of Buddha, or a tooth, or a particle of his robe, or some relic of one of his disciples. There also prayers are offered, and sacrificial offerings of flowers, candles, and incense, presented by the people, who, true to the fetichistic habits of their forefathers, ascribe miraculous healing powers to such relics. . . . . But suppose you retrace your steps through the various temples you have visited, you will find it interesting to have a look at the apartments occupied by the priests. They have most of them their own cells, but dine together in one large hall, which, together with the kitchen and its enormous rice-boilers, are worthy a visit. The abbot has his private rooms, apart from the cells of the priests. You may find him willing to receive you, but you will be astonished if you enter his rooms expecting to find there the same primitive simplicity and economy which you noticed when passing through the apartments allotted to the use of the priests, and which reminded you so strongly of the internal arrangements of a Roman Catholic monastery. A modern abbot takes it generally very easy. If his monastery is not too far from any centre of foreign commerce, he will show you with pride a collection of articles *de luxe.* He has watches and clocks of foreign manufacture, photographs of less than questionable decency, and he is generally not only a confirmed opium-smoker, but considers himself a good judge of champagne, port, and sherry. His attendants are invariably laymen, relatives of his own, who may have no intention whatever to take the vows. But the same abbot may also have a printing-press with movable types, likewise of foreign manufacture, and you may see it turning out neat reprints of the most popular portions of the Buddhist scriptures, or little tracts and pamphlets of local reputation.

" After a visit to the gardens, which are generally well kept and which abound in curious specimens of artificial training, after a passing glance at the place where the bodies of deceased priests are burned, and the tomb which covers their ashes, you return through the labyrinth of galleries and courts. In one of the latter you may now notice a series of little chambers, popularly called chambers of horrors, containing statuary representations of the various tortures supposed to be employed in the various compartments of hell. For your guide will tell you, with a sly hit at yourself, that all those who do not believe in Buddhism, or violate its commandments, will after death be reborn in hell. He will inform you that there are underneath our earth eight large hells of extreme heat, eight more of extreme cold, again eight hells of utter darkness, and on the edge of each universe ten cold hells; but as each of these hells has many antechambers and smaller hells attached, all being places of torture, there are in reality altogether over a hundred thousand of such chambers of horrors. A pleasant prospect to heretics like yourself, your priest will add.

"On passing out through the gate, your eye may perhaps be arrested by a crowd of people surrounding a number of pigs wallowing in the richest food thrown before them. You will also notice in a conspicuous position near these pigs a poor-box, into which the people drop their offerings of money. What is it all about? Look at the inscription affixed to that box in large staring letters, 'Save life!' The greatest Buddhist commandment is that which forbids the taking of life. All life, human as well as animal life, is absolutely sacred in the eyes of the Buddhist devotee. The killing of animals for the purpose of food is a heinous offence. Still more so is the love of cruelty which leads the strong to prey upon the weak, and enables the sportsman, the fox-hunter, the deer-stalker, the pigeon-shooter, in heathen and Christian countries, to derive a horrible enjoyment from the piteous sufferings of poor dumb animals. These pigs are therefore exhibited by the priests to remind the people of this greatest of all Buddhist commandments. . . . . But, on the other hand, it is ridiculous to compare this Buddhist commandment, 'thou shalt not take life,' with the religion of Him who would not break

the bruised reed nor quench the smoking flax, and to give
the palm — as some European admirers of Buddhism have
actually done — to this Buddhist ideal of charity. Just ask
your guide whether the Buddhist church, which so laudably
extends its charity even to the brute creation and assiduously
feeds sacred pigs in its monasteries, exerts herself to amelio-
rate the condition of poor suffering humanity. He will have
to acknowledge that no hospitals, no asylums for the blind,
the deformed, the destitute, have ever been founded by a
Buddhist community. Alms, indeed, are encouraged, but they
are to be bestowed on the worthiest, — on the priest, the clois-
ter, the church, — and thus the current of charity is diverted
from the destitute or outcasts of society, whose very destitu-
tion is, according to the Buddhist scriptures, a proof of their
unworthiness, to the worthiest on earth, to the community of
priests, who are bound to receive the gifts bestowed, in order
that the faithful may acquire merit, though forbidden by the
self-renouncing principles of their creed to retain them for
their private advantage. Thus it was brought about that the
Buddhist priests take to feeding sacred pigs. A Buddhist
Peabody, therefore, would be doing the correct thing if he
were to throw all his humanitarian efforts with all his money
— before the swine.

"Well, you have visited a fair specimen of the popular pan-
theon of Northern Buddhism. What is the result? . . . .
Ancient Buddhism knows of no sin-atoning power; it holds

out to the troubled, guilty conscience no prospect of mercy, no chance of obtaining forgiveness, no possibility of justification, allowing not even so much as extenuation of guilt under any circumstances whatever. . . . . It is a science without inspiration, a religion without God, a body without a spirit, unable to regenerate, cheerless, cold, dead, and deplorably barren of results."

October 21. — We call this morning on the American consul (our fellow-passenger on the *Great Republic*). He invites us to come to the consulate at three o'clock in the afternoon and be present at his formal reception of the Viceroy. As we have no right to wear an official costume, we are obliged to decline. We promise, however, to dine at the consulate on the morrow. We dine in the evening with Commissioner Hart, brother of Commissioner James Hart of Pekin.

October 22. — Colonel Lincoln, the American consul, has kindly invited us to come to his house at four o'clock this afternoon, and, in company with himself and family, to spend an hour on the river and return afterwards to dinner. All the foreign consuls have large, comfortable boats, with well-protected cabins; and the flags of the different countries float gracefully over the sterns. All thanks to Mrs. Lincoln, for the first time in my travels I see my country's representative surrounded by attendants appropriately dressed. Mrs. Lincoln has presented to the crew of her husband's official boat a very simple but tasteful uniform, of which they are very proud. It

consists of a white sailor's shirt with a broad blue collar on which are stars, blue trousers, and a broad-brimmed straw hat with *American Consul* printed on the ribbon. Besides these articles, each man has a handsome red sash tied around his waist. Small matters like these make a great impression on the Chinese mind. The common people judge largely of the importance of a foreign country by the size of its consulate, its interior arrangements, of which they hear through the servants, and by the appearance of the attendants of the representative when they accompany their master about the city. While other nations seem to recognize this, — as is proved by the marked dress of their servants, the spaciousness of their legations, and the precision with which their households are conducted, — America pays but little attention to the quarters or maintenance of those she sends abroad.

After a very pleasant row on the river and a visit to a large joss-house lately erected, we return to the consulate for dinner.

To-morrow we leave Canton and continue our journey to Macao. In Canton one sees thorough Chinese life. The people are more interesting than the inhabitants of the North. They are more agreeable and kindly to foreigners, their streets and dwellings are far cleaner, and they are farther advanced in the peculiar arts of their race. Pekin is a barbarous encampment on the frontier of civilization. Canton is a bustling city which brings continually before the mind thoughts of the past, the present, and the future.

CHAPTER XII.

CANTON TO BATAVIA.

Macao. — Fan-tan Gambling. — Hong Kong. — Singapore. — Crossing the
Equator. — Arrival at Batavia.

October 23. — At half past seven this morning we bid farewell to our kind hosts and go on board the steamer *Spark*, bound for Macao. Just before we start a graceful row-boat draws near, propelled by a neatly dressed crew and steered by a foreigner. It is Commissioner Hart, who has come to wish us good-speed. Soon our vessel is under weigh. Having passed Whampoa, I perceive that the door leading to the steerage is locked, while a native of Manilla, armed with pistols and a huge cutlass, walks up and down continually before it. An armed man, likewise, patrols the upper deck. I am informed by the captain that these precautions are necessitated by the quantities of pirates that infest the waters between Canton and Macao. He says, furthermore, that every Chinese passenger is searched as he comes aboard, and all suspicious-looking baskets, bundles, and packages are thoroughly overhauled, in order that any concealed weapons may be brought to light.

"About two years ago," says he, "the *Spark* one morning

left Canton with a large number of Chinese steerage-passengers bound for Macao. Whampoa was passed in safety, and the *Spark* had reached the broad portion of the river and was steaming rapidly along, when several junks were observed headed directly for the vessel. This excited no remark, however, but a blast of the whistle was given as a notification of the steamer's approach. It was noon. The captain was at dinner; the only passenger was sitting idly on deck, and the quartermaster at the wheel was steering the vessel easily through the calm water without need of assistance. Suddenly a body of natives rushed up from the steerage, poured over the upper deck and fell upon the foreigners without mercy. The captain was literally cut to pieces. The passenger was mortally wounded and left for dead, and several of the crew who resisted were killed by their fellow-countrymen. Immediately the junks (which were previously noticed) approached the *Spark*, and another score of rascals climbed over the side. The captors, however, were unable to make off with their prize. They were ignorant of the practical use of the machinery. Having therefore plundered and stripped the vessel from stem to stern, they decamped in the junks and made for the nearest land. The Chinese who were left on the *Spark* succeeded in bringing the vessel to Macao. The outrage was promptly reported to the authorities; the pirates were pursued, and several that were captured were executed. Since that time all steamers on these waters post a guard in bow and stern."

At 5 P. M., after a smooth and delightful trip, we reach Guia light, and come in sight of the curious pink, yellow, and brown buildings, which give to Macao such a strange appearance, — so different from anything we have seen for the past few months. As soon as we have landed we make our way to the Royal Hotel, followed by a string of Portuguese beggars, who are even more importunate than Chinamen. Macao was settled by the Portuguese in A. D. 1547; and though this nation has held it ever since, and filled it with her own citizens and soldiery, still China has always insisted that it is in reality under her dominion. A lovely place it is, with a long curved beach, and with boldly rising hills around, on whose summits fleecy clouds rest constantly. In front of the town are several islands. The typhoon of September, 1874, did great damage to the town and harbor, but the traces of the disaster are nearly removed.

The hotel is built on a long curved street, Praya Grande, which follows the bend of the beach. The trade of Macao has departed. The coolie traffic alone remains. In the Chinese quarter, however, the stores are as thronged as in Canton. Undoubtedly in time the whole place will have fallen into the hands of the Chinese. The few Portuguese officials who are obliged to reside here come with reluctance. A social circle scarcely exists. The place is lifeless in part, and the busy multitude of Chinamen only brings before the minds of the foreigners the terrible loneliness of their lot.

Soon after dinner we take sedan-chairs and visit the great *fan-tan* establishment. *Fan-tan* is a gambling game which is played continually in Macao, both by foreigners and Chinese. The Portuguese government receives one hundred and fifty thousand dollars a year as a license from the proprietors of the gambling-houses. Every Saturday evening the steamers from Canton and Hong Kong bring many foreigners to try their luck on the *fan-tan* table. Here all is eagerness, animation, and excitement,—a dangerous agent to banish loneliness and *ennui*.

The game is played as follows: a flat piece of lead, perfectly square and a foot in length and breadth, is placed in the middle of the table. The banker—a keen-looking Chinaman—thrusts his hand into a pile of "cash," and, grasping as many as he can, lays them down on the table in sight of the players. The players than stake certain sums on 1, 2, 3, or 4, laying their money opposite the sides of the square so numbered. Taking now two chopsticks, the banker slowly counts off the "cash," *pushing aside four at a time*, and the number of the last count which finishes the pile—four, three, two, or one, whatever may end it—determines the winning side of the lead square. As the banker evidently cannot be sure of the number of "cash" which he takes in his hand from time to time, and as moreover the stakes are not deposited till the handful of "cash" is placed on the table, it is hardly possible for the players to be imposed upon. When the bank pays, however, it gives three times the amount of the stake less a discount of eight per cent,—a commission which in the end must pay the proprietors very largely.

The foreigners play *fan-tan* in a room at the top of the house, while the Chinese (who are inveterate gamblers) remain down below. The same *fan-tan* table is used, however, by both parties. A basket is let down by a cord from the foreigners' room; the money is placed in the basket, with a ticket indicating the number which the player has selected, and the whole is then lowered to the table. At the conclusion of a play, if the foreigner has won, his gains are hoisted up in the basket.

We prefer to witness the game in the lower room, and we spend a half-hour with great interest watching the Chinamen of all grades betting eagerly on every play. Several coolies and common servants are here risking dollar after dollar of the only money they own in the world,—the result of weeks of saving. If they lose, having no more with which to play, they quietly withdraw; but if they win, their good fortune only incites them to higher stakes. Peering eagerly into the heap of "cash," as each division of four is swept aside, they determine accurately the number of the last count long before the banker himself announces it.

We are standing near a Chinaman,—probably a messenger or house servant,—who has been playing steadily for many minutes. He has lost continually, and has nearly arrived at the end of his resources. His money is all gone, but he places a small silver watch in the hands of the banker, who tells him it may represent one silver dollar. The player, being apparently satisfied with this estimate of its worth, lays it down by the side of the lead square marked 1 and awaits the result of the count. Several other Chinamen, thinking this man must have some good reason for trusting his last piece of property to this number, follow his example by placing their bets by the side of the watch. The banker slowly sweeps the "cash" from the table, four at a time, the owner of the watch following each movement of the chop-sticks with eyes almost starting out of their sockets. When more than half has been counted off, an expression of delight fills his face, and when, soon after, one odd "cash" remains from the lot and he receives back his watch and nearly three dollars besides, he is the picture of happiness and is congratulated loudly by the other players on his good fortune. Soon after this little drama we return to the hotel.

October 24. — After breakfast this morning we visit the large garden now owned by Lourenço Marques, containing the grotto of the poet Camoës, where he is said to have composed some of his best known works. Following a path which runs through thick tropical vegetation, we come to a little hill, on the summit of which is a grotto which overlooks the sea. In this grotto is a bust of Camoës bearing the following inscription: "Luiz De Camoës; Nasceo 1524, Morreo 1580." Outside the grotto are several tablets with various poetical inscriptions; one signed "Bowring, July 30, 1849," being particularly appropriate:—

SONNET TO MACAO.

"Gem of the Orient Earth and open sea,
  Macao! That in thy lap and on thy breast
  Hast gathered beauties all the loveliest
  Which the sun smiles (on) in his majesty!

"The very clouds that top each mountain's crest
  Seem to repose there, lingering lovingly.
  How full of grace the green Cathayon tree
  Bends to the breeze, and now thy sands are prest

"With gentlest waves, which ever and anon
  Break their awakened furies on thy shore!
  Were these the scenes that poet looked upon
  Whose lyre, though known to fame, knew misery more?

"They have their glories, and Earth's diadems
  Have nought so bright as genius' gilded gems."

After dinner we visit the church of Our Lady of Sorrows, situated on the top of a hill overlooking the town and harbor. A curious wooden cross stands in front of the church, said to have been erected by a sea-captain, who, being caught, many years ago, in a typhoon off Macao, vowed to plant a cross in front of this church made from the mainmast of his vessel, and carry the mast up the hill on his back, if he was permitted to reach the shore in safety. In the vestry of the church there is a picture which shows the ship in the storm and distress which occasioned the vow.

We next visit the Protestant chapel, where we find a tablet to the memory of James B. Endicott, a native of Danvers, Massachusetts; Mr. Endicott was long well known in Macao, and died here in 1870. In the neighboring graveyard rests Morrison, the first Protestant missionary who ever came to China. A stone near by bears the following inscription: "In memory of Lord John Henry Churchill, son of George, 5th Duke of Marlborough."

At sunset we make our way round the Portuguese fort to the high hill on which stands the lighthouse. At the foot of the hill we enjoy a refreshing swim; the water is warm and delightful. From here we scramble up to the top of the hill to the lighthouse, and are kindly shown over the premises by the Portuguese in charge.

October 25. — We leave Macao at half past seven this morning in the steamer *Po-wan*, and reach Hong Kong at noon. Hong Kong (Island of Sweet Water) was seized by the English in 1842 in return for the destruction of opium by the Chinese, and for various insults to British residents at Canton. Hong Kong is built on an island, and the town is planted at the base and on the side of the precipitous Victoria Peak, which rises perpendicularly for eighteen hundred feet. It is said that one can drop a stone from the summit into the main street of the town below. The population of Hong Kong is made up of different nationalities, and varies so continually that it is impossible to state it exactly. In round numbers, it is about one hundred and thirty-five thousand. The foreigners number about three thousand five hundred; the rest of the population consist of Chinese, Portuguese, and Parsees. The harbor is large and convenient, and is full of steamers and sailing-vessels from all parts of the world. The warehouses of the merchants are commodious and well built; the private residences and villas, nestling in different parts of the hill, form agreeable retreats after the toil of the day; to the left, a densely populated Chinese quarter recalls to your mind that you are still in the immediate vicinity of the Celestial Empire. Over the post-office, in the centre of Hong Kong, are these words: "As cold waters to a thirsty soul, so is good news from a far country."

October 27.—Except the ever-pleasant society of the foreign residents, there is very little in Hong Kong of special interest to the traveller. When he has climbed Victoria Peak, and visited the Happy Valley and the Public Gardens, he may continue on his way. We planned to start for Manilla at once, but a typhoon is raging on the neighboring waters, and furious wind and constant rain indicate to us its resistless power. The departure of the Manilla steamer is therefore postponed, and the thick weather obliges us to remain in-doors.

October 28.—Heavy rain continues without cessation. We dine in the evening with Mr. W. Seymour Geary, of Olyphant & Co., whose house is finely situated on the hill.

October 30. — The rain continues. We are very glad to meet one of our fellow-passengers of the *Great Republic*, who is a merchant here in Hong Kong. Thanks to his kindness, we have enjoyed for several days the hospitality of the new club-house, a fine structure in the Gothic style. We hear also of the three United States army officers who crossed the Pacific with us. They are expected here in about ten days.

On account of the rain and wind, the Manilla steamer is again delayed! If we wait longer we may be obliged to omit some portion of our proposed Indian travel; so we decide to continue our way to Singapore, and proceed from there to Java. The regular mail-boat of the Peninsular and Oriental Steamship Company has just left Hong Kong. Another will not start for a week; we take passage, therefore, on the steamer *Abbotsford*, bound for Singapore direct, and at 5 P. M. we move slowly out of the harbor of Hong Kong, with a voyage of fourteen hundred miles before us.*

---

* I take this opportunity to thank the American Consul, D. Bailey, Esq., for his many kindnesses, official and personal. I have something to say here in regard to the O. & O. S. S. Co. Having collected various Japanese and Chinese curiosities, I desired to have them reach my friends in Boston by Christmas. I therefore decided to send them by steamer to San Francisco, and have them forwarded across the continent by rail. This method is, of course, far more expensive than carriage on a sailing-vessel, but, as I have said, I wished the articles to reach my friends at Christmas-time. The agent of the O. & O. S. S. Co. assured me that the boxes *would not be opened* in San Francisco (as they were accompanied by a full consular certificate), but would be forwarded promptly in bond to Boston. Believing him to be reliable, I left the articles

October 31. — The sea is very rough, and we pitch and roll from morning till night, to the decided injury of the crockery and to the great annoyance of everybody. Captain Patterson, a thorough Scotchman, pays us the most continual and thoughtful attention, and the different officers of the ship exert themselves in many ways to make our voyage pass pleasantly.

November 5. — We are now within three hundred miles of Singapore. The sea is calm and still, the sky is clear, and the sun is uncomfortably warm. We are well into the tropics !

November 6. — At two o'clock this morning a fierce squall sweeps over us. Dark clouds suddenly cover the bright moon and clear sky. For an hour and a half our steamer struggles on against a fierce wind and heavy sea. The first officer is on the watch, and I come on deck and go up with him on to the bridge. Lightning flashes around us, the thunder rumbles, and at last a heavy rain falls. Soon the moon shines clearly forth again, the clouds roll aside, — the storm has washed itself away.

At 1 P. M. we pass the lighthouse which marks the entrance to Singapore Straits, and our course is immediately

in his hands. The result was as follows : On their arrival at San Francisco, the boxes were *opened, thoroughly overhauled, and laid aside.* In response to frequent letters from my friends in Boston (whom I had notified), they were finally started along. They reached Boston January 22d ! As an example of our present tariff, I will mention that my curiosities were valued at $ 250 ; the government exacted a duty of $ 100.50.

altered to the westward. At five o'clock we can see in the distance the large warehouses that front the harbor of Singapore. On our right hand are thick groves of cocoa-nut trees, surrounded by tropical vegetation that seems to shut out the very light itself. At six o'clock we reach our wharf, and long before the vessel is made fast it is surrounded by light canoes, paddled by small Malay boys who dart hither and thither, calling out to us in broken English to toss them small coins, for which they promise to dive. And dive they do! Hardly can a coin touch the water — thrown purposely a long distance from the canoes — before three or four have dropped from their boats, eager to seize the money before it sinks to the bottom. One even brought up a cent from the very bottom, which we had tossed in an unexpected direction.

November 7. — Singapore, the capital of the Straits settlements, is situated one degree north of the equator. It was founded in 1819, and transferred by the Indian government to the Crown in 1867. The population is about one hundred thousand, of whom eight hundred are English, Americans, and Europeans. Singapore is on one of the great highways of the world. Steamers from all directions touch here constantly, and it is a regular stopping-place for the mail-boats of the Peninsular and Oriental, and Messageries Maritimes Companies. Singapore contains representatives of nearly every race of men on the globe. Here one may see, besides English, Americans, Germans, and French, Chinese, Malays,

Persians, Arabians, Jews, Turks, and Indians. The business part of the town contains many fine buildings, and the large and comfortable dwellings of the merchants are pleasantly situated in the suburbs. The town possesses a large Episcopal church, several massive government buildings, and a spacious residence occupied by the governor. A strong fort over-looks the harbor. There are many beautiful gardens, and ex-cellent roads in the vicinity, while an unchanging and agree-able climate, luxurious tropical vegetation, and a profusion of delicious fruit combine to render Singapore a most enjoya-ble residence for man.

We visit the English church — it is called a cathedral — in the morning. In the afternoon we walk out to the Bo-tanical Gardens, situated about three miles from the centre of the town. These gardens contain tropical plants of various kinds, a menagerie of deer, monkeys, bears, and other animals, and an extensive aviary.*

November 9. — We are kindly introduced at the English club. In the evening we dine with the partners of Gilfillan, Wood, & Co., at their pleasant house in the suburbs.

November 10. — We receive permission from Mr. Whampoa, an influential Chinese merchant, to visit his large and curious

---

* We have had a narrow escape. The "P. & O." mail steamer which we just missed at Hong Kong reached Singapore after a dangerous passage in a typhoon. *The steamer for Java which connected with it is just reported lost.*

gardens, situated about two miles from the city. Mr. Whampoa is a man of importance in Singapore, being even a member of the Legislative Council. His gardens are laid out in strict Chinese style, but they contain many trees and plants well worth seeing. Here is the traveller's palm, which, being tapped, yields very drinkable water. Here too are banana and lemon trees; tea, coffee, aloe, and pineapple plants; pummelo and cocoa-nut trees, and many others.

In the evening we dine with the firm of Boustead & Co.

November 11. — At 10 P. M. we go on board the Dutch steamer *Banda*, which is advertised to start for Batavia at daybreak to-morrow.

November 12. — The sea is very smooth; the atmosphere, though very warm, is not oppressive; but a sort of tropical languor compels us to sit idly, watching the thickly wooded shore of the island of Sumatra, which seems to be ever gliding away.

It is 6 P. M. We are crossing the equator. Our captain tells us we are now *upon* it. I gaze over the ship's side in a vain endeavor to discover that black line which seemed such an absolute reality in the school-days of my earliest youth.

November 13. — The boats of the Netherlands India Steamship Company are decidedly uncomfortable. The state-rooms are small and stuffy, the food is rarely varied and is always carelessly prepared and uninviting. Each captain is allowed

a certain sum with which to provision his boat, and either
the sum is far too small, or a boat's *menu* is diminished in
direct ratio to the amount an economizing captain reserves
from the money advanced. Besides this, a corps of absolutely
untrained and stupid Malay boys attempt to wait on the
passengers, but only get in everybody's way. I hear that
some French steamers are soon to be put on the line between Singapore and Batavia. For the public's sake I hope
they will appear speedily.

November 14. — At noon to-day we come to anchor off
Java, and soon a small steamer comes alongside to take us
up the narrow canal which is the only approach to Batavia
from the harbor. The *Banda* is anchored two miles from
the town; and although we have bought tickets for Batavia,
(which we supposed would carry us there), we are obliged to
pay another fare to the small steamer, unless we wish to remain at a long distance from land. This is an outrage; and
although I heard several protesting against it, yet the nuisance has been suffered to continue so long, that no one is
willing to be the first to challenge it.

We are landed at the custom-house. Passing through, we
find a score of small barouches in waiting, drawn by small
but powerful ponies. We are driven through broad streets,
past spacious residences and warehouses. Horse-cars rumble
along by our side. A canal — the delight of the Dutch —
runs parallel with the principal street, in which multitudes

of Malays are bathing, or conducting a general laundrying establishment. Large numbers of handsome equipages are going in various directions, driven by Malay coachmen in stylish liveries, topped by curious gayly painted tin hats. Behind the vehicles two footmen stand, dressed in the same costume as the drivers; and as the turnouts rattle by at the tremendous speed for which the place is noted, the whole effect is very striking. Groves of cocoa-nut trees are scattered here and there throughout the city, and bread-fruit and other tropical productions grow in every other garden-plot. The Malays are a very healthy-looking race, and very few beggars are to be seen in the streets.

At six o'clock we walk to the parade-ground to hear the military band. We are surprised to find a large concourse of foreigners in carriages or on horseback, the ladies in elegant toilets, and nearly everybody without hat or head-covering of any sort, — for the sun always sets at six o'clock, and the city is then cool and delightful. On the parade-ground is a monument erected in memory of the battle of Waterloo, — a bronze lion on a high pedestal. The music is excellent, and we can hardly realize — with all the fashion and civilization that surrounds us, and with the strains of the " Blue Danube " in our ears — that we are on an island below the equator, far away from the chief habitations of men.

CHAPTER XIII.

JAVA TO CEYLON.

BATAVIA. — BUITENZORG. — AN INLAND TRIP. — EMBARKATION FOR CEYLON.
— ARRIVAL AT POINT DE GALLE.

November 15. — The population of Batavia is about one hundred thousand. It possesses, besides its many private residences and warehouses, an opera-house, several very ordinary hotels, a fine museum, and a handsome residence occupied by the governor-general. The climate is hotter than our very warmest summer day, and no one walks out in the middle of the day, for the sun has a very dangerous power. Many sorts of fruits can be obtained, and all may be eaten with safety, except the pineapple, which, in Java, is exceedingly hurtful.

We present a letter of introduction, this morning, to Dümmeller & Co. As there is very little of interest in Batavia itself, we plan to start for the interior of the island on the morrow. Messrs. Dümmeller & Co. give us much information in regard to our proposed inland journey, and, after some further conversation, we call at the adjoining office of the American Consul, P. Nickerson, Esq., of Boston. As we enter the consulate, we remark the absence of the American flag. Mr. Nickerson tells us that, at the special request of the Dutch government, no foreign flag is displayed by the different consuls; for the Dutch wish the natives to continue to believe that the Dutch flag alone is the emblem of power throughout the world.

In the afternoon we visit the large museum, where may be seen a collection of ancient Javanese gods, weapons, agricultural utensils, and so forth. In the evening we go to the opera. It is the opening night of a French company which has recently arrived. The theatre is not large, but is excellently ventilated and well-lighted. The orchestra is satisfactory, and the scenery is passable. Many ladies are present in full evening dress. A black frock or cut-away coat seems to be considered sufficient by the gentlemen, and our swallow-tails are therefore somewhat conspicuous. The ladies are not remarkable for beauty, but the majority are ablaze with jewels, and their toilets are as elaborate as one could find in any capital of the world.

The programme bears the following notice: "*Avec la permission de M. le Résident.*" The first piece performed is "Le Chalet"; this is followed by the excellent little opera "Les Noces de Jeannette."

November 16. — A railroad connects Batavia with Buitenzorg, distant thirty-seven miles. We leave Batavia at half past seven and reach our destination at ten o'clock. Buitenzorg, besides being itself a place of remarkable beauty, is the usual starting-point for Sing-dang-laya and the high mountains near by. The Hotel Bellevue at Buitenzorg is built on the summit of a hill, and, standing on the back piazza, the visitor sees before him one of the most beautiful views that the island affords. At the foot of the hill a winding river flows between tall groves of cocoa-nut trees, and through the very thickest tropical foliage; a cloud-topped mountain rises boldly in the distance. On its summit are found the curious bird's-nests which are so largely exported for food.

In the afternoon we visit the extensive gardens of the governor-general. These gardens contain a large assortment of tropical plants, a pretty lake, and broad lawns on which several hundred spotted deer wander about. Here is the deadly upas, and a large specimen of the rubber-tree. The governor's residence is a spacious white stone building with two wide wings running out from the central portion. Several paths are for the use of the governor alone, and conspicuous signs in Dutch command the visitor not to enter them. The palace and grounds are guarded by a garrison of Dutch soldiers, and as we walk along we meet that saddest of all processions, — a military funeral. To the soldier, in time of peace, death in this distant spot must be hard indeed!

November 17. — We rise at five, and soon are rattling over an excellent road in little carriages drawn by three ponies, bound for Sing-dang-laya. After travelling for about an hour through a well-cultivated country, we stop for breakfast at a small town called Gadok. Although the hotel is full of guests,

no proprietor can be found. The united efforts of our party in English, French, Italian, and German fail to obtain any response from the different people about the house, and, as we do not talk Dutch, we are almost in despair, when at last a young man appears who speaks English. This gentleman calls a native who seems to be manager-in-chief of the establishment, and we are soon properly served. After breakfast we continue our way. The road runs for miles through extensive coffee plantations. At eleven o'clock we stop for *tiffin* at a native inn kept by an old Malay woman called Ma-mina. Many travellers stop here in the course of a year, and the old woman cooks remarkably well after the Dutch style. Native and foreign officials, going to the interior or coming back to Batavia, halt for an hour at this inn. The dinner-table is completely covered with names and initials, and it is evidently the custom of travellers to leave these "footprints on the sands of time," in order that succeeding patrons, "seeing, may take heart again," when almost despairing over the long delay of the meal.

As we are about to leave, having finished *tiffin*, a native official, with gold-lace on uniform and hat, drives up. Having greeted us courteously in his own language, he calls for a glass of water. The servant who brings it to him stops with the tray at some distance off, and hands the water respectfully, bending his body almost to the ground with the most remarkable gesture of deference I have ever seen, as if a nearer approach would defile the magnate.

Leaving the inn we drive on for about a mile and stop at a little path which strikes through thick woods, and, having left the carriages, we follow a guide up the mountain-path, passing through the very ideal of a tropical forest. The foliage is so luxuriant that it seems superabundant; the ferns and grasses astonish us; and beautiful vines and masses of exquisite creepers, winding around the rich trees, bear witness to nature's productive power when unchecked by cold and frost. This fertility, however, is not confined to the vegetable world. Animal life keeps pace with it. Deadly snakes, small creeping reptiles, and poisonous insects lurk in the depths of the most beautiful plants; and man, dwelling in this lovely spot, finds himself opposed by multitudes of enemies which the very luxuriance of the favored latitude has brought forth.

After a half-hour's walk we emerge on to the bank of a small lake which covers the crater of an old volcano, extinct for the past eighty years. The lake is called Te Laga Varna. A wall of exquisite foliage, three hundred feet high, rises from its opposite shore.

Having returned to the carriages, we proceed for about six miles, and stop at two o'clock at a little hotel near Singdang-laya, where we intend to spend the night, in order to meet and talk with Mr. Carlo Ferrari, a great sportsman, who has lived in Java for many years. We are sorry to hear from Mr. Ferrari that we have come to Java in a very poor season for good sport; but he kindly offers to accompany us for a few days if we wish to make an expedition in search of a tiger.

About 11 P. M. a party of native dancers come to the hotel and perform to an interested audience. Three men, sitting cross-legged on the ground, furnish the music, which consists of a drum, a fife, and a pair of peculiar cymbals. A large torch is stuck in the ground, and the dancers, men and women, — the latter very strikingly dressed in many-colored native cloths, — circle round and round the light to the sound of the music, gliding towards each other, meeting, bowing low, swaying from side to side, and finally separating entirely, all the time chanting a peculiar refrain, which is even heard above the shrill and discordant sounds of the instruments.

Java, as I have said, abounds in deadly insects and reptiles. Besides the centipedes and scorpions, which are very numerous, there is a very dangerous worm, long and thin like a horsehair, which crawls into men's ears from pillows and elsewhere, and produces deafness and often death by its sting. If the worm can be extracted from the ear, no serious danger need be anticipated. If it has penetrated too far, however, the victim lingers for days in great pain, till death ends his sufferings. Large tarantulas are frequently found suspended over a bed, and there is a species of wasp whose sting causes excessive inflammation.

To a traveller making a tour into the interior of Java, the

following Malay words will be useful. They are, of course, spelled phonetically : —

Fork	Garfu.
Knife	Picho.
Spoon	Tsenoch.
Napkin	Tserbatr.
Water	Ire.
Plate	Peering.
Bread	Roti.
Rice	Nasci.
Egg	Tulor.
Sugar	Gular.
Milk	Susu.

November 18. — Two of our party, Mr. U. of New York, and our English companion, decide to accompany Mr. Ferrari on a tiger hunt. The prospect of sport, however, is so doubtful and the probability of discomfort so unquestioned, that F—— and I decline to accompany the others. As the hotel at Buitenzorg is far more comfortable than our present habitation, and as Mr. Ferrari assures us that we have already observed the characteristic scenery of the island, we do not wish to travel farther inland. F——, however, is anxious to ascend a neighboring mountain, and promises to follow me to Buitenzorg on the morrow. Bidding farewell, therefore, to the two who are to remain in the island, I set out for Buitenzorg, which I reach at noon.

November 19. — F—— arrives from Sing-dang-laya at 7 P. M., and we make preparations to return to Batavia early to-morrow morning.

November 20.—We reach Batavia at ten o'clock this morning. Our steamer starts at 8 A. M. to-morrow. The day is very warm, and after arranging for our departure, we keep indoors till the cool of the evening renders walking agreeable.

November 21.—At half past seven we go on board the steamer *Amboina*,* bound for Singapore, and think with dismay of the three days that we shall be obliged to pass in the hands of the Netherlands Steamship Company. The *Amboina* is fully as uncomfortable as the *Banda*, and the food is even less varied and more disagreeable.

November 23.—We arrive back at Singapore at 6 P. M., after a smooth passage from Java.

November 24.—I have a long talk with Major Studer, American Consul. It is the same old story. His salary is hardly sufficient to allow him to live like a gentleman. The consulate of the United States of America consists of two small rooms in a hotel!

November 26.—At 10 A. M. we embark on the fine steamer *Tigre* of the Messageries Maritimes Company. About forty-five passengers of different nationalities are on board. We start at noon on our voyage of fourteen hundred miles, for

* As we were in Batavia only for a few hours on our return from the interior, we were unable to bid farewell to Messrs. Dümmeller & Co., and to the American Consul.

F—— and I intend to leave the ship (which is bound for Marseilles) at Point De Galle, to visit some of the chief points of interest in Ceylon.

November 28. — At 5 P. M. we pass Acheen Head, a promontory which marks the limits of the Straits of Malacca, now the scene of a war between the natives and the Dutch, and soon after our ship is rolling from side to side under the influence of the long swell of the Indian Ocean. The *Tigre* makes an average day's run of three hundred miles, and we expect to reach Ceylon December 1.

November 30. — A grand concert, vocal and instrumental, was given by several of the passengers this evening, in aid of a poor Scotch widow who is travelling home with two children, whose entire capital consists of two pounds sterling. Selections from a few well-known operas were pleasingly rendered, after which a magic-lantern amused the company for a while, and at the end of the evening a collection was taken up, which amounted to somewhat over twenty pounds, —a very god-send to its recipient. The officers deserve great credit for their kind efforts, and the performers may well feel that they have done a good action.

December 1. — At eleven o'clock this morning we come in sight of the coast of Ceylon, which stretches far away to the right. Thick groves of cocoa-nut trees cover the shore for miles, and the luxuriant foliage of the land closely resembles Sumatra and Java. At 4.30 P. M. we can plainly see, far

ahead, the shipping in the harbor of Point De Galle, and soon
after, having obtained a pilot, we drop anchor off the town,
just as the guns from the English fort announce the arrival
of the Prince of Wales at Colombo, a town seventy miles to
the north. As the steamer rounds the green promontory which
marks the entrance to the harbor of Point De Galle, a most
beautiful picture presents itself. On the right, groves of cocoa-
nut trees, surrounded with thick foliage, afford refreshing shade
to a little cluster of native huts, which, with their thatched
roofs, look tropical and primitive. On the left, a tall lighthouse rises boldly from a high ledge of rocks over which the
sea tumbles and breaks, leaping upwards every little while in
high clouds of spray. In front lies the town, running from
the sea-shore to the summit of a hill, and sheltered completely
behind the guns of the English fort, which cover every approach to the harbor. In the distance is Adam's Peak, which
rises to a height of seven thousand four hundred feet.

The native inhabitants of Ceylon are Singhalese and Tamils.
As soon as a steamer comes to anchor it is surrounded by
multitudes of long, narrow boats called *catamarans*, each with
two huge outriggers, to which is attached a thick log, which
moves along near the surface of the water, and steadies the
whole craft. Indeed, these canoes are so narrow that, without this balancing-log, it would be impossible to navigate
them.

CHAPTER XIV.

CEYLON.

December 2. — Point De Galle — so called by the Portuguese when they had possession of the island — contains a population of about seven thousand. Besides the beautiful scenery in the vicinity, there is very little of interest to the traveller. We wish, therefore, to press on to Colombo, but, on account of the unexpected arrival of the Prince of Wales, it is impossible to obtain places in the regular stage which runs between the two towns. The Prince and suite have changed their route, owing to reports of cholera from the southern coast of India, which they had planned to visit before coming to Ceylon. The steamer *Socotra*, of the British India Steamship Company, is fortunately in the harbor, bound for Bombay *via* Colombo, and we promptly engage passage for the latter place. As the boat will not start till 5 P. M., we have the day to look about us.

Soon after breakfast we take a carriage, and drive for an hour over a fine road running through groves of cocoa-nut and palm-trees, with beautiful ferns and flowers on all sides. On our way back we stop at the foot of a hill on whose summit stands a large Catholic church. As we are walking up the hill on our way to the church, we pass a small schoolhouse in which about fifty Singhalese boys are studying English and the usual elementary branches under the care of a benevolent-looking old gentleman, himself of Singhalese descent. As we pause a moment at the door, the old gentleman comes out and invites us politely to step in and witness a recitation, — an offer which we gladly accept. The class is engaged in a reading-lesson, and the old master, placing us behind his desk, — on which lies a pliant rattan, — hands us the book, — the Third Reader, — and opening at the well-known story of Solon and Crœsus, calls on the head boy to begin. The Singhalese boys read very correctly and intelligently, and at the conclusion of the exercise the master examines them on the subject-matter of the lesson. Although several of his questions touch on broad principles of ethics, the boys show excellent appreciation of the text, one bright little fellow doing uncommonly well. Soon after this we take our leave, and having visited the new church, we return to the hotel. About five o'clock we go on board the *Socotra*, which starts immediately for Colombo.

December 3. — At five o'clock this morning we come in sight of Colombo, and at seven o'clock we anchor off the town, within a stone's throw of the steamer *Serapis*, which is carrying the Prince of Wales on his travels. The *Serapis* and the companion steam-yacht *Osborne* lie inside of a half-circle of English gun-boats which attend them,— the *Undaunted, Raleigh, Narcissus, Inamortalite,* and *Newcastle.*

We call a native boat and are rowed quickly ashore. On landing at the jetty we find it completely decorated in honor of the Prince's arrival. The whole wharf is one mass of flags, mottoes, and insignia, placed on a background of green plants in which various kinds of fruits have been cleverly entwined. Tall green arches span the streets, each proclaiming the town's welcome to the Prince, and declaring the people's loyalty to the royal family. All the chief buildings bear gayly painted sentences of welcome, "God bless the Prince of Wales," "Welcome to Albert Edward," and so forth. The day is a holiday, no business is transacted, crowds fill the streets; and although the Prince left this morning for Kandy (seventy-four miles inland), the enthusiasm does not seem to have abated. The hotel is packed with a mass of thirsty Englishmen, all calling for the cooling brandy and soda to which they are so accustomed at home; and the popping of soda-water bottles, mingling with the many different voices, produces an absolute din. We succeed, however, in obtaining rooms at "royal visit prices," and, as we are too late to catch the afternoon train to Kandy, we spend several hours in walking about Colombo.

Colombo, the capital of Ceylon, is situated on a peninsula,

surrounded on three sides by the sea. It has a population of one hundred and twenty thousand. The town contains many fine business blocks and large warehouses. The
residence of the governor, Right Honorable W. H. Gregory,[*]
is especially noticeable. Outside the walls are the dwellings
of the Dutch and Portuguese. On the right of the town is
the Pettah, or black town, occupied by the natives. To the
left stretches a beautiful beach, over a mile long, beside which
runs an excellent carriage-road. Colombo is well garrisoned,
and several batteries face the sea. The climate of Ceylon is
very warm, but much cooler than that of Java.

December 4. — At 2 P. M. we drive to the railroad station,
and soon are on our way to Kandy. The railroad was started
in 1859 by the late governor, Sir H. Ward. It runs through
the thickest vegetation of the island, and for twelve and a
half miles ascends an incline of one in forty-five, rising to
an altitude of seventeen hundred feet at a station called Kadu-
ganava. The journey to Kandy occupies nearly five hours.
This time is required, as the train must go very slowly for
the last third of the way. The cars wind over mountains,
through long tunnels, and along the verge of apparently inaccessible heights, from which one can look far down into the
valleys below. Indeed, this portion of the line somewhat resembles a part of the Central Pacific Railroad of California.
The day is rainy, and we can look down on to the tops of

* Now Sir W. H. Gregory.

large clouds which are floating over the valleys beneath us.
On each side of the road is a sort of fence, recently constructed,
formed of plants with different fruits placed at little distances
apart; and every station is hung with flags and mottoes, wel-
coming the Prince of Wales, who yesterday passed over the
road with his suite.

We reach Kandy at seven o'clock in a pouring rain; and
as all the carriages are engaged elsewhere by the crowds who
have followed the Prince, we are obliged to hire two Singhalese to carry our valises, and we ourselves, having borrowed
a native umbrella, follow our guides to the hotel.

On our arrival at the Queen's Hotel (a wretched inn, an
outrage on the name it bears), we learn that the Prince has
departed for an elephant hunt, farther inland, and will not
return to Kandy, but is to be received by the people of Colombo next Monday afternoon. To-day is Saturday, so we
decide to spend Sunday in Kandy, and return to Colombo in
time to witness the passage of the Prince through that city
on his way to open the Agricultural Grounds.

December 5. — Kandy, the old residence of the native kings
of Ceylon, is situated in a valley surrounded by beautiful
hills, and on the bank of a small lake. It now contains
many European dwelling-houses and public buildings. The
governor's palace, the library, and the English church are the
most important. It contains a population of ten thousand.
Yesterday, in the old Hall of the Kings, the descendants of

the conquered princes paid homage to the son of their queen.

After breakfast we visit "Lady Horton's Walk," a wide path which winds up a neighboring hill, from whose summit a fine bird's-eye view of Kandy may be obtained. From here we go the Dalada, or the Temple of the Tooth, a curious Buddhist structure, built to protect a veritable tooth of the great Buddha, which is here carefully preserved by the priests. This tooth is only exhibited once a year at a great religious festival; and though it was yesterday brought out for the inspection of the Prince of Wales, it has already been returned to its secluded resting-place, and the priests refuse to exhibit it to us. The Temple of the Tooth is a curious piece of architecture and well worth a careful study.

December 6. — We take the seven-o'clock train for Colombo, which, on account of the numbers who have come to Kandy to see the Prince and are now returning, is unusually long and crowded. Twenty-eight cars and two engines — the longest train ever on the road — toil slowly down the mountain, and it is fully one o'clock — an hour and a half behind time — when we reach the station at Colombo.

On our arrival at the hotel we find that the Prince is delayed in camp, and will not enter Colombo till to-morrow afternoon.

After lunch we walk to the sea-shore, and engage a *catamaran*, and balancing ourselves on its narrow seat, we order the Singhalese to row us out to the *Serapis,* the Prince's ship. As soon as we set foot on board, we send our cards to the officer of the deck with a request to be permitted to visit the "royal apartments." A polite and affirmative answer is at once returned, and a seaman is detailed to conduct us to the door of the Prince's dining-room and put us in charge of the Prince's steward, who alone has charge of the apartments during the absence of the royal party.

The steward conducts us first over the dining-room. This is a large apartment in the stern of the ship, luxuriously furnished, out of which lead several smaller chambers, two of which are for the exclusive use of the Prince. The dining-room contains a beautiful table and handsome sideboard. All the furniture is marked with the Prince's crest and the letters A. E. The steward leads us around the table, saying, "The Prince of Wales sits there, the Duke of Sutherland there, Sir Bartle Frere here," and so on. Passing now into the parlor (which is, indeed, only separated from the dining-room by a mast of the ship), we see before us a large picture of the Queen, and near by a most beautiful one of the Princess of Wales. Around the room are fine maps, and on the tables are the latest books upon India and Ceylon. A mail has evidently been lately received, for a score of letters are lying on a little secretary, the majority of which are directed to Sir Bartle Frere.

Our guide shows us next through the private apartments

of the Prince. We examine with interest his famous swivel-bed. In his little parlor adjoining is an Indian dagger, covered with jewels, which was presented to the Prince by some native ruler. Books and pamphlets of travel and science are scattered about, showing that the royal visitor endeavors to post himself thoroughly in regard to the different countries he is passing through.

Having paused a moment in the room of the Duke of Sutherland, we follow our conductor to the smoking-room. This apartment is a gem. It is situated on the main deck, elegantly furnished, and enclosed by large plate-glass windows, which command an extended view in all directions. Having retraced our steps to the outer door of the dining-room, we are again put in charge of the seaman who has waited for us, and the steward instructs him to show us over the other portions of the ship.

We visit the stables where the fine horses of the Prince are kept. Each animal has his name painted over his stall. Near by are the cattle and poultry for the use of the Prince, and opposite is the kitchen where his own food is specially prepared.

After examining the quarters of the regular officers and seamen of the vessel, we take our leave, and return to Colombo. Viewed from the water, the *Serapis* presents a huge appearance; but it is necessary to walk through the ship and examine it in detail, before a just idea of her immense capacity can be formed.

December 7. — In company with Captain V. Hoskioer, of the Royal Danish Engineers (our fellow-passenger on the *Tigre* from Singapore, and bound also to Calcutta), we visit this morning an old Hindoo temple of most curious architecture, situated in the Pettah. This building is well worth a visit, but seems to be little known by the European inhabitants. From here we drive to the large coffee warehouses of Armitage Brothers, and are very politely shown over the establishment by the overseer, who explains fully, as we walk about, all the details of the process required to bring the coffee into a condition for market. The coffee-berries are first spread out over large "barbecues," — wide, flat surfaces hardened with asphalt, — to be dried by the sun; after which they are placed in a sort of mill called a "peeler," where large wheels strip off the two skins that cover each berry, — the outer skin and the silver skin. When these have been removed, the coffee-berries are thrown into "feeders," which blow away all dust and chaff that remains, after which "sizers" receive them. These "sizers" are sieves of different sizes which separate the large berries from the small, and also remove any gravel or foreign matter that may have become mixed with them.

When all these operations are finished, the coffee is placed in bags, and is once more poured out, to be examined by native women whose business it is to search for and remove all imperfect berries that can be found. This being done, the coffee of the best quality is ready for the market. The imperfect berries, however, are collected together and sold also, but of course at a much lower price.*

On our return to the city we go to the office of the British India Steamship Company to inquire about the Calcutta steamer. The office, however, is closed, and the agents have very carelessly omitted to put up a notice in regard to their boat. On inquiring at the post-office we are told that the steamer has arrived, and is to leave in half an hour, and that the mails have just been sent aboard. This seems conclusive, so we return at once to the hotel, give up our rooms, and having placed our luggage in charge of coolies, make our way in company with Captain Hoskioer to the wharf. Having engaged a boat at "royal visit prices," we spend half an hour in the fierce tropical sun endeavoring to find the steamer *Patna*, which we finally discover has not yet arrived in the harbor! We are obliged to return to the hotel (after engaging another squad of coolies for the trunks), and we arrive there hot and tired, only to find that our places have been filled by others. The head steward, however, very kindly gives us his room, and we accept it with thanks, being entirely upset in our arrangements by the neglect of the agent to inform us of the steamer's movements.

* The total product of the coffee crop of the world for 1874 is estimated at about 900,000,000 pounds, of which amount the United States imported, in 1875, over a third, or 317,970,665 pounds.

The Prince of Wales has returned to Colombo, having left his hunting-grounds at an early hour this morning, and at half past four this afternoon he is expected to pass through the city to open an agri-horticultural exhibition, for which great preparations have been made. The decorations along the streets, which were erected in honor of his landing, have been added to and improved; new arches have been built, fresh greens have been placed here and there, and everything possible has been done to make the second welcome even more cordial than the first. By three o'clock the street leading from the governor's house (where the Prince resides during his visit) to the Agricultural Grounds is lined with thousands of people, Europeans and natives, all eager to see the Prince as he passes by. A remarkable crowd it is! Here one can see a group of Singhalese or Tamils, in the very scant costume of their race, side by side with a little knot of Londoners in frock-coats and tall hats; while near by are some native women in all the glory of silk dresses, Indian shawls, and bare feet! Police inspectors gallop up and down, thunder angrily at natives who straggle through the lines, and endeavor to hide their excitement and embarrassment in the heights (rather than the depths) of their pith helmets. At last, at about five o'clock, four lancers appear, followed by two carriages, in the foremost of which, dressed in cool light garments and surrounded by some of his suite, sits the Prince of Wales, raising his hat from time to time in response to the cheers which greet him on all sides. The immense concourse of natives, however, do not utter a sound. The outspoken welcome comes entirely from the Europeans. The Singhalese and Tamils gaze wonderingly at the Prince's carriage, look into each other's faces, and turn half disappointedly away. A gentleman in the crowd who understands the Singhalese language discovers the cause. The natives (who associate great outward adornment with the name of prince) expected that the son of their Queen would come to them in a gorgeous chariot, with a crown of gold on his head, and arrayed in splendid robes. Instead of this he appears like any other of their European masters. Their hearts are loyal to him, but their eyes are not satisfied.

CHAPTER XV.

CEYLON TO CALCUTTA.

Negapatam. — Pondicherry. — Madras. — Masulipatam. — Coconada. — Vizagapatam. — Bimlipatam. — Gopolpore. — False Point. — Diamond Harbor. — Arrival at Calcutta.

December 8. — The steamer *Patna*, bound for Calcutta, arrives early this morning. We go on board at noon with Captain Hoskioer, and at two o'clock bid farewell to Ceylon.

December 11. — At noon to-day we sight the southern coast of India, and at one o'clock our ship drops anchor off Negapatam, a place of very little interest to the traveller, which came into the possession of the English in 1783. Having received a little cargo, brought from the shore by natives in large, clumsy scows, we continue our way.

December 12. — At daybreak this morning we arrive at Pondicherry. This town is the capital of the French East Indian territory. It is situated eighty-eight miles south of Madras, and has a population of thirty thousand. Our ship is to receive the French governor, and carry him to Madras to pay his respects to the Prince of Wales, who is now on his way thither. As the governor will not embark till evening, we have ample time to land and examine the town. Calling a native boat, we are soon set down on a fine beach, near which runs a hard, wide avenue. The town itself is well laid out and pleasantly situated, its excellent roads being especially noticeable. We find here hotels, cafés, an opera-house, a Catholic cathedral, forts, a dock-yard, and lighthouse. The governor's residence is in the centre of the town, and is a spacious building. Multitudes of little carriages are about the streets, propelled by natives from behind, and used here as the *jinrikisha* in Japan. This vehicle is called a *pushpush*.

At noon we return to the steamer, and at five o'clock a salute from the fort announces the departure of the governor for our vessel. Soon a large row-boat comes alongside, with the French flag at bow and stern, and the governor, — a pleasant-looking old gentleman, — his aide-de-camp, private secretary, and several servants, leaving the boat amid "tossed oars," are received at the gangway by our captain (himself an old naval officer) with all due etiquette and ceremony. In a few moments we are under weigh.

December 13. — At five o'clock this morning we anchor off Madras, and, early as it is, the governor of Pondicherry, in full court dress and accompanied by his suite, leaves the steamer, and is rowed quickly ashore by the servants of one of the English officials. It is necessary for him to land thus early, as the Prince of Wales is expected to arrive at the railroad station at eight o'clock, and the governor is one of the Committee of Reception.

A resident of Madras, who comes aboard our steamer, tells us of an amusing mistake recently made by the English officials in regard to the arrival of the governor of Pondicherry. It was believed in Madras that the governor would take passage in the regular mail-boat of the French Messageries Maritimes Company. When that vessel appeared, therefore, two days ago, a salute was fired from the English fort, and a company of soldiers were drawn up on the wharf in readiness to receive the governor. Soon a little boat left the steamer and was rowed rapidly towards the town. On its arrival a gentleman stepped out and walked slowly up the steps of the wharf. The soldiers presented arms, the commanding officer advanced respectfully, and the cannon roared from the town. The gentleman who had just landed was evidently surprised. Pausing near the commanding officer, he raised his hat with a polite and interrogating "Monsieur?" The Englishman in his turn was mystified. Then, suspecting some mistake, he said, "Are you not the governor of Pondicherry?"

"No, sir," replied the stranger in excellent English, "I am the purser of yonder vessel, and his Excellency is not on board." The cannon ceased quickly, the soldiers retired, and all Madras laughed.

Madras, formerly called Fort St. George, is the capital of the Madras presidency, and contains a population of four hundred thousand, of whom four thousand are Europeans. Madras is distant seven hundred and sixty-four miles from

Bombay and one thousand and sixty-two miles from Calcutta. An immense number of vessels arrive at Madras in the course of a year, and the yearly imports and exports of the city average eight million pounds.

Calling a Masullah boat, we are rowed skilfully through the high surf to the beach. The town presents a very gay appearance. All the chief buildings are hung with flags and adorned with mottoes of welcome to the Prince of Wales, and the streets are filled with crowds of natives and Europeans eager to catch sight of his Royal Highness. Great arches have been erected, similar to those in Ceylon, but more elaborate and costly. Our steamer is to remain till afternoon, and we have the morning before us. Taking a carriage we visit some of the chief objects of interest in the city. We drive first to the People's Park, a large public garden containing an extensive menagerie. Here are monkeys of all kinds, lions, panthers, leopards, wild-cats, hyenas, a tiger, and a rhinoceros. From the gardens we proceed to the Central Museum, founded in 1851, which contains a large collection of ancient Indian stone work, old agricultural implements, and extensive ornithological cabinets. After lunch we visit a large Juggernaut car. The English have forbidden the natives to use them as of old.* On our return to the steamer we find our passenger-list considerably increased. Among the

* In a bookstore in this city we found for sale Dr. John Todd's Student's Manual.

late arrivals is Mr. Ashbury, M. P., and the Marquis of Kildare, eldest son of the Duke of Leinster, grandson on his mother's side of the second Duke of Sutherland, and grandnephew of Lord Francis Egerton.

December 14. — The sea is very high to-day, and our ship runs through frequent storms of rain. At 7 P. M. we anchor off Masulipatam, three hundred and fifteen miles north of Madras. This town was taken by the English in 1759. The place contains no harbor, and the neighboring waters are so shallow that steamers are obliged to lie nearly three miles from land.

December 15. — We remain off Masulipatam till 4 P. M., while our steamer is unloading and receiving cargo.

December 16. — We reach Coconada, our next stopping-place, at 8 A. M. Coconada, situated near the Godavery River, contains a population of eighteen thousand. Its harbor is rapidly filling up with immense quantities of silt, brought down by the river. Continual dredging is necessary, and even now steamers are obliged to anchor nearly four miles from land. A canal, ninety miles long, joins the neighboring deltas of the Godavery and Kistna Rivers. Coconada contains extensive cigar manufactories and castor-oil works.

Our steamer is to remain till evening, and several of us engage a large native boat and sail to the town, the voyage occupying over an hour. Ascending the canal for a short distance, we disembark at the house of the agent of the

British India Steamship Company, who also is the American Consul. This gentleman receives us very politely, furnishes us with a guide to conduct us over the cigar and castor-oil establishments, and kindly invites us to *tiffin* with him on our return. Leaving the agent's house, we follow our guide to the cigar manufactory near by, where we are shown the different processes of cigar-making. Afterwards, we visit the castor-oil works. All the details of this business are fully explained to us, and we see the oil itself pouring out from the press in which the beans are placed, and running into large casks. After a thorough boiling it is ready for shipment.

After *tiffin* we engage carriages, and drive to a large Hindoo temple about four miles distant, which, in its outward adornment, is ample evidence of the religious sanction which was given to debauchery of the wildest description.

On our return to the town we find the Steamship Company's steam-launch about to start for our vessel, and we are thus saved a long and tedious cruise in a native boat. At midnight we resume our course.

December 17.— At noon to-day we anchor off Vizagapatam, four hundred and ninety-one miles from Madras. The town is built at the base and on the side of a hill, near the summit of which is a curious mosque. The inhabitants adorn boxes and other articles with porcupine quills, which they offer to strangers.

Proceeding on our way we reach Bimlipatam at six o'clock.

This town is sixteen miles from Vizagapatam. It contains little of interest to the traveller.

December 18. — At 4 P. M. we leave Bimlipatam and continue our journey.

December 19. — At four o'clock this morning one of the passengers rouses me, and we go on deck, where we obtain a fine view of the constellation of the Southern Cross. At eight o'clock we anchor off Gopalpore, a small settlement in a sandy plain. We go ashore and spend an hour at the bungalow of the Steamship Company's agent.

December 20. — We reach False Point at noon to-day; and after taking on board several passengers and a small amount of cargo, we leave for Calcutta.

December 21. — At 5 P. M. we come to anchor in the Hooghly River off Diamond Harbor, thirty miles from Calcutta. We are obliged to lie here all night, as the tide will not allow us to ascend the river till to-morrow.

December 22. — We continue our voyage at daybreak, and soon are meeting continually steamers and sailing-vessels bound in all directions. The Hooghly runs for one hundred and twenty-five miles from the Ganges to the sea. At its mouth its width is eight miles. Above Diamond Harbor, however, it is not more than three quarters of a mile wide. In several places the shores are quite high and picturesque. At ten o'clock we pass the palace of the King of Oudh, who is kept here as a political prisoner by the English. The buildings are lofty and the grounds extensive. After turning around a little bend in the river just above the palace, we come suddenly among a fleet of vessels, representing, I may almost say, all nations. The amount of shipping around us is astonishing! Soon, as our steamer picks her way carefully along, we see ahead, above the multitudes of masts, the tall spires and domes of the buildings in the city; and higher up the river, the wide bridge across the Hooghly, thronged with men, horses, and vehicles, gives us the final assurance that we have arrived at one of the great commercial centres of the world.

I cannot take leave of the *Patna*, in which I have travelled so long, without offering my grateful acknowledgment to Captain Street for the uniform kindness and attention which he showed us, and for his continual efforts to make the voyage pass pleasantly,—a result which I can assure him he accomplished.

On landing at Calcutta, we go at once to the Great Eastern Hotel, and find accommodation awaiting us, as we have telegraphed for places several days previously, knowing that the arrival of the Prince of Wales (who is to reach Calcutta to-morrow) will produce the usual crowd and confusion. This settled, we drive to our bankers for our letters (which await us in goodly numbers), and afterwards set out to present several letters of introduction. The Prince of Wales (as I have said) is expected to-morrow, and the streets are full of arches

and festoons of welcome, and grand preparations are on foot
for the illumination which is to take place Christmas eve.
Besides this, large placards announce the holiday attractions
of Calcutta's three theatres, and I see the veteran actor
Charles Matthews advertised to appear in several of his
specialities.

Soon after our return to the hotel, General Litchfield, the
American Consul, comes to our room and invites us infor-
mally to dinner. We pass a very pleasant evening at the
consulate, and are very glad to meet again Generals Upton
and Forsythe and Major Sanger, with whom we crossed the
Pacific and from whom we parted in Japan.

CHAPTER XVI.

CALCUTTA TO BENARES.

December 23. — Calcutta (called so from Kali, a goddess; and Cuttah, a temple) is situated on the west bank of the Hooghly, about one hundred and ten miles from the mouth. The place has been in the possession of the English since 1664. The middle of the city is in the form of a square, with the Maidan, or Park, in the centre. Here is Government House, the residence of the Viceroy. Near by is the Town Hall, Hospital, Court House, and the new Post Office, the latter situated on the site of the famous *Black Hole*. The native quarter is thickly inhabited, and contains bazaars, Hindoo pagodas, and Mohammedan mosques.

At the north end of the town are jetties for sea-going steamers. The streets of Calcutta are wide and clean, and the whole city, including the native quarter, is excellently drained. The entire population amounts to one million, of whom twenty thousand are Europeans. The thermometer rarely falls below 52°, and seldom exceeds 100°.

The leading English papers published in Calcutta are *The Friend of India, The Englishman, The Indian Daily News, The Calcutta Observer, The Indian Public Opinion, The Charivari.* Besides these there are several native papers and periodicals.

The residence and grounds of the Viceroy occupy twelve acres. Here are statues of Wellesley, Dalhousie, and Hardinge. Near by is a column to the memory of Sir David Ochterlony. Across the Maidan is Fort William. The city is well lighted with gas, and reservoirs at Barrackpore furnish an ample supply of water.

Calcutta possesses many colleges, a University founded in 1857, and the Imperial Museum, where the Industrial Exhibition of 1869 was held. One third of the entire trade of India is done in the city of Calcutta.

After breakfast this morning we visit Fort William, and are greatly pleased with the excellent barracks provided for the soldiers. After a walk through Eden Gardens we return to the hotel, and find a ticket awaiting us, kindly sent by General Litchfield, admitting us to Prinsep's Ghât, where the Prince of Wales is to land at four o'clock this afternoon. As F—— is suffering from a severe cold, and as I am engaged to dine at six o'clock with a Boston merchant, we do not make use of it.

December 24.—The Prince of Wales arrived yesterday afternoon, and the streets are crowded with natives and Europeans, hurrying this way and that, and the authorities are giving the last touches to the various parts of the coming illumination. Countless rows of little glass lamps, of various colors, full of cocoa-nut oil, have been suspended on every public building; all the private dwelling-houses are likewise adorned; and the tall arches covered with emblems, the frequent transparencies that are to be seen in all directions, and the masses of lamps and gas-jets wreathed in different devices, all assure a most brilliant effect. It has been arranged that the Prince and party shall leave Government House at dusk, and drive through the principal streets to witness the illumination; and as soon as the Prince is well on his way, all other carriages may follow in procession.

General Litchfield has most kindly offered F—— and me seats in his carriage; and as F—— is unfortunately unable to leave the hotel on account of his cold, I walk out, about half past five, in company with Dr. Von Scherff, a gentleman who is making a tour of the world, and we make our way past a long line of vehicles filled with a most brilliant assemblage, waiting for the royal party to appear. We soon find the carriages of General Litchfield. In the large barouche are seated General Litchfield and wife, Generals Upton and Forsythe, and Judge M'Crae of California. Room is found here for Dr. Von Scherff, and Major Sanger and I take seats in the little brougham behind.

It is now dusk, and we have hardly taken our places,

when, through the rapidly increasing darkness, the different buildings begin to shine out with their broad borders of light. The effect is magnificent! The evening is perfectly calm and still; hardly a breath of air is stirring; and as building after building rises forth out of the darkness, — all the doors and windows and roofs indicated by dazzling lines of light, — we seem to be gazing on some strange aerial city whose houses are mere outlines, like imaginary geometrical figures utterly devoid of substance.

Promptly at six o'clock the Prince and suite drive by, followed by a company of Sepoys in brilliant uniforms, riding at full gallop with drawn swords. After waiting about ten minutes, all the carriages fall into line, and we drive for over an hour through the principal streets, lined with myriads of wondering natives, past countless brilliant devices, and building after building all ablaze with light. The rich costumes of Indian princes, the jewelled trappings of their horses, the handsome equipments of the native soldiers, and the curious costumes of the common people, all combine to form a scene from fairy-land, a picture from the Arabian Nights!

Calcutta is remarkably well situated for an exhibition of this sort. The city contains so many broad, open squares, that the many tall buildings when illuminated can all be seen to good advantage, and at the same time the eye can take in the general effect of the whole. It is hard to say where the most pleasing results were produced, but I think it is generally conceded that the new Imperial Museum outshone everything else. This tall building is not yet completed, but the deficiency was temporarily made good by the erection of a skeleton mansard-roof, which was hung with rows of lamps. The front of the structure bore in large letters of light, " God bless the Prince of Wales." The Ochterlony monument seems to me to deserve the next place. The base was surrounded with rows of lamps; a single string of lamps was wreathed gracefully round the column from bottom to top, like a circlet of roses; and two brilliant electric lights blazed forth from the little gallery at the summit.

After witnessing the illuminations, we drive to the house of one of the leading American merchants, to spend the remainder of Christmas eve. Nearly all the Americans in the city are present. Soon after twelve we wish each other a "merry Christmas," and perform a solemn toast to our distant friends.

Since my arrival in Calcutta I have been frequently to the American Consulate, and have had considerable conversation with General Litchfield in regard to it. The building is of good size and well situated. Indeed, it is the least objectionable of any consular residence that I have yet seen. The establishment, however, needs a large staff of servants. Calcutta contains so many English, and other foreigners, that social festivities are very frequent. Travellers from all parts of the world arrive constantly, and the representatives of their countries must entertain them at least to some degree. In short, the city holds such an important position, politically and commercially, that all nations should give their chosen representatives full power and means to administer their interests in the best possible way. General Litchfield informs me that the salary of the consulate is quite insufficient to enable him to discharge the various social obligations which are continually arising.

O, for our country's sake, may future travellers find a change! Legislators who vehemently support propositions of retrenchment in the consular service think, no doubt, that they are working the United States a benefit by thus effecting a "saving." I have seen with my own eyes that the country *loses* the money *fifty times over*. When a congressman gives his vote for such a measure, he is doing incalculable harm, not only to the consular body itself, but also to every citizen of the United States who values his country's reputation in foreign lands.

December 25. — Christmas day! and everything about us like summer. What is Christmas without snow? There can be no Santa Claus here for children, no sleigh-rides, no softly falling flakes which cover all unsightly spots and make the earth look clean and pure. Such festivals must make the dwellers in this distant land long all the more for home.

At 7 A. M. I join, by appointment, several American gentlemen whom I met last evening, who have promised to show
me some "jungle riding." I am furnished with a large Aus-
tralian horse. The others, similarly mounted, lead the way.
Off we dash, straight into the jungle, across ditches and low
walls, which are easily cleared by my companions, but which
demand a style of riding which I have never practised in
America. However, I manage to keep up with them fairly
well, and we return about ten o'clock, after a very enjoyable
airing.

F—— and I have decided to push on to Benares. There
is but little in Calcutta of peculiar and special interest to the
traveller. Benares, the most holy city in India, teems with
curiosities. General Litchfield has kindly offered to procure
us tickets for the ball at Government House, and for the
approaching Chapter of the Order of the Star of India. To
witness these we shall be obliged to remain here another week.
Dr. Von Scherff starts to-night for Benares, and we are glad
to accompany him. Having therefore bade farewell to our
kind friends, we drive across the river to the Howrah station,
and leave Calcutta on the night mail at half past ten, on the
East Indian Railway.

December 26. — We rush along all day at a tremendous
speed, past small villages and broad fields stretching far away
on either side. We pass great numbers of fat snipe and wild
pigeons, which are very tame, and which do not seem to be

at all disturbed by our rattling express. Great hawks, too, perched on the telegraph-poles, look at us half sleepily, as if certain of not being interfered with. At every station several natives walk up and down by the cars, shouting, "Panee, panee" (water). The accommodations on the East Indian Railway might be far better. Even the first-class coaches are dirty and uncomfortable.

After a tiresome day's travel, at six o'clock we reach a station called Mogul Serai, where it is necessary to change cars for Benares, which is six miles distant on a branch road. Having shifted our various parcels, we start again in about an hour; and when we have safely accomplished five miles of the six, our engine breaks a connecting-rod and the train comes to a stand-still. We are told by the guard that another engine has been telegraphed for, but it is not probable that it will arrive before an hour. As we feel sure we can accomplish the remaining distance in much less time on foot, we leave the train and walk into Benares, like the countless pilgrims who annually visit its holy precincts. We have hardly reached the station, however, when the train slowly draws up, the engine having in some way recovered itself. We take carriages (*gharis*), and crossing the Ganges on the Bridge of Boats, are soon installed at Clark's Hotel.

December 27. — Benares is situated on the left bank of the Ganges, four hundred and seventy-five miles, by rail, from Calcutta. Its population amounts to about one hundred and

seventy-four thousand. It is regarded by the natives as the
most holy city in India. Multitudes of pilgrims flock to Benares annually, and aged priests, expecting soon to die, hasten
hither to rest their bones in the city's sacred soil. Indeed,
men guilty of the foulest crimes believe that a visit to Benares,
and a solemn worship at some of its numberless shrines, will
bring forgiveness for their sins and will assure the safety of
their souls hereafter.

As far back as the middle of the sixth century Benares
must have been a city of importance in many ways; for it
was to the Tsipattana Vihâra, or monastery, now called Sârnâth, that Shâkyamuni, the Great Buddha, came at that time,
and, seating himself under a tree, preached for the first time
the famous doctrines of Dharma and Nirvâna, which have
been since embraced by four hundred millions of people.
Before this period Benares was the centre of Hindooism and
chief seat of its authority. "Benares is a city of no mean
antiquity. Twenty-five centuries ago, at the least, it was famous. When Babylon was struggling with Nineveh for su-
premacy, when Tyre was planting her colonies, when Athens
was growing in strength, before Rome had become known, or
Greece had contended with Persia, or Cyrus had added lustre
to the Persian monarchy, or Nebuchadnezzar had captured
Jerusalem, and the inhabitants of Judæa had been carried
into captivity, she had already risen to greatness, if not to
glory. Nay, she may have heard of the fame of Solomon, and

have sent her ivory, her apes, and her peacocks to adorn his palaces; while partly with her gold he may have overlaid the Temple of the Lord."*

Soon after breakfast we engage a guide and make our way to the Màn-Mandil Ghât and ascend some steps near by which lead up to the Observatory, erected by Raja Jay Singh towards the end of the seventeenth century. On our way we pass several ancient idols, some being in the form of monkeys representing the god Hanumàn. A flag floats from the top of a high staff near by, in honor of the Raja of Jeypore,— the present proprietor of this part of the city, and the descendant of Raja Jay Singh. In the lane leading from the Ghât is the temple of Dàlbhyeswar, the god who controls the rain. The image is at the bottom of a cistern in the middle of the temple; for the people believe that the god must be continually drenched with water if a favorable answer is expected to their prayers for rain. This deity is also known as the Poor Man's Friend, and it is said that needy men, by visiting his shrine, will have their wants relieved. The great poverty throughout the city is an unfavorable evidence of the power of the god. Near by is Sitàlâ, the goddess of small-pox.

On entering the Observatory, the first instrument we see is the Bhittiyantra, or Mural Quadrant, which consists of a wall eleven feet high and nine feet one and a quarter inches broad, in the plane of the meridian. This is used to ascer-

---

* Rev. M. A. Sherring, M. A., LL. B.

tain the sun's altitude and zenith distance; also the sun's greatest declination, and the latitude of the place. Near by are two large circles, one made of stone, the other of lime; and also a large stone square. It is said that these were used for the purpose of ascertaining the shadow of the gnomon cast by the sun, and the degrees of azimuth; but every mark upon them is destroyed.

Another immense instrument is called Yantrasamrât (prince of instruments), the wall of which is thirty-six feet in length and four and a half feet in breadth, and is set in the plane of the meridian. One extremity is six feet four and a quarter inches high, and the other twenty-two feet three and a half inches. By this instrument the distance from the meridian, the declination of any planet or star, and the sun, and the right ascension of a star, may be discovered. Here, also, is a double mural quadrant, and, to the east, an equinoctial circle of stone. At a little distance off is the Chakrayantra, an instrument used for finding the declination of a planet or star. Near this is another large instrument called Digansayantra, by which the degrees of azimuth of a planet or star may be found. To the south is another equinoctial circle.

Having inspected the Observatory, and returned to the Mân-Mandil Ghât, we procure a boat and are rowed slowly along in front of the vast number of curious buildings which rise from the various Ghâts to a height of fifty or sixty feet, and contain five, six, and sometimes seven stories. This view of the city from the river is picturesque to the highest degree. The different towers, temples, mosques, and palaces, of Hindoo and Saracenic styles, stretch along the river-bank, and rise to the summit of a lofty cliff over a hundred feet high. In the holy waters of the Ganges hundreds of people are bathing; while others, who have performed their morning ablutions, are worshipping at some of the numerous shrines in the vicinity, or are conversing with pious Brahmins, — called Sons of the Ganges, — who, seated under immense palm umbrellas, exhort the people or expound theological dogmas. Near our boat a dead body is floating slowly along on the surface of the water, and a greedy vulture, perched upon it, is tearing it to pieces with evident enjoyment. Opposite, on the shore, a family is making preparations to burn a father or brother lately deceased; near by several stone altars mark the spot of the now abolished *suttee*.

Looking at this varied scene, as our boat glides slowly along with the current, we involuntarily forget the present, and are transported in thought into the past. Here modern progress does not seem to be known. The presence of the railroad and telegraph is forgotten; steamboats may never have been; we are witnessing peculiar rites and ceremonies, which have been continued by generation after generation for hundreds and hundreds of years.

In regard to the dead body floating down the Ganges, the

explanation is easy. When a poor man dies, if his family or friends cannot afford to purchase wood for his burning (which is very expensive), they singe the upper lip or the face of the dead, and throw the body into the Ganges. It is firmly believed that the body of the dead must have some contact with fire, or the soul will not be at rest. This became so frequent, that the English government were obliged to forbid it for sanitary reasons; but in spite of the prohibition the nuisance still continues to some degree.

We stop our boat opposite the Burning Ghât, where, close to the water's edge, the dead are burned. We have arrived at the beginning of the funeral ceremonies of a man. The body, wrapped in white cloth, is carried by the relations on a rude litter, and is thrust, feet foremost, into the muddy waters of the Ganges. When it has been completely submerged in the sacred stream, the cloth over the face is removed, and a relative carefully shaves the deceased. After this, it is placed on a funeral-pyre, and wood is piled around and over it. The nearest relative then takes a large handful of straw and light twigs, and kindling the bunch at the sacred fire kept ever burning by the Domra near by, he walks slowly round and round the corpse, touching it on the forehead each time as he passes, in token of farewell. Having circled it thus for five times, he thrusts the torch amongst the loose wood of the pyre, and soon after the whole mass is in a blaze. When the body is consumed, the ashes are scattered in the

Ganges, and the soul of the departed is at rest. The cremation of women is similar, in general, to the above, but a colored cloth is always used to cover the body. Leaving our boat, we proceed to Manikarnikâ, the famous Hindoo well. It is said to have been dug by the god Vishnu with his discus, and the deity, instead of water, filled it with the perspiration of his own body, and called it Chakrapushkarinî. Soon after, the god Mahâdeva arrived, and, looking into this well, beheld in it the beauty of many suns, which so delighted him that he promised Vishnu to grant him whatever gift he might desire. Vishnu replied that his wish was that Mahâdeva should always reside with him. Mahâdeva was so pleased with this request, that his body shook with joy, and from the violence of the motion an ear-ring called Manikarnaka fell from his ear into the water of the well. From this occurrence the well is called Manikarnikâ. On each of the four sides of the well is a series of steps leading down into the water. The seven lowermost steps are said to have been made by the god, and to be without juncture; and although several joinings are visible, it is held by the Brahmins that these are only superficial, and do not penetrate the stones. In a niche on the north side is a figure of Vishnu; and on the west side, near the mouth of the well, is a row of sixteen little altars on which pilgrims lay offerings to their ancestors. The water of this well is believed to possess the power to wash away every sin. It is a stagnant pool, full

of waste and decay, and the odors which constantly arise
from it are sickening. The sinner, descending the steps,
throws some of the liquid over his body, and comes forth
forgiven. Even murderers are thus fully absolved from their
guilt.

Our guide next shows us a large round slab, called Cha-
rana-pádukâ, which projects from the pavement. In the
middle of it is a stone pedestal, the top of which is inlaid
with marble, and contains two indentations, which are said
to be the impressions of the feet of the god Vishnu when
he alighted to worship the god Mahâdeva.

From here we make our way past Sindhia Ghât and the Raja
of Nagpore's Ghât (the former of which is continually sinking
into the bed of the river), and then, re-entering our boat, we
are rowed to Panchgangâ Ghât, where we dismiss it. This
Ghât is often thronged with pilgrims, for it is believed that
five rivers meet at this spot, although only one can be seen.
We ascend the Ghât, and arrive at the lofty mosque of
Aurungzebe. This is the highest building of the city, and
its tall tapering minarets invariably arrest the eye. These
minarets, eight in number, are one hundred and forty-seven
feet in height (reckoning from the floor of the mosque), and
eight feet in diameter at the base. They lean fifteen inches
from the perpendicular. They were originally some fifty feet
higher than they now are, but they were shortened in consequence of exhibiting signs of weakness and insecurity. From

the summit of one of the towers we obtain a fine view of Benares and its suburbs.

Leaving the river-bank, we push our way through the narrow streets, thronged with natives of all castes, — all with curious marks on their foreheads, placed there daily by the priest of the temple at which they worship, — past venerable Brahmins, and numbers of sacred bulls who wander hither and thither unchecked. Indeed, travellers are foolish if they endeavor to hinder them, for the bulls are believed to be deities, and to oppose a deity would soon create great disturbance. After five minutes' walk, we enter the principal business street, called Purânâ Chank, and make our way to the store of Baboo Debi Parsâd, to inspect his extensive stock of shawls and cloths, magnificently embroidered with gold and silver. Proceeding, we enter the long narrow street called Chank-hambha, where beautifully enchased vessels of brass and copper are to be found.

We finish the morning with a visit to the Nepalese Temple, which rises from the banks of the Ganges not far from the Mân-Mandil Ghât. This temple is so peculiarly Indian, that it is utterly unfit for a lady to visit.

After *tiffin* we set out again, and visit first the elephants of the Raja of Vizianagram, whose palace is in Benares. We are told by our guide that if we will send our cards to the Raja's secretary, we shall be permitted to ride one of the elephants; but we have so much else to accomplish, that we decline. We proceed first to the temple at Durga Kund. The neighboring buildings, the temple grounds, and the walls and housetops in the vicinity literally swarm with monkeys. These are believed to be gods and goddesses, and are carefully fed by persons specially appointed. Before we reach the temple grounds, multitudes of them come scampering along the wall, and, sitting down in a line, chatter at us in token of welcome. We stop at the entrance-gate to purchase a few handfuls of grain, and, passing in, we are soon surrounded by the diminutive proprietors. What a nuisance they must be in the neighborhood! Indeed, the magistrate of Benares removed a large number of them to the jungle, a few years ago. It is said that they steal constantly in all directions, and injure the surrounding property in various ways. The whole place is given up to these creatures, and they certainly seem delighted with their lot.

We now retrace our steps to the city, and stop at the famous Well of Knowledge, called Gyân Kûp, in which, as the natives believe, the god Shiva resides. Multitudes visit this well, and cast in flowers and other gifts, and the odor which comes from this putrid mass is disgusting. We soon after arrive at the Golden Temple, or Bisheshwar, dedicated to the god Shiva, whose image is the *lingam*, a conical stone set on end. The god of this temple is the supreme deity of Benares, and holds sway over all other gods in the city. The dome and tower are covered with thin plates of gold, spread over thick plates of copper overlaying the stones beneath. This decoration was furnished by the late Maharaja Runjeet Singh of Lahore. The temple itself was built by Ahalyâ Bai, Maharanee of Indore.

Passing once more through the narrow streets of the city, we next visit the famous Well of Fate, called Kâl-Kûp. In the roof of the temple which surrounds this well is a square hole, and the rays of the sun, passing through this opening at twelve o'clock, strike upon the water in the well below. At noon, multitudes of people visit the well; and any who cannot trace their shadows in the fatal water will surely die within six months from that instant. "The general ignorance respecting the explanation of this daily phenomenon does not speak much for the scientific knowledge of the Hindoos, or even for their common-sense."[*] As the afternoon is now far advanced, we return to the hotel for dinner.

December 28. — Soon after breakfast we set out for the famous ruins at Sârnâth, situated about four miles from the city. These ruins are universally believed to be portions of buildings erected in the sixth century before Christ, and they are said to have been standing during the early ministry of the Great Buddha. These ruins consist of two towers, — situated about half a mile apart, — and of walls and foundations of other structures, which have been lately excavated. "The great Stupa, called Dhamek, is a solid round tower,

[*] Rev. M. A. Sherring.

ninety-three feet in diameter at base, one hundred and ten feet in height above the surrounding ruins, and one hundred and twenty-eight feet above the general level of the country. The foundation or basement, which is made of very large bricks, has a depth of twenty-eight feet below the level of the ruins, but is sunk only ten feet below the surface of the country." *

There is one other tower at Sârnâth. It is situated about two thousand five hundred feet to the south of Dhamek, and was once called Chaukandi, but is now called Lori-ki-kûdan, or Lori's Leap, for a Hindoo named Lori leaped from its summit and killed himself. The ruin consists of a mound of solid brick work, seventy-four feet in height, on the top of which is an octagonal building twenty-three feet high, built to commemorate the ascent of the mound by the Emperor Humayun, son of the great Baber, who began his reign A. D. 1531.

We return to the hotel for *tiffin*, and at 2 P. M. we leave Benares on the Oudh and Rohilkund Railway, bound for Lucknow.

---

* For full information in regard to this interesting ruin, see Report of Major-General Cunningham, printed in the Journal of the Asiatic Society of Bengal, Volume XXXII.

CHAPTER XVII.

LUCKNOW, CAWNPORE, AND DELHI.

December 29. — We reach Lucknow at half past six this morning, after a most uncomfortable night on the road. The outer air was very cold, and the "accommodation" in the first-class cars scarcely deserves the name. We drive at once to Hill's Hotel. The cold is intense, the atmosphere is excessively damp and penetrating, for the sun has not yet risen. Hill's Hotel is kept in a large rambling building built by Nasir-ud-Din Haidar for the son of his Prime Minister, Roshan-ud-Daulah, who was Commander-in-Chief of his Majesty's army. The dining-room is long and lofty, and bears traces of elaborate decoration.

Lucknow is situated on the banks of the Gumti, a river which empties into the Ganges beyond Jampur. The city is about three hundred and fifty feet above the level of the sea. It is distant seven hundred and eighty-one miles from Calcutta by rail, and contains a population of two hundred and seventy-three thousand; it extends over thirteen square miles.

Lucknow was founded by the Hindoos. In A. D. 1160 the city was captured by Sayad Salar, a Mohammedan. The modern town contains three quarters, — the native portion, built by Akbar the Great in the middle of the sixteenth century; the court suburb, built by Asoof-ud-Dowlah in 1775; and lastly, to the north and west, the country-houses of the ex-king (deposed in 1856, and now confined at Calcutta), the residences of the English officials, and the cantonments of the troops.

Immediately after breakfast we procure a guide and proceed to the ruins of the Residency, situated about half a mile from the hotel. This is one of the most historically interesting spots in India, and stands as an unchanged memento of the mutiny of 1857; bearing witness at once to deeds of the most heroic courage and endurance, and to sufferings rarely equalled in the history of the world.

The native revolt did not spread to Lucknow till the 29th of June. On the morning of that day Sir Henry Lawrence learned that a body of rebels was advancing upon the city, and on the following morning a picked portion of the garrison marched out to meet them. This force consisted of 500 infantry, 40 mounted volunteers, 120 native troops, a detail of artillery manned by native gunners, and an eight-inch howitzer drawn by an elephant. Having marched six miles from

the city, the Englishmen were astonished to find a complete
army, composed of an irresistible force of all arms, drawn up
in order of battle. The native artillerymen, on the side of the
English, at once deserted their guns; the howitzer was immediately captured by the enemy; the small British force was
speedily surrounded; Colonel Case of the Thirty-second and
nearly a hundred of his men were killed; and, but for the
continual efforts of the mounted volunteers, and the strange
omission on the part of the enemy to seize or destroy the
Iron Bridge, every man would have been slain. One hundred
and seventy-two Europeans were killed or wounded, including
thirteen officers, — more than half the entire number, — and
the survivors had scarcely time to blow up the Machi Bhawan
Fort, when they found themselves completely besieged in
the grounds of the Residency. The siege began on the 1st
of July. The garrison consisted of nine hundred and twenty-
seven Europeans, and seven hundred and sixty-five natives,
two hundred and thirty of whom soon deserted. On the
4th, the brave Lawrence expired, killed by a shell thrown
from his own lost howitzer, which entered a room in the
Residency where he was writing a despatch. The sufferings
of the besieged were terrible. Deaths occurred from day to
day. When, on the 26th of September, Havelock arrived to
their relief, the entire garrison numbered only eleven hundred and seventy-nine, the loss having been chiefly among
Europeans. Of nine officers of the Bengal artillery, five had

fallen; eleven ladies and fifty-three children had been slain, or had died of sickness and privation; and from this time till the 17th of November (the date of the final relief by Sir Colin Campbell), one hundred and twenty-two more of the old garrison and four hundred of Havelock's men died. The ladies and non-combatants left on the 19th of November; and on the night of the 22d, the Residency and grounds were evacuated in silence, and the different positions on the road to the Dilkusha abandoned in turn. On arriving at the Dilkusha the women were hospitably received, the sick were tenderly nursed, and here poor Havelock, worn out with care and fatigue, soon after died, leaving Sir James Outram to watch the rebels in the Alum Bagh. Sir Colin Campbell conducted the survivors in safety to Allahabad, which they reached on the 7th of December.

The above is a hurried narration of the bare facts; but it is impossible for the pen to fill out the sad picture. "Gazing to-day upon the peaceful garden-scene, one cannot realize the terrors and tumult of those frightful months. One must be content with imagining the roar of artillery and the rattle of small arms, kept up incessantly from before sunrise for more than three hours daily by an investing swarm of a hundred thousand relentless savages; the lull of the weary noonday; the resumption of hostilities in the long afternoon at a season when Europeans in India are wont to shield themselves from the depressing glare or plunging rain, and rest within cool houses; the sallies, the rallies, the mines and countermines; the explosions of roofs, the downward rushes of crumbling masonry; and, worst of all, the slow decay of wounds and epidemics, sustained in crowded rooms, amid a plague of flies, with insufficient food; finally, the incessant monotony of daily funerals. Small-pox was prevalent; women brought forth children only to bury them; Polehampton, the chaplain, after being shot through the body, died of cholera, which seems to have been chronic, especially among non-combatants; officers were on several occasions shot by the sentries inadvertently; some few even committed suicide. But despair was the exception; and the general endurance deservedly received the admiration of the world." *

Leaving the main road, we pause at the gate of the Residency, called the "Baillie Guard," from Colonel Baillie, one of the old British Residents, who built it as a defence to the Residency in the early part of the present century. The stones of the archway are riddled with shot and shell, bearing witness to the fierce and incessant cannonade which was poured upon the whole place. Passing in, the large ruined building on the right is the Residency proper, in which Lawrence received his death-wound. In the cellars underneath many women and children lived during the whole siege. Adjoining is a watchtower where man after man was shot down. On the left is Dr. Fayrer's house, the under-

* H. G. Keene's Handbook to Lucknow.

ground rooms of which also harbored women and children. These buildings, with the exception of portions of the walls, are completely battered to pieces. Near by is a cross erected to the memory of Sir Henry Lawrence. This monument is very unsatisfactory in itself, and, considering that the whole place as it stands to-day is a glorious remembrance of the hero, this little decoration, perched on the highest hill in the grounds, is unnecessary and in bad taste.

To the north stood the Redan battery which commanded the Iron Bridge (already mentioned). This was held throughout the whole siege by Lieutenant Lawrence of the Thirty-second Foot. The next house was occupied by Mr. Martin Gubbins, C. S., and was defended by Major Ashton, Forty-first N. I. Near by is the Brigade Mess-house, and, to the right, the famous Sikh Square, blown up by the rebels.

We now come to the Cawnpore battery. This was exposed to the hottest fire of the enemy, and was considered so dangerous that it was held by volunteers, or by men detailed from day to day according to the roster. A neighboring post was guarded by sixty-five boys from the Martinière school.

In the adjoining cemetery rests Lawrence. His tombstone bears the following inscription : —

Here Lies
HENRY LAWRENCE
Who tried to do his duty.*
May the Lord have mercy on his soul.
Born 28 June 1806. Died July 4 1857.

---

* These were his last words. The succeeding sentence seems out of place.

Leaving the Residency we call a *gurry* and are driven to Hosenabad. Passing under a curious gate, built in the Saracenic style, we enter a large quadrangle, at the upper end of which is the main building. This is a large edifice with polished marble floor and vaulted dome. It contains a great collection of mirrors, chandeliers, and all sorts of glittering ornaments. To the left is a white building intended as a copy of the famous Taj of Agra.

From here we proceed to the Lall Baradari. This was the Public Hall of Reception of the old native rulers. On the death of the old King Nasir-ud-Din, in July, 1837, the Queen Dowager declared that a youth named Munna Jan was the heir to the throne. This the British denied, and insisted that the succession devolved upon the uncle of the late king, an old man named Mahomed Ali. The Queen Dowager and the pretender, accompanied by multitudes of followers, entered the Lall Baradari and ascended the throne. The English commander, Colonel Low, with his soldiers, surrounded the building, and sent word to the Begum that if the hall was not evacuated in fifteen minutes the soldiers would be ordered to storm the premises. No notice of this was taken, and a company of the Thirty-fifth dashed into the hall. As they advanced with fixed bayonets they saw themselves reflected in a large mirror hanging behind the throne, and, believing that an opposing band was charging towards them, they poured a fierce volley into the looking-glass. This put the mob to flight.

The Begum and her *protégé* were arrested and the old uncle was proclaimed king. To the Lall Baradari, also, came Lord Canning to meet the Talukadars of Oudh, and to announce to them the forgiveness of the Queen of England and the terms of their future allegiance.

We visit next the curious Chattar Manzal, or Umbrella-house, so called from a grotesque gilt ornament which crowns the summit. This was the harem of the King Nasir-ud-Din. In the time of the mutiny it was surrounded by a high wall, which was originally intended to secure the retirement of its inmates. During Havelock's advance it was the scene of a severe cannonade. The best rooms are now used for the United Service Club, the Theatre and Assembly Rooms, and the Public Library.

We now arrive at the Kaisar Bagh. Passing under a gate over which are the double fish, the family arms of the founder, we cross a court-yard and soon reach the group of buildings erected in 1850 by Wajid Ali Shah, at a cost of eight hundred thousand pounds sterling. As to the architecture, the effect of the whole is spoiled by the gaudiness of the decorations. Mr. Keene calls it "a stucco Louvre, in which Italian and Moorish styles blend in a manner that is more grotesque than graceful; and where gilding and ochre and whitewash tend to give a strange appearance of the theatre to the 'residency' of this Oriental Gerolstein."

We visit now the Kadam Rasul, a plain tomb-like struc-

ture covered with a dome. It is called Kadam Rasul, or
Apostle's Step, from the fact that it is said to contain a stone
marked with the sacred footprint, and brought from Mecca.
It was built by the first king of Oudh, Ghazi-ud-Din Haidar.
In the mutiny it was held first by the rebels, but was captured without difficulty by General Campbell. Our guide
thus laconically describes the scene: "English out of sight,
rebels walk about; English come up, rebels run away."

Continuing our way we reach Sikandar Bagh, a large walled
enclosure called after the Sikandar Begum. To the right of
the gate is a place where the wall was breached during the
advance of Sir Colin Campbell, on the 16th of November,
1857. The Ninety-third Highlanders, with some British and
Sikh Infantry, rushed in and bayoneted the enemy. Near
by is Wingfield Park, called after Sir Charles Wingfield, M. P.,
a former Chief Commissioner.

We next visit the Martinière. This is the former residence
of General Claude Martin, a native of Lyons, who, after a
very varied career, died in Lucknow in 1800, leaving over
four hundred thousand pounds, the larger portion of which he
bequeathed to the cities of Lucknow, Lyons, and Calcutta, for
the foundation of schools. General Martin also left special
directions that his tomb should be erected in one of the apartments of this building, knowing that Musulmen would then
never violate the premises. His body rests in a vaulted
chamber in the basement. The building is used as a boys'

school. It is a large and curious structure, with numerous statues on the outside. In front, near a lake, is an Ionic column.

The Dil Kusha, or Heart's Delight, is our next stopping-place. This was built for a residence by the Nawab Saadat in the early part of the century. It was captured from the rebels in 1857 by Colonel Hamilton of the Seventy-eighth. To this place (as I have said) the rescued garrison were carried from the Residency.

We finish our tour of the city by visiting the Alum Bagh. This was erected by King Wajid Ali as an occasional residence for a favorite wife. It consisted of a large pavilion and several adjoining buildings. It was captured by Havelock from the rebels on the 23d of September. It then became a convalescent depot. Here Havelock was buried; and here Sir James Outram remained, after it was found necessary to evacuate Lucknow, till the final relief in March, 1858.

On our way back to the hotel we walk through the principal business street of the town. Here we find several articles for which the place is noted, — caps and slippers exquisitely embroidered in gold and silver, and a pattern of "bangles" which is only produced in this city.

We leave Lucknow at 8 P. M. and reach Cawnpore at midnight.

December 30. — Cawnpore is situated on the Ganges River, six hundred and eighty-four miles from Calcutta and forty-two miles from Lucknow. It contains a population of one hundred and sixteen thousand. It is now an important military station, and carries on an extensive trade. A railroad bridge over the Ganges is soon to take the place of the present bridge of boats.

The story of Cawnpore in the mutiny days will always give a sad but deep interest to the place.

In the year 1852, Bajee Rao, the last Peishwa of the Mahratta confederacy, died, leaving all his property to his adopted son, Dhoondoo Punth, commonly called Nana Sahib. The government of Lord Dalhousie, however, at once announced that the titular dignity had ceased, and, though Nana Sahib should inherit the property, the pension and official salute of the Peishwaship would be discontinued. For the next five years Nana used every effort to change this decree, and, smarting under a sense of wrong, he heard of the outbreak at Delhi with joy, and, being on intimate terms with the English, knew that he was in a position to obtain as complete revenge as his long-continued and un-noticed injuries seemed to demand.

On the morning of the 6th of June, 1857, the native troops mutinied and marched out to Kalianpur, the first stage on the Delhi road, evidently with the intention of eventually joining the main body of mutineers. The English garrison, under the command of Sir Hugh Massey Wheeler, consisted of the following force: one battery of six guns, with fifty-nine men; sixty of the Eighty-fourth Infantry; seventy-four invalids of the Thirty-second; and fifteen of the First Madras Fusiliers. The native troops consisted of the Second Cavalry, the First, Fifty-third, and Fifty-sixth N. I., and the native gunners attached to the battery. The entire European population numbered seven hundred and fifty souls.

Sir Hugh Wheeler took his followers, combatant and non-combatant, into a refuge that he had prepared for them in the depot-barracks, standing where the new church is now built. These consisted of two long barracks of one story each, each built for the accommodation of one company. One was thatched, both were surrounded with verandas, and the inner walls were of brick, a foot and a half in thickness. Around this shelter a trench was dug, and the earth thrown up to form a parapet about five feet in height. The guns pointed through openings, and were entirely without protection. The whole place was about two hundred yards square, and was armed with ten field-pieces of different calibres. Provisions had been obtained calculated to last for thirty days.

It was now the Nana's turn. Although he had been for the last few years continually petitioning for a restoration of his predecessor's honors, he had always used such tact that the English, so far from regarding him as an enemy, put him in charge, at this critical period, of the arsenal, magazine, park, and treasury! Thus extraordinarily favored by fortune, his revenge was easy. Following the rebels who had departed to Kalianpur, he quickly persuaded them to return and attack the British at once, instead of proceeding to their fellow-mutineers at Delhi. On the very day that Sir Hugh Wheeler entered the entrenchment, the Nana declared his rebellion. Summoning an overwhelming body of natives, he surrounded the little band of Europeans on all sides, and formally opened the siege on the 7th of June.

For three dreadful weeks the little garrison struggled on. With many sick and dying, without medicines or hospital stores, and short of ammunition, they were subjected to a continual bombardment from without, and to hunger and distress within. The brave men, however, did not suffer themselves to be simply besieged. Many sorties were made, and several of the enemy's guns were spiked and captured. Deaths, however, occurred frequently. Men, women, and children sank under the prolonged sufferings; and when, on the 26th, the Nana offered to treat, the survivors accepted the proposition.

It was agreed that the Europeans should depart, under the Nana's escort, to Allahabad, and boats were provided to convey them thither. The scenes that followed are well described by Keene: "On the fatal morning of the 27th of June, the survivors proceeded to embark. It is not possible to dwell upon the events connected with this episode with calmness. The facts far exceeded all that the imagination could conceive. Immediately on the embarkation of the deluded and now helpless people who left the enclosure in the early dawn of the morning, there followed the most dastardly piece of treachery that has perhaps ever been perpetrated. Only a portion of the party had taken their places in the boats, when, by previous arrangement, the boatmen set the thatched coverings of the boats on fire, and rushed on to the bank. A heavy fire of grape and musketry was then opened on the Europeans. Out of thirty boats, two only managed to start; one of these was shortly swamped by round-shot, but its passengers were enabled to reach the leading boat. Of those on board the other twenty-eight boats, some were killed, some drowned, and the rest brought back prisoners. Of the fugitives who quitted their weak position but a few hours before, only fifty had contrived to escape for the time, though it was in the case of the larger portion only to die shortly after. The boat they occupied was under an incessant galling fire from both banks, but it pursued its course till it grounded at the distance of six miles. All the night of that eventful and trying day continued the struggle for life, amid hopes and fears of which we can form but a very slight conception. Early on the following morning the miserable occupants of the frail bark managed to push on till the boat again grounded. They were again attacked, and a number were killed; but the assailants were driven off, and retired to Cawnpore. The Nana then immediately despatched *two complete regiments* in pursuit. As it was found impracticable to move the boat, a party of *fourteen* landed to drive back their assailants, which they did most effectually. Of these fourteen but four survived, — one now Colonel Mowbray Thompson, — to tell 'the story of Cawnpore'; those left in the boat were brought back and shared the subsequent fate of all the others. . . . . At last came the order to cease from slaughter, and the miserable survivors were driven off."

How different the scene of this massacre, as it lies before us to-day! The little temple near the water's edge (near which was the ambush) still stands, riddled with bullets, as if bearing witness to the dastardly deeds; near by, however, are several neat bungalows; the Ganges flows peacefully along on its course; natives are leading cattle to drink in its waters; a party of boatmen are chanting their peculiar monotone as they endeavor to pull their boat out of the stream; and the calm quiet and serenity which seem to pervade the spot are greatly in contrast to the rattle of artillery, the groans of the wounded and dying, and the exultant shouts of the treacherous natives, the remembrance of which will always bring a pang to every civilized nation in the world.

On the site of Wheeler's entrenchment now stands the Memorial Church. This edifice is in the Romanesque style, and is built of brick and stone in the form of a cross, with a tapering belfry at one end. The interior contains a beautiful wheel-window and one or two memorial windows; and

many tablets are placed on the walls, erected to different
victims of the mutiny. In short, the church is both pleasing
and displeasing; satisfactory in part, and yet disappointing
in several details. It was originally intended to defray the
cost by private subscription, but a large portion of it has
been paid by the government. H. H. the Maharaja of Jodh-
pur has contributed white marble slabs for the flooring of
the chancel; a handsome brass lectern has been given by
Mrs. W. C. Plowden; and the employés of the East Indian
Railway have presented a sum of money in memory of those
of their body who fell in the siege.

Two tablets in the interior of the church should be mentioned; one for its peculiar sadness, the other for its appro-
priateness. The first reads: "In memory of Mrs. Moore,
Mrs. Wainright, Miss Wainright, Mrs. Hill, forty-three soldiers' wives, and fifty-five children murdered in Cawnpore in
June, 1857." The other tablet commemorates the death of a
score of officers and soldiers, and underneath it are the words,
"Vengeance is mine, I will repay, saith the Lord."

The last act in the Cawnpore tragedy remains to be told.
Of all the multitude that started down the river in boats,
four only, as I have said, escaped. The other survivors were
driven to the quarters of the Nana. The women and children were placed for the time in a building called the
Savada Kotee; the men were shot on the parade-ground.
About ten days later there was a general move nearer the

town. The Nana took up his quarters in a house used as a hotel; the women and children, with some officers who had been lately captured elsewhere, were put into a house near the bank of the river, called Beebeeghur. Coarse food and furniture were given them, and the women were ordered to grind corn.

Here they remained till the 15th of July. The sufferings of these poor creatures can only be imagined. A Bengalee apothecary attended them for a few days, and his journal (afterwards found) proves that births and deaths were frequent among them. A thorough subsequent investigation satisfied the English officials, however, that dishonor was not added to the other horrors of those fearful days.

On the 11th of July, the prisoners were joined by other unfortunates. Colonel Smith of the Tenth N. I., with a party of refugees of both sexes, was captured the day before at Bithoor, passing down the river in a boat from Futtehgurh. These, to the number of fifty-five (chiefly women and children), were put in the palace at Bithoor for the night. On the next day they were obliged to march over twelve miles in the fierce sun, to receive sentence from the Nana at Cawnpore. Colonel Smith and Judge Thornhill, with the women and children, were thrown into the Beebeeghur, already crowded with the other captives. The rest of the men were immediately shot.

The Nana's triumph, however, was nearly over, and he

signalized the close of his power by one of the most frightful acts of vengeance that has ever been chronicled in history. Soon after the capture of Colonel Smith, the English obtained possession of Futtehpore. On the morning of the 15th, a fresh disaster to the natives occurred at Aoung. The news of the steady advance of the avenging British was brought to the Nana early in the afternoon of the same day. The Nana and his suite gathered in council to determine what disposition should be made of the prisoners. The matter was soon decided; the captives were to be put to death. At sundown four of the male prisoners were (at the special order of the Nana) taken out of the Beebeeghur and murdered on the high road. Then the general slaughter was begun. Volleys were first fired into the Beebeeghur through the doors and windows; and then the savages, rushing in among the captives with drawn swords, completed the fiendish massacre. At length the work was finished, and the doors were closed. The Nana was living in an old hotel within fifty yards of this house. It is said that he ordered a *nautch*, and passed the night in feasting and revelry. At daybreak he ordered the Beebeeghur to be cleared. It is estimated that it contained nearly two hundred dead bodies. These were stripped, and the majority cast into a well near by. The remainder were hurled into the Ganges.

Mr. Sherer, who arrived at Cawnpore soon after the suppression of the rebellion, says in his report: "Thence we were directed to the Beebeeghur and well.   And then broke upon our eyes that dreadful spectacle, over the very idea of which there are still broken spirits and widowed hearts mourning terror-stricken in distant England. . . . . There were no dead bodies, except in the well.   The well was narrow and deep; and, looking down, you could only see a tangled mass of human limbs entirely without clothing."

As soon as order was restored, Lord Canning resolved to erect a memorial on this sad spot.   Mr. C. B. Thornhill, at that time Commissioner of the Division (who had lost two brothers in the mutiny), was placed in charge of the work. He was commanded to devise a structure that should protect the fatal well and preserve its site; while the Viceroy, at his own expense, ordered a memorial statue of Baron Maro-chetti.   The result is as follows: on a pedestal built over the well is a large figure of the Angel of Pity.   A Gothic wall with iron doors surrounds the premises.   Near by is a well-kept garden.

The statue is pleasing and appropriate, but the curious wall around it is cheap looking and unnecessary.   Over the portal of the door is this inscription: "These are they which came out of great tribulation"; and around the well are these words: "Sacred to the perpetual memory of the great company of Christian people, chiefly women and children, who near this spot were cruelly massacred by the followers of the rebel Nana Dhoomdoo Punth of Bithoor; and cast, the dying with the dead, into the well below, on the 15th day of July, 1857."

We leave Cawnpore at half past two on the East Indian Railway.

December 31. — At seven o'clock this morning we come in sight of Delhi. The first view of the city from the railway is very picturesque. Before us are the high walls of strong fortifications, tall columns, and bulbous domes. Indeed, the railway itself, after crossing the Jumna on a strong girder-bridge, and passing directly through the old fort of Suleem-gurh, rushes close to the great Red Castle of Shahjuhan, and finally lands the traveller in the neighborhood of the Queen's Gardens.

The present city of Delhi was founded in 1631 by Shah-juhan. It is built within red granite walls, forty feet high, and seven miles in circumference. The city is situated on the Jumna River, one thousand and nineteen miles north-west of Calcutta, and eight hundred and seventy miles from Bombay. It contains a population of one hundred and fifty thousand. The city was ravaged by Nadir Shah in 1739, who took one hundred and twenty million pounds of spoil back to Persia. The fall of the nominal sovereigns of Delhi was succeeded September 1, 1858, by a proclamation of authority from the Queen of England.

After breakfasting at the United Service Hotel, we set out for a tour of the city, accompanied by Baboo Budree Das, one of the proprietors of the hotel, a very intelligent Hindoo of high caste, who speaks English perfectly, and is thoroughly posted on all points of interest in and around Delhi.* Passing out of the southeast or Delhi Gate, we drive southward, with the Jumna River on our left, bound for Feerozabad. After a drive of a half-hour we arrive at the *Kotila* of Feeroz Shah Toghluk, with the stone pillar. This is situated in the midst of ruins, and is a single shaft of sandstone, about forty-two feet high, and covered with inscriptions. The ruins of the palace of Feeroz surround it. The old city of Feeroz was about six miles long and two broad, and is said to have contained a population of one hundred and fifty thousand. From here we proceed to another portion of Feerozabad, called Indraput.

We visit next Homayoon's tomb. It was begun by this emperor's widow, Hajee Begum, and completed by his son; it is said that two hundred workmen were employed upon it for sixteen years, and that its total cost was fifteen lacs of rupees ($750,000). It is built of red stone in the form of a square, with a fine marble dome, and contains a large central hall. Here, in 1857, Major Hodson and Lieutenant Macdowell shot the two sons of the Ex-King Bahadoor Shah,

---

* Let me, however, warn travellers not to advance this man any money for expenses on the road, but to pay all such themselves, for the way the Baboo distributes rupees among the populace must give them the idea that those he is serving are princes in disguise.

who had taken refuge in this place after the mutiny. The
side chambers contain the tombs of several of the house of
Timoor.

Continuing our way we arrive at the tomb of Shah Niza-
moodeen. In regard to this man there is much uncertainty.
He served under the Emperor Ala-ood-deen Khilji towards
the end of the thirteenth century. He is said by some to
have been a sorcerer; by others, a member of the dangerous
Secret Society of Khorasan; and it is even alleged that he
was the founder of Thuggism.

The first building in this cemetery contains the tomb of
the foster-brother of the great Akbar. It is a fine marble
hall supported by pillars, which form graceful groined arches.
On each side is a carved screen of white marble.

Next comes the tomb of Nizamooden. This is surrounded
by a veranda of white marble, and the sarcophagus is enclosed by a marble screen. At the head of the grave is a
stand with a koran.

Not far off is the tomb of Juhanara Begum. The sarcophagus is likewise enclosed by a marble screen. Juhanara was
the daughter of the Emperor Shahjuhan. She is said to have
been a woman of remarkable talents and virtues. She was
the sister of Dara Sheko, heir-apparent to Shahjuhan, who
was murdered by his younger brother Aurungzeb, who then
deposed his father and proclaimed himself emperor. Juhanara
refused to reside at the court of her wicked brother, but re-

mained with her father at Agra. It is believed that she was removed to Delhi and murdered at the command of Aurungzeb. On her tomb are these words, said to have been written by herself: "Let no rich coverlet adorn my grave; this grass is the best covering for the tomb of the poor in spirit, the humble, the transitory Juhanara, the disciple of the holy men of Cheest, the daughter of the Emperor Shahjuhan." The top of the grave is covered with a growth of coarse grass. The carved marble screen around it is an exquisite piece of workmanship. Near by is the Bowlee, or well-house, a large, deep tank of water, into which little boys jump from great heights, for small coins.

Turning now to the east, we set out for Toghlukabad. After riding for a little distance in the carriage, we are obliged to change our conveyance, as the road is only suitable for native bullock-carts, called *teujahs*. These vehicles are drawn by two bullocks, who travel at the rate of ten miles an hour; but the *teujahs* are but little better than the terrible Chinese carts, and I advise travellers who wish to visit Toghlukabad to accomplish the last part of the way on horseback.

Toghlukabad, the massive citadel of the Emperor Toghluk Shah, was begun A. D. 1321, and finished two years later. The fort is built on rising ground, and is a half-hexagon in shape, with three faces of three quarters of a mile in length each, and a base of one mile and a half, the whole circuit being nearly four miles. It is constructed of immense blocks of stone, is surrounded on several sides by water, and the rampart walls are pierced with loop-holes for light and defence. The fort has thirteen gates, and contains a well cut in the solid rock to a depth of eighty feet; inside the walls, too, are the ruins of the founder's palace, and many ruined houses.

Standing on the citadel, one realizes the important position the fort held in the past. In the distance is Delhi; and at our feet a beautiful grassy plain, where, indeed, the Prince of Wales is to hold a grand review in about two weeks. Opposite us is the tomb of Toghluk Shah.

Leaving the fort, we cross over to the tomb. The two are connected by a causeway six hundred feet long. The tomb itself is built of stone, ornamented with white marble. It is a square of sixty-one and one half feet exteriorly; the walls are twenty-one and one half feet thick, thirty-eight and one half feet high, with a slope of seven and one half feet from top to bottom. The total height to the top of the domed roof is seventy feet, and the pinnacle is ten feet more. Each of the four sides has a lofty doorway with a pointed arch. Within are three tombs, said to be those of the old king, his wife, and his son and successor. The latter was a very cruel and unjust monarch; and his successor, the good Feeroz Shah, obtained, after long efforts, a paper signed by all whom his predecessor had wronged, declaring their full forgiveness. This he deposited in the late king's tomb near his right hand, that, in the resurrection day he might appear with it before the judgment seat. The following are the words of Feeroz Shah himself in regard to it: "I have taken pains to discover the surviving relations of all persons who suffered from the wrath of my late lord; and having pensioned and provided for them, and for those who had been maimed by order of the late Sultan, have caused them to execute deeds, declaring their satisfaction, duly witnessed; these being placed in a chest have been deposited at the head of the tomb of the said Sultan, in the hope that God of his infinite mercy will take compassion on my departed friend."

As the sun is sinking fast, we turn our faces towards Delhi, and after another dose of bullock-cart, we rejoin our carriage and arrive at the hotel in time for dinner.

Before leaving the hotel in the morning, we gave orders to the proper persons to prepare a *nautch* for us this evening, as we wished to witness this curious dance. At 8 P. M. we leave the hotel, and, accompanied by the Baboo, make our way through a labyrinth of streets to a hall brilliantly lighted, containing a sort of stage, on which chairs are placed for us. The native musicians sit at one end, several Indians with torches are standing near by, and the dancing-girls are grouped at the side. Their dresses are elaborately embroidered with gold and silver, and countless bangles of gold and silver are on their wrists and ankles. Silver rings, connected by silver chains, are worn on their toes. Long veils, beautifully embroidered, are thrown loosely over their heads or twisted around their bodies.

Now the musicians strike up a slow, mournful refrain. The torchbearers advance, and throwing the fitful light on the dancers, cause the bright dresses of the latter to sparkle like masses of jewels. The dance is begun with a measured, graceful step; the glittering figures wind in and out, advance, retreat, and move from side to side, their dark faces and barbaric garments forming a weird scene. Now one of them steps before the others, and, placing a cup on the ground, circles round and round it, now rushing towards it with eagerness, then, with hand outstretched to seize it, moving back hurriedly with an expression of fear on her face. The music is rapid and shrill, and wild bursts from time to time seem to call on the dancer to taste the fatal draught. It is "Temptation" enacted. At last the girl leaps forward, throws her veil from her, and dances towards the cup. The music grows even more rapid, her bosom heaves, and, with uplifted arms, she sinks within the charmed circle, grasps the cup with utter abandonment, and drains it to the bottom.

1876, January 1. — We start this morning for the Fort and Palace of the Moguls. This fortress was built at an expense of fifty lacs of rupees ($2,500,000), and was not finished for twenty years. It is about a mile and a quarter in circumference, and contained originally about a dozen buildings, of which the most important still exist.

We go first into a large hall open at three sides, and supported by rows of red sandstone pillars. On the right-hand side (as we stand looking up the hall) is a marble staircase leading up to a throne, covered with a canopy which is supported on four pillars of white marble. The throne is raised about ten feet from the ground. The wall behind the throne is covered with mosaic work in precious stones, the majority of which have been removed. This work was done by Austin de Bordeaux.

Continuing our way to the left we enter the exquisite Hall of Audience, which once contained the celebrated Peacock Throne, worth six million pounds sterling, which Nadir Shah took away in 1739. This hall is supported by graceful marble pillars, beautifully inlaid with precious stones in floral designs; and the upper sections, the ceiling, and the cornices are gilt. The room is long and wide, the marble columns are massive and finely wrought, and the decoration is most elaborate. I do not believe it has its equal in the world.

The white marble platform on which the Peacock Throne rested is still here. On the cornices at each end can still be deciphered the famous inscription, in flowing Persian characters: "*Ugur furdauss burra-i-zumeen ust, humeen ust, humeen ust, humeen ust*" (And, oh, if there be an Elysium on earth, it is this, it is this, it is this").

"The Palace of Shahjuhanabad, in the short space of its existence, has witnessed many startling scenes, mostly tragic.

Here, in 1716, the Scottish surgeon, who cured the Emperor Furrokh Shur on the eve of his marriage, was rewarded by that permission for his employers to establish a factory and to maintain a territory of thirty-eight towns on the banks of the Hooghly, which was the foundation of the 'Presidency of Fort William,' and all that has since sprung therefrom. Gabriel Hamilton was thus the *homme nécessaire* of the British Indian Empire. Here, on the 31st of March, 1739, the degenerate Muhumud Shah entered the Throne-room with the fearful Nadir Shah of Persia, and sipped his coffee on the Peacock Throne. Next day, the invaders massacred the citizens before 'the dark and terrible eye' of their leader, as he looked on from the roof of Roshun-ood-dowlah's Mosque. The Peacock Throne was then broken up, and Nadir returned to Persia with plunder valued at eighty millions sterling in the value of the day. Less than ten years after, the Abdalee Chief of Cabul, Ahmud Khan, repeated the cruel lesson and despoiled the palace of much of its remaining wealth. In 1759 the work was completed by the Mahrattas, under Sudashea Rao Bhao, marching to their ruin at Paniput; when . . . . . the plating was torn down from the ceiling of the Throne-room. In 1788 the sanctity of the imperial halls was further violated by the cannon-shot of Gholam Kadir, and shortly after by his actual presence. Here he lay and smoked his *hookah* on the faded substitute of the Peacock Throne; and here he, with his own hands, shared in the torture of the royal family and the blinding of the helpless old Emperor Shah Alum. Here, on the 15th of September, 1803, as the sun was setting, the long cavalcade of Lake defiled into the Am-Khas, where the blinded chief of the house of Timoor was found 'seated under a small tattered canopy, the remnant of his royal state, with every external appearance of the misery of his condition.' And lastly, here in May, 1857, the last representative of the Great Moguls, a not unwilling tool in the hands of the Company's mutinous soldiery, consented to the butchery of helpless women and children."*

We go next to the Jama Musjid, the great Mosque of Delhi, and the finest in India. It is built on a rocky height to the westward of the Palace, and is constructed of white marble and red sandstone, with three domes and two minarets. It stands in a splendid court-yard, four hundred and fifty feet square, and is reached by handsome marble steps. The mosque itself is two hundred and one feet long, one hundred and twenty feet broad, and one hundred and fifty feet high. The roof is supported by beautiful marble pillars, and the marble floor is divided into spaces for the worshippers. At each end are marble screens behind which the women knelt.

It is said that five thousand workmen were constantly employed on this mosque for six years. It was completed A. D. 1658, the same year in which its founder, Shahjuhan,

---

* Keene's Handbook to Delhi.

was deposed.   In a building near the mosque we are shown various relics, — a shoe of Mahomet, a hair from his beard, and a very old Koran.

On our way back to the hotel we pass through the famous Chandnee Chouk, or Street of Light, where the chief shops are situated.   Here we find a profusion of beautifully embroidered shawls, jackets, cloaks, and caps, for which Delhi is noted.   The jewellers' stores are well worth visiting, and we examine with interest a saddle-cloth, intended for the Prince of Wales, which is covered with precious stones of all kinds.

After *tiffin* we set out for the Kootub, a wonderful tower about eleven miles distant from the centre of the city.   As we ride along we pass first the Juntur Muntur, or Observatory, constructed for the Emperor Mohummud Shah in A. D. 1730, by Jay Singh, Raja of Jeypore.   Farther on, on the other side, is the tomb of Sufdur Jung ("Piercer of Battle Ranks").

The Kootub is a red stone tower two hundred and thirty-eight feet high, and sloping from a diameter of forty-seven feet at the base to one of scarcely nine at the summit.   It is divided into five stories, of which the first and last make up one half, the second, third, and fourth the other half, of the total height.   The three lower stories are surrounded with carved scrolls containing verses from the Koran, and the name and praises of the founder.

The literal meaning of Kootub is Polar Star. The tower was begun by Kootub-ood-deen Aibuk, the lieutenant of the Ghorian conqueror of India, towards the end of the twelfth century. It was not completed, however, till the middle of the reign of his successor. The tower is exquisitely proportioned. A winding staircase leads up to the top, whence an extensive view may be obtained.

Near the Kootub is a remarkable gateway built by Ala-ood-deen in the fourteenth century. The façade is covered with delicate chiselling, and, viewed from a little distance, the tracery is wonderfully beautiful. Near by is a plain iron pillar, twenty-two feet high, with six Sanscrit lines cut upon its western face, indicating that it was erected in the fourth century of the Christian era. Several other interesting ruins are in the vicinity.

Retracing our steps we reach Delhi in time for dinner.

A few words in regard to the mutiny in this city. Early on the morning of the 11th of May, 1857, the revolted troopers of the Third Bengal Cavalry crossed the bridge of boats and entered the city. The entire native garrison quickly joined them, and the foreigners were at once attacked. Simon Fraser, the Resident, Captain Douglas, Commander of the Palace Guard, with the Chaplain and his daughter, were killed at the main gate of the citadel; Colonel Ripley and other officers of the Seventy-fourth N. I. were shot in front of their own men; the magazine was captured; and the Europeans, men, women, and children, were pursued by a frantic mob and shot down as they ran. The magazine, however, was bravely exploded by Willoughby and Forrest, and many Europeans escaped across the Jumna and arrived safely at Meerut.

On the 8th of September operations were begun to retake the city. Troops under John Lawrence had arrived, and, best of all, came the great John Nicholson. For five days the gunners of England beat upon the northern walls without ceasing. On the evening of the 13th two practicable breaches were reported by the Engineer officers, one at the Cashmere Bastion, the other at the Water Gate. At daybreak of the 14th the roar of artillery suddenly ceased. According to previous agreement the Sixtieth Rifles sprang forth with a cheer to cover the advance, and Salkeld and Home of the Bengal Engineers stepped forward with non-commissioned officers, buglers, and powder-carriers, to blow up the Cashmere Gate. The scene that followed is thus described by an eye-witness, Colonel Medley, R. E. : " Followed by the storming party, one hundred and fifty strong, Home and his party reached the outer gate almost unseen. With difficulty they crossed the ditch, and having laid their bags, retired unharmed. It was now Salkeld's turn. He also advanced with four other bags of powder and lighted port-fire, but the enemy had seen the smallness of the party and the object of their approach. A deadly fire was poured upon the little land from the open wicket not ten feet distant. Salkeld laid his bags, but was shot through the arm and leg, and fell back on the bridge, handing the port-fire to Sergeant Burgess, bidding him light the fuse. Burgess was instantly shot dead in the attempt. Sergeant Carmichael then advanced, took up the port-fire, and succeeded in the attempt, but immediately fell mortally wounded. Sergeant Smith, seeing him fall, advanced at a run, but finding that the fuse was already burning, threw himself into the ditch. . . . . In another moment a terrific explosion shattered the massive gate, the bugle sounded the advance, and then with a loud cheer the storming party was in the gateway, and in a few minutes more the Cashmere Gate and Main Guard were once more in our hands."

All the survivors were recommended for the Victoria Cross. Salkeld, however, died of his wounds; and Home, coming out unhurt from this terrible ordeal, fell soon after in a small engagement. General Nicholson, after leading his column over the breach by the side of the Cashmere Gate, was shot while urging his men towards the Burn Bastion. On the fifth day, however, the whole city was in the hands of Sir Archdale Wilson.

January 2. — We leave Delhi at half past eleven this morning, and reach Agra at 7.30 P. M. We drive at once to Harrison's Hotel.

CHAPTER XVIII.

AGRA AND BOMBAY.

January 3. — Agra is situated on the west bank of the
Jumna River, one hundred and thirty-nine miles southeast
from Delhi, nine hundred and six miles from Calcutta, and
seven hundred and fifty from Bombay. It contains a population of one hundred and forty-three thousand, and has a
considerable trade in cotton and salt, which are sent down
the Jumna in boats to Mirzapore and Calcutta.

The city was named from *agur*, a salt-pan, much salt having been made in the place by evaporation. It was founded
by Akbar the Great in the middle of the sixteenth century,
and is particularly interesting to travellers on account of the
Fort, the Taj, and the Pearl Mosque.

We begin our day's tour with a visit to Sikundra, the
tomb of Akbar the Great. This is a square building of red
stone with five stories, the upper one being of white marble,
and crowned by four small kiosques. The tomb was built
by Jahangeer, the son and successor of Akbar. It is said to

have cost fifteen lacs of rupees. A beautiful garden surrounds it, full of orange, banana, tamarind, mango, palm, and peepul trees. A high, red stone wall encloses the grounds, with a lofty gateway in the centre of each of its sides.

On the summit of the mausoleum is a white marble sarcophagus, exquisitely sculptured, and placed in the centre of a large chamber open to the sky. Ninety-nine titles of the Creator are on the tombstone, and at the head and foot are the salutations of the school or faith of Akbar, "Allaho Akbar! Jilli Julali Hoo!" The real tomb which covers the remains is in a vault below the floor of the building. The hall is about thirty-eight feet square, and the ceiling is of blue and gold plaster.

Stand at a little distance from the building, opposite the main gateway. From here one can appreciate the beauty of the whole. On either side of the wide stairway are two minarets. The different red stone stories rise one above another, surmounted by the beautiful chamber of white marble; at each corner of the upper terrace are two marble turrets with gilded domes which flash and glitter in the sun; around us is the luxuriant garden, filled with bright sunlight and patches of shade, while a deep and impressive silence pervades this abode of the dead.

We next visit the Fort situated in the town. This is a lofty structure of red stone, with walls about seventy feet in height and a mile and a half in circumference. It is said, however, that their strength is more apparent than real, and that the stone of the works is only veneered over banks of sand and rubble. Passing over the moat on a drawbridge, we pass through a curious gateway, and crossing a court-yard enter the Dewan-i-Am, or Public Audience Hall. This chamber is one hundred and ninety-two feet in length and sixty-four in breadth. The traces of the emperor's throne are still to be seen, and near by is a slab of marble on which Akbar stood when administering justice. At the side, over-looking the river, are beautifully decorated chambers, formerly occupied by the ladies of the court. The remains of an ex-tensive system of water-pipes are still shown; and underneath a little building near by is a large *bowlee*, or well-house, whose interior walls are covered with little mirrors. These well-houses were designed for cool retreats during the heat of the day. The fort was captured by Lord Lake in 1803.

The Motee Musjid, or Pearl Mosque, is the most beautiful building on the premises. It is of white marble, standing on a lofty sandstone platform, and has three delicate domes of white marble. "It is a sanctuary so pure and stainless, revealing so exalted a spirit of worship, that I felt humbled as a Christian to think that our noble religion has never inspired its architects to surpass this temple to God and Mahomet." *

From here we drive to the Taj. Arrived at the premises,

* Bayard Taylor.

we pass through a splendid gateway of sandstone, covered with inscriptions from the Koran in white marble. Proceeding, we enter a beautiful garden with rich trees, shrubs, and flowers, and many fountains. At the farther end, above the rich foliage, rises a marble building of dazzling whiteness. Its proportions are so graceful that it seems to be but lightly resting on its foundations, and its dome is so delicate that it is almost transparent. While gazing on the structure the eye assures the mind that this is absolute perfection.

We ascend some wide marble steps and reach a white marble platform. Crossing this, we arrive at the door, a gem of delicate carving and tracery. We descend into the vault containing the sarcophagi of Shah Juhan and his queen, — Moomtaz-i-Mahal, The Light of the World. The tombs are exquisitely adorned with bloodstone, agate, carnelian, and jewels, inlaid with great taste. They are surrounded with an octagonal screen of marble, covered with different designs worked with precious stones. The roof and walls of the chamber are pure white blocks of marble, and the echo that is returned here is wonderful.

I have seen many different buildings, many handsome structures, many varied styles of architecture; never have I beheld one which fills me with such delight as this Taj Mahal.

January 4. — We leave Agra at half past five this morning, with a long railroad journey before us.

January 6. — I reach Bombay at half past eleven this morning. F—— left the train at Jubbulpore to spend a night at the "Marble Rocks." He is to rejoin me to-morrow. After obtaining my letters I drive to the Esplanade Hotel, an immense iron structure lately erected.

Bombay is distant fourteen hundred and seventy miles, by rail, from Calcutta, and seven hundred and seventy-five miles from Madras. The English obtained the place as part of the dowry of the Princess Katherine of Portugal, when she was married to Charles II. This monarch ceded it to the East India Company in 1669. It contains a population of about seven hundred thousand, and carries on an extensive trade. The city now contains many handsome buildings, wide streets lighted with gas, and a horse railroad. It is excellently drained; and Malabar Hill, overlooking the town, is covered with picturesque bungalows. Multitudes of Parsees, with tall black-paper hats, are constantly seen on the streets. They are very thrifty and industrious, and many of them have amassed large fortunes.

January 7. — F—— arrived to-day. In the afternoon we visit the curious and repulsive Tower of Silence, the strange cemetery of the Parsees. On the top of a lofty hill, remote from the town, is a garden surrounded by a high wall. A long flight of steps winds up to the summit of the hill. In the centre of the garden is a low, square building without any roof. It contains one chamber, in which is a sort of iron altar formed of round bars of iron joined together. When a Parsee dies the body is taken solemnly to this Tower of Silence, strapped upon the iron altar, and left entirely exposed to the air in the open chamber. These people do not follow the custom of cremation or of burying, but believe that the body should be placed above ground, and suffered, undisturbed, to return to the elements of which it was made. Therefore, having secured it to the iron altar, they leave it in the open air, and, shutting the outer gate, allow Nature to deal with their dead as she will.

Their theory, however, is never carried into effect. Scarcely is a body fastened to the altar when, from all the neighboring trees, multitudes of vultures spring into the air, and, scenting their coming banquet from afar, wheel round and round the summit of the hill in a thick, dark flock. As soon as the outer gate is shut, they swoop upon their senseless prey, and, tearing off pieces of flesh, group themselves on the neighboring wall, and finish their repast at their leisure before the very faces of the relatives of the deceased.

This shocking scene is repeated so frequently, that the British government has decided to command the Parsees to bury their dead in the usual way.

None but Parsees can enter the garden. Royal visitors and high officials are, however, admitted. The custodian informs us that we cannot pass the gate. He says that the Prince of Wales was the only foreigner who has obtained admission for years. Assuming a dignified air and raising my voice, I reply, "We have travelled a long way from home. We are Bachelors of Arts and we wish to see the inside of your cemetery." The Parsee is puzzled. He sees we are strangers, and has evidently never heard of our declared rank. Seeing a smile on F——'s face, he suspects something. Shaking his head, he declares that we must send our names to the secretary of his Sect, and inform him that we are Bachelors of Arts. This, he says, may admit us. It is needless to say that we do not follow his advice.

At 6 P. M. we meet, by appointment, Mr. E. Lord, of Lyon & Co., who drives us along the beach road to the centre of Malabar Hill, where he has a delightful house. A fine sea-view is obtained here, and the air is cool and refreshing.

January 9. — Having engaged a small steam-launch we start about seven o'clock for the Caves of Elephanta, situated on Garapuri Island, about eight miles from Bombay. This is a specimen of the numerous cave-temples found in various parts of India. Here we see large chambers hollowed out of the rocky cave, regular rows of sculptured pillars, and rude statues of various divinities. The chief object of interest in Elephanta, however, is the Hindoo Trinity, an immense head with three faces, cut out of a single piece of rock, representing Shiva, Vishnu, and Buddha. When the Prince of Wales was in Bombay this cave was illuminated, and the effect must have been very picturesque.

January 10. — Two steamers are lying in the harbor bound for Suez. One is the regular mail-boat of the P. and O. S. S. Co., which is due at Suez in twelve days; the other is an Italian steamer, very comfortable in appearance, and said to be an excellent boat. She does not, however, run on schedule time, and on this account the fare is much less than by the mail-boat. I prefer, however, to take the fast steamer, while F—— champions the other. He reminds me that we are in no hurry to reach Egypt; assures me that the Italian boat will arrive at Suez but a very few days after the other; and tells me that we will make quite a saving in our fare, — a powerful inducement to a traveller. To this I answer that we have already travelled many thousand miles on the sea. I am anxious to accomplish this voyage as speedily as possible. To do this I am willing to pay a higher fare. Moreover, it is quite uncertain when the Italian steamer will reach Egypt. She may stop for cargo or passengers along the Red Sea, and take several weeks to accomplish the voyage.

All that I say is of no avail. F—— remains firm in his preference. We both see that our arguments are powerless with the other. We fix matters as follows: F—— is to embark on the Italian steamer, and I on the mail-boat. His steamer is due (as far as is now known) at Suez two days after mine. I promise to wait for him in Cairo, when we will continue our tour.

At 3 P. M. we bid each other farewell. I embark on the

English steamer and F—— goes on board of the Italian. At five o'clock we weigh anchor. Behind us is F——'s steamer, which has not yet started. India disappears in the distance. Once more I am on the water with a long voyage before me, but, for the first time, with no fellow-countryman at my side.

CHAPTER XIX.

UP THE RED SEA TO CAIRO.

January 11.—The *Pera* is the flag-ship of the Peninsula and Oriental Squadron, her commander, Captain Methven, being the oldest officer in the company's service. She is a fine large vessel, and the captain pays the most continual attention to the comfort of passengers intrusted to him. Besides this, he keeps a most watchful eye upon every portion of the ship, and satisfies himself by thorough and frequent inspections that his orders are carried out and proper care taken. We have but few passengers, for people seldom return to England in the cold weather after living for a year or more in the warm climate of India. I am the only American on board, and I am obliged to endure continual (good-natured) allusions to the "Bird of Freedom," "the Stars and Stripes," and "The Ideal Yankee."

January 17.—After a swift run across the Arabian Sea, we reach Aden at daybreak this morning; and while the steamer is coaling the passengers have time to visit the town. Aden is situated on a rocky peninsula near the entrance to the Red Sea. It is owned by the English, and would be an important naval station in case of war. It has a population of about twenty-one thousand, the majority of whom are natives. A small trade is carried on with the interior of Arabia and with the opposite ports in Africa. It is a stopping-place for the Peninsula and Oriental boats, and for the steamers of the Messageries Maritimes Company. Hardly a tree is to be seen in the place, and the neighborhood is lonely to the last degree. The natives present a very curious appearance. They stiffen their hair with a sort of yellow earth, which gives the head the exact look of a large mop. Ostrich-feathers and coral may be bought here in large quantities, but no one should think of giving the prices demanded.

We leave Aden at **11** A. M., and at **7** P. M. are opposite Perim, in the Red Sea.

January 18. — At noon to-day the strong, favorable wind dies completely away, and leaves us gasping for breath. No one who has not experienced it can imagine the heat which frequently prevails on the Red Sea. There seems to be absolutely no air to breathe. The steamer's smoke rises slowly, and hangs about the smoke-stack in a dense cloud, moving neither to the right hand nor to the left. The sun beats down fiercely upon the awnings stretched over the decks; the passengers are all siezed with a burning thirst, and soda-water and ale are in great demand. I can now appreciate the story, often told, that ships navigating this water in July or August are sometimes obliged to turn round and run backwards to get a little air! How we should enjoy some of the January blasts that are probably now whistling over America!

January 20. — We are revived! A fresh breeze is blowing in our faces, tossing up great waves against the ship, and considerably retarding our progress; but better, far better withal, than the furnace-heat of yesterday.

January 22. — At five o'clock this morning one of the passengers kindly comes to my state-room, and calls to me to come on deck and look at the range of mountains among which is Sinai. Going up stairs, I find several of the passengers already assembled, the majority provided with glasses, or small telescopes, all earnestly gazing at a group of snow-capped hills which rise boldly from the desert. The beams of the rising sun shine full on the white summits, and cast a beautiful rosy light over the whole. A more intensely desolate place I have never beheld. Besides the mountains, only a wide expanse of blue water and far-stretching sand is to be seen, and an eternal silence seems to hold possession of the spot.

At midnight we arrive off Suez, but are obliged to wait till daylight before going up to the dock.

January 23. — At daybreak this morning we are again in

motion, and at nine o'clock the ship is securely tied to the
wharf. All of us are thankful to be once more on land.
Those of us who are bound for Cairo find that we shall be
obliged to wait till to-morrow before proceeding on our
journey, as the only train from Suez has started. We therefore decide to spend the time at the Suez Hotel. As soon
as we set foot on shore we are surrounded by swarms of
Arabs, dozens of whom urge us to make use of at least fifty
donkeys at once; while whole platoons and relays insist upon
bearing off all our baggage, and, having made a most minute
division of the whole among themselves, we are dragged to
the hotel by a regiment of guides, while the vast army of
baggage-carriers moves on in front, and we make our way
through streets lined with natives all demanding *backsheesh*
at the same time. I am rejoiced to reach the hotel, and,
shutting the door of my room as quickly as possible, I listen
with dismay to the loud chorus of voices outside roaring
forth the terrible word *backsheesh*.

Suez is situated on a sandy tract of land at the head of
the Red Sea. It is distant thirteen hundred and eight miles
from Aden, and twenty-nine hundred and seventy-two miles
from Bombay. It owes its present size entirely to the canal,
which has necessitated the erection of warehouses and dwellings, and has attracted thither a much larger European population than the place ever would have obtained otherwise.
The inhabitants number about fifteen thousand. In the im-

mediate vicinity of Suez is shown the spot where (it is said) the Israelites crossed the Red Sea. Excursions may be made also to the Well of Moses, Mount Sinai, and Mount Horeb. At best, however, Suez is uninteresting and desolate.

Later in the day, when the throng outside my window has dispersed, I take a long walk with a fellow-passenger through the town and across the desert. We pass a large camp of Nubian soldiers, waiting for transport-ships to take them to the seat of war in Abyssinia. A dress-parade is in progress; and although the manual of arms is not very well mastered by the majority, still the many different companies of dusky soldiery uniformed in white with red fezes form a picturesque scene.

January 24. — We start at eight o'clock this morning for Cairo, distant two hundred and twenty-four miles. The cars of the Egyptian Railway are very dirty and uncomfortable, and very little attention is paid to the specified running time. Just before we start, our compartment is surrounded with the usual multitude of Arabs howling for *backsheesh*, to whose demands we, of course, pay no attention. Suddenly, however, a determined-looking Arab forces his way to the window, and gaining the attention of one of my companions, stretches out his hand for alms, prefacing his request as follows: "You kicked me yesterday, — backsheesh!" It seems that my friend was yesterday wearied most to death by this fellow's importunities, and finally, refusals producing no effect, kicked him out of his path. The Arab then vanished without a word, but appeared this morning, as I have related, to urge his claim for *backsheesh*, to which he considered himself entitled, owing to his previous maltreatment. As the fact is indisputable, my friend tosses him a sixpence, which entirely satisfies him, and having salaamed he departs, his countenance beaming with joy.

The railroad runs directly across the desert, and the journey is very uninteresting. After changing cars and lunching at Zagazig, we continue our way, reach Cairo at 5.40 P. M., and drive at once to Shepheard's Hotel. The different hotels in Cairo send carriages to the station to meet the daily trains, and it is the custom for travellers to hand their baggage-receipts to the hotel people, who assure its speedy arrival at the chosen hotel. I advise everybody, however, to collect their baggage themselves before leaving the station, as one of my companions was obliged to circulate around the city in search of a stray valise, thereby losing his dinner, his peace of mind, and probably his temper.

January 25. — Cairo (Italianized from El Kahirah, The Victorious) contains a population of three hundred and seventy-five thousand, of whom twenty thousand are foreigners. The Khedive has greatly improved the city, and the European quarter contains many handsome residences, hotels, a public garden, and a fine opera-house.

Soon after breakfast I jump on a donkey, and having ob-

tained an intelligent dragoman to act as my guide and interpreter during my stay in the city, I make my way through
the narrow streets to my bankers, where I am glad to find
several letters. From here I proceed to the Citadel, the largest
mosque in Cairo, built on the highest ground in the city, from
which a splendid view is obtained in all directions. This
mosque was founded by Saladin in 1176, and its domes and
minarets can be seen from almost every part of the city.
Standing on the front balcony, a splendid panorama is spread
out before me. Far away to the left the dark waters of the
Nile can be distinguished, winding through fertile fields; at
my feet is Cairo; while in the distance the Sphinx and the
"everlasting Pyramids" rise boldly from the boundless desert.
The interior of the mosque is plain, and in short the whole
building is not to be compared to the exquisite structures in
India; and to one familiar with the latter, the Egyptian are
decidedly disappointing. Passing into the neighboring gardens,
I am shown the spot where Emir Bey leaped his horse over
the wall to avoid being killed, with his brother Mamelukes,
in the massacre of March, 1811. Two other mosques worthy
of a visit are the mosque of Kaït-Bey, and of Emir Akhor.
A cannon is fired from the Citadel every day at noon.

After lunch I pay a visit to the bazaars. Here everything
is very Oriental in appearance. The streets are full of tall
men with flowing garments and long beards, who exactly
resemble one's idea of the old patriarchs. The remarkable

costume of the peasant-women who walk the streets so completely covered that only their eyes are visible; the elegant carriages rattling along, through the half-closed blinds of which a woman of some Pacha's harem, closely veiled, can be seen; the throngs of donkeys, and the multitudes of men with red fezes, — all form a moving panorama which holds the attention of the stranger far longer than one might suppose.

Shepheard's (now Zech's) Hotel is the most largely frequented of any in Cairo, in spite of its new and pretentious rival, — an immense structure lately erected opposite the Public Gardens. At dinner at Shepheard's one may see a most varied and cosmopolitan gathering. The English are largely in the majority, but close by a lord or duke a "free American citizen" is often located, while Frenchmen, Italians, and Germans are scattered in various directions. An incident occurred here which well illustrates the different lights in which Americans are regarded by their English cousins. The conversation among a party of English had turned upon America, and one young man declared in a loud tone of voice that "no American can be a gentleman." Before any of our nationality could reply, a very beautiful Scotch girl, who was sitting directly opposite the oracle, overwhelmed him with a storm of righteous indignation. "How can you say such a thing?" said she. "Some of the most perfect gentlemen I ever met are Americans!" This sudden reproof, coming from such a beautiful source, completely silenced our traducer, who soon after withdrew from the table. A vote of thanks was tendered our country's champion for so heroically defending our reputation, and we assured her that her name should be preserved in the archives of the State Department.

I was present this evening at a representation of "Aïda" at the opera-house, which, in point of scenery and costume, was really marvellous. The scene of "Aïda," as is well known, is laid in the vicinity of Cairo, and the costumes must, therefore, be Egyptian. Here, however, the dresses were gorgeously *red*, the scenery was exquisite, and the effect of the whole was astonishingly beautiful. The opera-house itself is built on the Continental plan; but four boxes in the second tier, heavily curtained with lace, behind which some of the inmates of the Khedive's harem may be dimly seen, recall the fact that although I am in the midst of some modern culture and refinement, I have not yet left behind me one of the most disgraceful customs of antiquity.

January 26. — Soon after breakfast, to-day, I procure a donkey and set out for Boulac, the port of Cairo, one mile distant, which contains a large museum of Egyptian antiquities and curiosities. Here also are the mosques of Sinaneeyeh and Abu-l-Ela, the latter remarkable for its picturesque minarets. Boulac itself is about one mile long and one half mile broad, and is a very dirty town, containing about twenty thousand inhabitants.

I remount my donkey, and proceeding to the Nile am

ferried across in a native boat to the Nilometer opposite. The point where we land is said to be the spot where Moses was found in the bullrushes. The Nilometer is an instrument for measuring the depth of the Nile. It consists of a square tank connected with the river by a narrow canal. The sides of the tank are marked off into divisions, and from the height of the water in the tank at any time an estimate is made of the average depth of water in the river at that particular season.

Leaving the Nilometer, my guide leads me through a labyrinth of narrow, dirty streets, and, having at last arrived at the end of a particularly unclean alley, we dismount and make our way into a curious and very old Catholic church, full of ancient paintings, and containing also a most interesting old Bible. Having examined this place, we retrace our steps and I return to the hotel for lunch. I spend the afternoon in wandering through the bazaars, where the ever-changing crowds afford me continual amusement.

January 27. — No news from F——! His steamer should have arrived at Suez two days ago.

At nine o'clock this morning I set out with two other gentlemen for the Pyramids. The Khedive has built a broad and good road thither, and the distance — about ten miles each way — can be accomplished in one of the numerous barouches which are always to be found in the vicinity of the hotels. The road is shaded with trees, and passes over the new bridge across the Nile near the ferry at old Cairo, a neighborhood thronged at all hours with multitudes of men, women, and children, camels and donkeys, while the various groups around the different cafés form a striking picture.

When we are about four miles from our destination, our carriage is surrounded by squads of Arabs of all ages and heights, who, running at full speed, accompany us on our way, all eager to help us ascend the Pyramids. As we proceed, the number of our self-appointed menials is continually increased, and, finally, we descend near the base of Cheops in the midst of a swarming army of desperate-looking sons of the desert, all clamoring loudly for the wished-for employment. Having arrived at the foot of the Great Pyramid, we are obliged to parley with an old Arab Sheik, who — for what reason no one seems to know — enjoys a sort of royalty from every traveller who ascends to the top. Having promised the Sheik that his demands shall be attended to on our return to earth, and having selected four of the frantic multitude who surround us, we are marched in triumphal array towards Cheops, two Arabs in front dragging each of us along, while two more follow close behind in readiness to push us up on to the enormous blocks of stone of which the Pyramids are composed. Mark Twain well says, that each stone "is as large as a dinner-table"; and it actually takes the combined exertions of the four Arabs, pushing and pulling, to get the visitor to the top. After enduring this torture for about five minutes, I am so completely exhausted that I am obliged to rest, and sinking down on to a broad stone, I look down at my companion, an old gentleman of over fifty years of age,— for my other comrade, having ascended once before, utterly refused to submit to the pummelling again, — whom I see toiling bravely up from stone to stone, pausing at frequent intervals to rest. My drooping spirits having been revived by a few swallows of water administered by a small boy who accompanies us with an earthen bottle, I once more am put into motion by my attendant demons, who haul me over stone after stone, chanting at the same time the following suggestive chorus, "Arab very good man! Arab very good man!" As I am too weak to dispute this at once, I allow them to remain for the time in the belief that I acquiesce in their assertion. At last, after a further ten minutes' work, and a slight rest, I surmount the topmost stone, and with a wild whoop, the Arabs set me down on the summit. This is a flat surface, thirty-two feet square. It is covered with the names and initials of travellers from all parts of the world, and the monogram of the Prince of Wales is very conspicuous. The view from this point is very fine. Directly in front, only a little distance off, is the smaller pyramid of Cephrenes; near by is the Sphinx; while in the distance stretches on one side the burning sands of the desert, and on the other the fertile valley of the Nile.

Having surveyed the prospect at my leisure, I begin to

wonder why the old gentleman does not appear, and, going to the edge, I look down towards the base. Far below me I see a group of figures, who resemble dwarfs, slowly descending, while one in the middle, with a long white rope tied round his waist, is being lowered down from stone to stone by the others. I conclude from this that the old gentleman has given up the ascent in despair, and, indeed, so it proves.

While standing on the summit, the Arabs beseech me to allow them to run down the Great Pyramid and up the side of Cephrenes, — a feat which they promise to accomplish in an incredibly short space of time if sufficient inducement is offered. I decline, however, and express a wish to descend. This operation is far less arduous than the ascent, but even in this the assistance of the Arabs is necessary. Having reached the foot, aching in every bone, I signify my desire to enter the pyramid and explore the inner chamber where the sarcophagus was originally deposited. This also is a task of no slight discomfort. The entrance itself is only between four and five feet high; and after stooping low and passing in, I find a series of worn foot-holes, by which I descend rapidly down a narrow passage one hundred and seven feet long. This passage is perfectly dark, but the guides light a couple of candles (after obtaining a promise of extra *backsheesh*), which serve to show the cavities in which one must place his foot. Having arrived at the end of the descent, I am pushed and pulled by the Arabs over a huge bowlder which seems to have been the seal to the inner chamber, and from here an ascent begins, part of which must be accomplished on hands and knees. At last I find myself in a long narrow apartment, called the Great Gallery. Here I discover the old gentleman, leaning against the wall, looking very faint, and fanning himself with his hat, and surrounded by a bevy of Arabs, who are taking advantage of his exhaustion to fiercely demand *backsheesh;* and so persistent are they, that the old gentleman is obliged to give them something to make them leave him for a few moments in peace; and on my arrival I find him recklessly dealing out shillings to the rascals, who receive each donation with a whoop of fiendish delight.

Proceeding a little farther, I reach the Queen's Chamber, the roof of which is composed of huge blocks which have been most ingeniously joined together. In the eastern end of this room is a niche, where the stones have been broken by Arabs in search of treasure. Returning to the Great Gallery I am shown a narrow, funnel-shaped passage called the Well. This leads down to another chamber, where the body of the builder is believed to have been originally laid. As the old gentleman wishes to get into the outer air as soon as possible, and as I have had enough crawling for one day, we do not descend to this spot.

Having returned to our carriage we come to a financial settlement with the old Sheik and his minions, and after much useless conversation at last make matters satisfactory. We then visit the Sphinx, which does not quite answer my expectations; and after spending a few moments inspecting a ruined tomb near by, we return once more to our carriage, where lunch is awaiting us. While discussing our meal we are pressed upon from all sides by Arabs who offer to sell us all sorts of "antiquities" (large quantities of which are manufactured in England), and who urge us also to allow them to "run up the Great Pyramid and down again for one shilling," — a feat which they promise to accomplish in eight minutes or forfeit the money. As we hardly believe it can be done in this time, we give the word to a fine-looking, athletic fellow, and off he starts. It is wonderful to see the agility with which he rises from stone to stone, and he reaches the top, apparently with the greatest ease, in just four minutes. His descent is as rapidly accomplished, and he arrives back at our carriage in seven minutes and a half from the time of his start !

We now turn our horses towards Cairo, and after retracing our steps for some time, stop near the banks of the Nile and leave the carriage to inspect a *dahabeyeh*, or Nile boat, in which parties ascend the river. These are long wide crafts, fitted up with some degree of comfort; but a large and merry party must be required to make the time pass pleasantly. Continuing our way we reach the hotel in time for dinner.

January 28. — Still no news of F——. It is probable that his steamer has been detained at some port to receive extra cargo or passengers.

I go to-day to the Tombs of the Mamelukes, which are by
no means equal to the stately marble cenotaphs of the old
Indian Rajas. At three o'clock I pay a visit to the temple of
the Dancing Dervishes. Passing up a narrow alley I emerge
into a small court-yard, on one side of which is an insignifi-
cant-looking building with a small door at one end, by which
my guide bids me enter. I find myself in a room about thirty
feet by twenty, with a gallery running round the walls, part
of which, separated and covered by a wooden lattice-work
screen, is devoted to any ladies of the harems who may wish
to observe the sacred rites. Nearly the whole floor of the
temple is enclosed by a wooden circular railing, inside of which
are standing about thirty men of all ages, with long flowing
garments, shaved heads, and curious hats. About twenty-five
spectators from the world at large are standing round the railing, on the outside, waiting for the worship to begin.

In about five minutes a tall, very old man with a long beard
enters the room from a side door, and marches slowly into
the mystic circle. All the other priests remain standing till
he has seated himself on a Turkish rug at the upper end of
the apartment. As soon as the chief priest is seated, the rest
all sit down around him, — the whole assemblage forming a
large circle, — and bowing their heads low over their laps
they remain thus motionless for nearly five minutes. Finally
the chief priest rises, and making one solemn bow to the
others, walks slowly round the room, all the rest bending low

as he passes. Having completed the circuit of the room, the old fellow starts on another round, this time followed by all the other priests, each one falling into line as the procession passes him. When the chief priest has once more reached his rug, he leaves the others to proceed without him, and sitting down, sinks his head on his breast and relapses into deep meditation. The other priests walk completely round the room twice more, after which they all return to their places and stand motionless for several minutes. At last the priest who is on the right of the patriarch steps forward, makes him a low bow, and crosses over to his opposite neighbor, to whom he performs a similar obeisance. He then stretches both arms straight out before him and suddenly begins to spin round and round, his long petticoats standing out like a bell around his feet. Scarcely is he well under weigh when the priest next in order goes through the same ceremonies, and, like the first, is soon twirling round and round with extended hands. All the priests, likewise, are soon in motion, with the exception of the patriarch, whose years evidently prevent him from joining in the dizzy whirl.

After witnessing this incessant spinning for some time, and learning from my guide that there is nothing further of interest to be seen, I call a carriage and set out for Heliopolis, the ruins of the ancient On, situated about seven miles from the city. On the way we pass the tomb of Malek Adel, the brother of Saladin. Near Heliopolis a very old sycamore-tree may be seen, under which the Holy Family are said to have rested on their flight into Egypt; but this legend has been pronounced impossible by naturalists, who declare that the tree is only two hundred years old. The only trace of Heliopolis is a solitary obelisk, sixty-two feet high, covered with curious hieroglyphics.

January 29. — As F—— has not yet arrived, and as there is no office of the steamship company in Cairo, I decide to push on to Alexandria to make inquiries of the agent. Leaving Cairo, therefore, at eight o'clock this morning, I reach Alexandria, distant one hundred and sixty-two miles, at noon, and go to Abbat's Hotel.

CHAPTER XX.

ALEXANDRIA TO FLORENCE.

January 30. — Alexandria, situated on very low, sandy
land, has a population of two hundred and fifty thousand,
nearly one half of whom are foreigners. The native quarter
of the city consists of narrow, dirty streets, lined with multitudes of wretched houses. Near the shore of the new harbor,
where the Europeans dwell, are fine large warehouses, handsome residences, hotels, and churches. The site of the ancient
Pharos is now occupied by a modern lighthouse. The celebrated library, which contained seven hundred thousand vol-
umes, stood near the present British consulate. Cleopatra's
Needle, Pompey's Pillar, and the Catacombs are objects of
interest for the traveller of to-day. Here St. Mark was
martyred, and here, too, some of the most eminent fathers of
the Church were born.

Soon after my arrival yesterday, I went to the office of
the Austrian Lloyd Steamship Company to inquire about the
vessel on which F—— took passage. I was told by the

agent that the steamer reached Aden two days late, but nothing has been heard from her since that time. She is therefore long over-due at Suez. In conversation last evening with an Englishman at the hotel, I was assured that it would be foolish to set out for the Holy Land at present, as the rainy season is not yet over, and tent-life would be unendurable. Moreover, the telegraph reports snow and rain at Constantinople; and as I have so lately come from the tropics, I dare not expose myself to cold weather. In short, my future movements are entirely uncertain, and I know not what to decide.

I attend the English Church this morning, and hear a sermon from Bishop Gobat of Jerusalem. In the afternoon I procure a donkey and a guide, and set out for Pompey's Pillar. This is a shaft of red granite, sixty-eight feet high, and nine feet in diameter at the bottom. Two British naval officers and an English lady are said to have ascended to the top by means of a strong kite and a succession of ropes, but the story can hardly be believed. Why the pillar bears Pompey's name has never been determined. From here may be seen Lake Mareotis, which connects the Nile with the Mediterranean.

I now proceed to Cleopatra's Needle, situated near the coast. This is a single red granite block, seventy feet high, and seven and a half feet wide at the base. Its four faces are adorned with three lines of hieroglyphics. The central bears the name of Thothmo III. It is said that the lateral lines were sculptured in the time of Sesostris. This pillar is one of four erected originally at Heliopolis, and brought hither by one of the Cæsars. Another is now in Paris; and a third, given to the English, has not yet been removed, but is lying neglected in the sand.

January 31. — I call this morning at the steamship office. No further news has been received from F——'s steamer. What shall I do? I do not wish to stay longer in this city; the fleas alone are sufficient to urge my departure. I am unable, as I have said, to visit Palestine or Constantinople at present. I decide, therefore, to cross over to Italy. The steamship *Pera* (which carried me from India) has been delayed in the Suez Canal, but is to leave for Brindisi to-morrow, and I conclude to continue my journey in the care of her good captain. I leave a letter for F—— explaining my departure, and urging him to inform me promptly of his arrival in Egypt.

Before going aboard the steamer, I visit the Catacombs, situated about three miles from the city. Having arrived at my destination, I descend (accompanied by several officious Arabs with pine-torches) into a spacious circular chamber from which a series of subterranean galleries extend on all sides into the hill. The recesses for the mummies are plainly to be seen, but the mummies themselves have been removed.

On my return to the hotel I collect my luggage and go

on board the steamship *Pera*, which is anchored off the town.

February 1. — We start at eight o'clock this morning, and are soon out of sight of land. Among the passengers are Lord and Lady Francis Cunningham, Captain Hoskiœr (from whom I parted in Calcutta), and Mr. and Mrs. Charles Matthews.

February 3. — We run, to-day, close to the island of Candia, which with its snow-capped hills looks exceedingly picturesque. Towards evening the sea becomes very rough, and the ship tosses about incessantly. A cold head wind greatly impedes our progress.

February 4. — At daybreak this morning the flat shores of Italy can be seen, and at nine o'clock we enter the harbor of Brindisi, the ancient Brundisium, at the end of the old Via Appia. The modern town contains about twelve thousand inhabitants. At half past one I leave on the special express for Bologna, where I must change cars for Florence, to which city I am bound. For many miles the railroad runs parallel to the blue waters of the sea. Our train rushes past groves of olive-trees, and through picturesque towns musical with chiming bells, with ancient monasteries and old castles perched on the topmost crag of overhanging hills. At Foggia, where we stop for supper, several of our fellow-passengers leave us to branch off to Rome or Naples. We reach Ancona at midnight.

February 5.—At five o'clock this morning our train moves into the long covered station at Bologna, where I alight for breakfast. At seven o'clock I am again on the road, with seventy-one miles still to accomplish. The weather is cold and disagreeable. Flurries of snow dash against the car-windows, and swift streams, running down the mountain-side, add sharpness to the air. The scenery around us is most beautiful, but long tunnels continually break the view. At last, at noon, the train leaves the hills and moves slowly out on to a plain. A fair city lies before us. It is *bella Firenze* with its Duomo, its Campanile, and its slowly flowing Arno.

CHAPTER XXI.

ITALY TO FRANCE.

FLORENCE. — NAPLES. — ROME. — VENICE. — MILAN. — TURIN. — ARRIVAL
AT PARIS.

February 12. — For a week I have wandered about this interesting city, ever finding fresh delights on all sides. Edward Everett says: "There is much in every way in the city of Florence to excite the curiosity, to kindle the imagination, and to gratify the taste." True indeed. The Campanile, the Duomo, and Santa Croce; the Pitti and Uffizi galleries, with their wonderful paintings and sculpture; the curious Palazzo Vecchio; the venerable Ponte Vecchio, and the other graceful bridges that span the Arno; the quaint houses and ever-varying street scenes, — all afford continual amusement and instruction. In the afternoons I walk slowly along by the Arno, and watch the gay crowds hurrying to the Cascine Promenade. There is a young noble, the representative of a long line of ancestors whose names are written in history, driving a splendid equipage at full speed. Behind him follows sedately the heavy carriage of an old countess, with the family crest emblazoned on the panel. There goes an American guiding ten horses hitched tandem; while on the foot-path in front of me are senators, officers, and peasants.

Later, when the sun is nearly out of sight, I walk up the hill to the old church of San Miniato. At my feet are the thickly clustered houses of Florence, with the Arno and its bridges; in the distance are beautiful hills studded with monasteries and old fortresses; afar off, the snow-capped Apennines shine dazzlingly forth against the pure blue sky. On my way back I pass several Dominican monks hurrying along to their evening service at a neighboring chapel, whose bell sounds clearly through the evening air. Below in the city, I stop and wait for a few minutes with uncovered head, while a dead man is carried by on a bier, followed by a long procession of Brothers of Misericordia with their long black cloaks and masks. A peasant-girl, closing the shutters of an humble shop near by, is chanting, half unconsciously, an evening hymn. The gas-lamps on the Lung' Arno form glittering lines of light. The rattling cabs are at rest; while the drivers, standing near their vehicles on the street-corners, are giving the horses their feed, or are discussing with animated gestures the latest news from the Vatican, or the last action of the Italian senate. A mantle of repose has descended upon the city, and the massive walls of its ancient palaces are covered with silence and gloom.

February 15. — To-day I received a letter from F——! His ill-fated steamer has at last reached Suez. In regard to his voyage he says: "I have not yet told you the cause of our delay. On our arrival at Aden the captain found orders awaiting him to go up to Jeddah (in the Red Sea) and take aboard some pilgrims returning from the feasts at Mecca. So up to Jeddah we went and stopped there a day, and took five hundred of these creatures on our deck. You may imagine that there was not very much room for the first-class passengers to walk about; and when a storm came on, and the forward part of the deck was almost constantly under water, the wretches had to be moved aft, and then the captain's bridge was the only thing left to us for two days. In addition to this, on account of having pilgrims on board, we were obliged to go into quarantine at a small town called Wedge (about two hundred miles from Suez), and there we stayed for four days. . . . . We really ran a great risk; for although we had no cholera, we had small-pox on board. . . . . We were allowed to leave on the morning of the fourth day." F—— is now making preparations to start up the Nile, and it is doubtful if I rejoin him.

March 2. — I leave Florence at half past seven this morning for Naples.

March 3. — I reach Naples at daybreak, this morning. I am unable to obtain accommodation at the Tramontana Hotel (well situated on high ground), but I am received near by at the Nobile, a new hotel. Here I find two college friends, G. W., of Boston, and W. C. S., of Brooklyn. They arrived last evening, and we agree to explore the neighborhood together. After breakfast we set out. We visit Baiæ, Pozzuoli, the villas of Cæsar and Cicero, old Roman temples, Mount Solfatara, the Baths of Nero, Lake Avernus, and the Cavern of the Sibyl. In an old ruined temple we witness the *tarantula* dance. On our way back we stop at Virgil's tomb.

March 4. — We set out this morning for Pompeii and Castellamare. Leaving the railroad at Torre Annunziata we visit Pompeii, where we remain till afternoon. At four o'clock we continue our way, and reach Castellamare at sunset. The Quisisana Hotel, situated on a high hill overlooking the town, is a healthy and comfortable residence.

March 5. — We drive, this morning, to Sorrento on the fine road which runs along the bluffs close to the sea. The view on all sides is superb. On our arrival at Sorrento we find it is useless to embark for Capri, for a fog is rolling in from the sea. We explore the town and return to Castellamare in the afternoon.

March 6. — We spend the day in the Museum at Naples.

March 8. — Yesterday my friends embarked for Athens and Constantinople.* They urged me to accompany them, but I have had enough of the sea for the present. I leave, to-day, for Rome. With Naples and her environs I am charmed. The inhabitants of Southern Italy are more interesting than

---

* As they were returning to Italy, some weeks afterwards, their steamer collided with an English steamer and sank immediately. My friends, however, were saved.

their fellow-countrymen of the North. Here one sees more
picturesque costumes and more beautiful faces. The laughter
and animation of the people accords well with the blue skies
and the bright sunlight. I leave Naples at half past two, and
reach Rome at 8 P. M.

March 13. — Modern fashion makes of Rome in the winter
season a cosmopolitan dwelling-place, a gay city, whose immense hotels afford shelter for the multitudes who meet each
other at balls and parties, and who visit, *en passant*, the rich
antiquities around them.

Stand in the centre of the Forum; before you are two
great establishments whose walls are but a stone's-throw from
the historic ground. Along the neighboring street roll handsome equipages with liveried footmen. Thus surrounded, it is
hard to repeople this spot in imagination, — to recall the senators hurrying over this very pavement to the senate-house;
the consuls with their attendants; and the multitudes who
once stood in this very place listening to the wonderful elo-
quence of Cicero. Never have I seen a city of the past suffering such continual transformations from the hand of the
inexorable present.

I have visited the chief objects of interest in the city. I
continue my way northward to-morrow. Returning to my
hotel I pass the church of the Capuchin monks. I enter, and,
accompanied by one of the brothers, I descend to the vaults
beneath, filled with a ghastly assemblage. Here are ranged

the skeletons of brothers long dead. Wrapped in the robes of their order, with their cowls drawn over their grinning skulls, and their bony fingers clutching their rosaries, they stand as hideous sureties to the monks of death's never-failing memory. Around the walls are patterns formed of bones. "Shall you be placed here when you die?" asks another visitor of our conductor. "Yes," he replies stolidly (and pointing among the horrible group), "we shall all lie there."

March 14. — Leaving Rome this morning at ten o'clock, I reach Florence at seven.

March 16. — I continue my journey and reach Venice at 5 P. M. The cars leave me on the brink of a broad canal, in which many long, narrow, black gondolas are hurrying up and down, while a score lie close to the station waiting, like so many cabs, to convey passengers and their luggage to the different hotels. I enter one, and in a minute more I am in the middle of the Grand Canal, skimming along with the most delicious sensation of ease that can be imagined. Soon we turn off into another "street," and, moving almost on a level with the lower stories of the houses, draw up at last by the broad stone steps reaching from the hotel door into the water. It is astonishing how still the city is. There are of course no horses or carts, and the only sound is the monotonous "swish" of the gondoliers' paddles, accompanied from time to time by warning shouts as the sharp prows turn suddenly round the corner of an old palace.

Soon after dinner I step from the hall of the hotel into a gondola, and am soon deposited at the foot of the steps leading to the Teatro Fenice, and in a moment more I am on the floor of one of the largest theatres in Italy. The opera is "Hamlet"; the audience is numerous, well dressed, appreciative, and critical.

March 17. — Having obtained an intelligent guide, I spend the day in visiting the well-known points of interest in the city. I wander over the Piazza S. Marco and the Doge's palace; I pause in the great square, and see the pigeons coming in myriads to be fed at a window, and in the square itself; then I proceed to the mosaic manufactory, stopping on the way at the church of Santa Maria Gloriosa di Frari. From here we go to the palace of the present Prince Jovanelli, after which I visit the churches of Gli Scalzi (the barefooted Carmelites) and Santa Maria della Salute. Finally I ascend to the chamber at the top of the Campanile, whence a grand view can be obtained of this wonderful water-city.

There is something about Venice, with its old palaces, its canals and gondolas, its stillness, — almost intense, — that makes it seem truly like a city of the past; modern fashion has not yet — to outward appearance — invaded it, and swept away, as from Rome, the mysterious atmosphere of antiquity.

March 18. — I leave Venice at eight o'clock this morning, and reach Milan at 5 P. M. The new Hotel Confortable is a credit to its name.

March 19. — To-day is Sunday, and I visit the great Cathedral, — immense, beautiful, impressive. As I stand in a distant corner, under a magnificent stained-glass window, a procession of priests and choir-boys is marching slowly round near the high altar, chanting a solemn Lenten miserere. I cannot see the singers, but the clear voices (without organ accompaniment), the interior dimness of the Cathedral, relieved only by the soft light admitted by colored windows, and the various groups of peasants bowed low before the different shrines, — together produce in my mind a feeling of perfect calmnesss and awe. From the Cathedral I proceed to the old Dominican Priory (used by the Austrians, at one time, as a stable), where is Leonardo da Vinci's "Last Supper."

Leaving Milan at 4 P. M., I arrive at Turin at half past eight.

March 20. — Continuing my journey, I leave Turin at 9 A. M. The cars are crowded, and when we arrive at Modena, and change into others, the accommodation is quite insufficient, and we are packed in like bales of goods.

March 21. — Passing through the Mont Cenis Tunnel, we reach Paris at eight o'clock this morning.

CHAPTER XXII.

PARIS, LONDON, AND BOSTON.

April 21. — I have been living for a month in a French family near the Arc de Triomphe. I have improved my knowledge of the language, and have obtained a little insight into the life of these remarkable people. How different are their manners and customs from our own! Small matters of frequent occurrence in America are not *comme il faut* here; yet these, I think, are more than overbalanced by abominations which would not be permitted for a day in our country. The excessive politeness of the multitude is only on the surface, and these courtly manners are often far more deceptive and dangerous than the disagreeable but honest brusqueness of a New England farmer. The moral sense of the people is strangely distorted. Sin is called by another name, and vice is concealed under such apparent refinement, that he who applies a harsh term to it is deemed a boor.

The family in which I have been living, however, is composed of people who are highly cultured and thoroughly agreeable; and yet, withal, their ways are not ours. I have heard and read much about the French boys. I witnessed the other day in this family an occurrence which testifies well to at least one little representative of the nation.

Edmond is a boy of seven years of age. Several weeks ago I promised him that he should accompany me some evening to the American circus. Since that time he has had it continually before his mind, and all day yesterday (the time finally agreed upon) he was in a state of the most intense excitement. Now, Edmond's father is a physician; and when we sat down to dinner last evening, he told his wife in German (which Edmond does not understand) that he could not allow his son to expose himself to a cold fog, which had spread itself over the city. How to break this doleful news to his little boy he could not determine; he knew that it would almost break the child's heart, for he had looked forward to the entertainment for weeks. For his own sake, however, something must be said to him at once. Instead of telling him bluntly (as some parents do) that he could not go, and assigning no reason therefor, he called the child from the dinner-table to the piazza outside. The rest of us remained in silence, awaiting the result of the conversation. The father was evidently explaining his reasons to his son. The firm low tones of the one contrasted with the tremulous but respectful inquiries of the other. At last the father finished, leaving the decision of the matter in his son's hands.

Together they returned to the dining-room. The little boy's lip was trembling, but his teeth were firmly shut together. He was making a manly effort to appear calm. There was silence for a minute; then the mother spoke: "Have you told Edmond why you do not wish him to go?" "Yes," replied her husband; "and what do you decide, my child? Will you give this up and go some other time?" For a moment he hesitated. Then brushing the tears from his eyes he answered in a low despairing tone, "*Oui, mama*." Upon this the old grandfather speaks: "*Mon enfant*," he says, "*vous avez bien fait, et je vous donnerai un franc pour votre petit porte-monnaie*." "I will add one, too, my child," says the father; and I also join in the reward. The boy takes the money and puts it in his little purse. Even then, however, the remembrance of the lost circus causes his eyes to fill with tears; but turning quickly to us, he says, "*Merci grand-papa, merci papa, merci monsieur*" (to me); then holding his purse up to his mother, he cries out, "*Regardez, mama, regardez!*" His disappointment is forgotten, and his present pleasure compensates him for his pain.

Paris is covered with the exquisite beauty of spring. The skies overhead are deep blue, the sunlight pours over everything, and the streets are thronged with gay promenaders and handsome equipages. All the world goes to the Bois in the afternoons, and the different theatres offer most varied entertainments for the evenings. The cafés are crowded, and the Boulevards are lined with little tables where people sit and drink coffee, and discuss the news of the day.

There is something about this Paris life which is wearisome. The whole place seems given up to pleasure, and the goddess of Gayety perpetually rules supreme.

May 8. — I leave Paris at 8 P. M. for London *via* Calais and Dover.

May 17. — I have been constantly occupied since my arrival in visiting the well-known objects of interest in the city. To-day I witnessed a debate in the House of Commons. Calling on Mr. Russell Sturgis, I was introduced by him to Mr. Kirkman Hodgson, M. P., who kindly gave me his card, which admitted me to the lobby, where Mr. Hodgson met me, and conducted me to the gallery. I was astonished to see the members sitting with their hats on; but the speakers were attentively listened to, and the quiet and decorum that prevailed was a contrast to the confusion that one often finds in the House of Representatives at Washington.

May 19. — Leaving London at ten o'clock this morning, I reach Liverpool at 1 P. M.

May 20. — The Cunard steamship *Russia* is advertised to sail at noon, and passengers are requested to be on board the steam-tender with their baggage at ten o'clock. Leaving the Adelphi Hotel shortly before that hour, I find many passengers and much baggage already on the little steamer, waiting to be conveyed to the larger vessel, which is anchored off the city. At ten o'clock we leave the wharf, and are soon alongside of the great ocean steamer. Now the confusion begins. The passengers pour over the ship's side in haste, with bags and bundles in their hands, and rush precipitately to the cabin to find their state-rooms. The sailors from the large steamer descend into the tender, and, grasping the passenger's trunks, carry them to the deck of the *Russia*, and toss them down in a heap, with a carelessness that would put to shame an American baggage-smasher. A very expensive gun which I carried on board in a case I found lying underneath a heavy trunk, which had been thrown upon it by some thoughtless seaman. At last we are under way, and a comparative amount of order is established.

May 21. — We reach Queenstown at nine o'clock this morning, and remain off the town till 1 P. M. Having received the late mails and a few passengers, we continue our voyage.

May 24. — For four days I have watched with delight the wonderful discipline which has been impressed upon the navigators of this ship. For four days I have endured with ever-increasing disgust the disorder that reigns in the dining-cabin at meal-times. On deck the sailors perform their duties with a quiet precision which assures the traveller that the company fully appreciate the responsibility of the many human beings committed to their care. Captain Cook himself is perpetually on the watch, and nothing is left undone that human efforts can accomplish. The interior management of the ship is, as I have said, far from satisfactory. We have by no means our full complement of passengers, and yet at table it is difficult to get attention. Besides this, the food — of good quality itself — is often carelessly prepared and uninviting. The waiters hurry hither and thither noisily, drop plates and dishes with loud clatter, and do not seem to work with any system or under any directing eye. The Chinese waiters on the Pacific Mail Steamers, governed by an American head-steward, put these English assistants to shame. The dinners, instead of being served slowly in courses, are put for the most part upon the table in a disorderly heap, and a mere pretence is made of pausing between the fish, meat, and dessert. In short, the company has obtained such a just reputation for excellent seamanship, that they care very little about the comfort of passengers. Any complaints made in regard to the minor details of the ship are answered with the remark that safety is placed before ease. " In long years of navigation on the dangerous Atlantic," they say, " we have never lost a passenger. We cannot allow considerations of comfort to interfere with the proper care of life."

It seems to me that these two departments are by no means inconsistent with each other. In all my travels round the world, over many oceans and seas, I have never seen steamers more carefully navigated than the boats of the Cunard Company; I have only seen their system equalled in one case, — the *Pera* of the Peninsula and Oriental Company, commanded by Captain Methven. But, on the other hand, I have only once seen their equal in bad table management, — on the boats of the Netherlands India Company, running from Singapore to Java. There is no reason why the excellent care of the deck should be the only recommendation of the Cunarders. If the comfort of the passengers was more regarded, these steamers would be the patterns of the world. As it is, they are far from deserving the title.

May 30. — We are in sight of land! Early this morning America was seen by the lookout. At one o'clock we pass Sandy Hook. Continuing our way we see beautiful green fields, and pleasant-looking houses perched on the neighboring hills. We see our country's flag floating over buildings in the distant city, and flying from the countless crafts which pass up and down by our side. At 5 P. M. we reach the dock, and, soon after, I am once more in my native land.

June 5. — Having visited the Exposition at Philadelphia, I leave New York this morning at ten o'clock for Boston. The journey is quickly accomplished. At 5.40 the train moves slowly into the station, and comes to a stand-still. I have travelled around the world, and, thank God, have reached my home in safety.

THE END.